Ivy Linden

and the

Treasure

of

Skull Island

Also by Donna Esposito

Flying Time: A Novel

Ivy Linden

and the

Treasure

of

Skull Island

Donna Esposito

Cordata
Press
Schenectady, New York

Ivy Linden and the Treasure of Skull Island

This book is a work of fiction. Any references to historical events, real people, or real places are used fictitiously. Other names, characters, places, and events are products of the author's imagination, and any resemblance to actual events or places or persons, living or dead, is entirely coincidental.

Cover and interior design by Donna Esposito
Images of dragonfly, skull, *Rafflesia*, and triton courtesy of Biodiversity Heritage Library
http://www.biodiversitylibrary.org
All other images produced by the author

ISBN-13: 979-8-9886782-0-5 (paperback)

Cordata Press
Schenectady, New York
www.cordatapress.com

For the Chalfont Hike and Trail Club

Chapter 1

I closed the book with an abrupt snap. I was more than a little satisfied when two young men in the front row were jolted awake and looked around sheepishly. The last class of the year was complete. I could hardly blame the boys for dozing. After the long Ithaca winter, spring had finally arrived. Warm air wafting in through an open window had made the lecture hall stuffy. My students had gazed outside absently at the greening trees while I spoke. Clearly they longed to be free, and so did I. Just the final exam to administer and then they, and I, would no longer be prisoners of these ivy-covered walls.

I didn't know what diversions my students had planned for the summer, but I knew I would be headed back to the sort of vine-cloaked environment I most prefer: the forest and jungle.

The botany students filed out the door, some pausing to say goodbye, most sprinting past without giving me another glance.

"Professor Linden," a serious young man with heavy, horn-rimmed glasses said as he paused at my desk, "I thought your class was swell. Much better than your father's last semester."

"Thank you, Mr. Jones. I hope you learned a lot in both classes. But why do you say that?"

"Oh, I don't know," he replied, looking down and beginning to blush. "I guess there was something about your class that held my attention better." He darted out the door as I began to scowl.

My father, Reed Linden, had been a botany professor at Cornell University for twenty-five years. This was just my third year as a professor with a specialty in ethnobotany. Of course, there weren't many universities with female professors – or even female students, for that matter – so I was pleased to become a faculty member here. I could tell things would change in this decade. After getting the right to vote eighteen years ago, we were finally making some strides in equality. But I realized I was still something of a novelty. Fortunately, my father had never thought there were only certain careers appropriate for women, so he encouraged me to follow in his leaf-strewn footsteps as a botanist. But I was also fascinated by other cultures, and after I heard Margaret Mead speak at Columbia, I knew I wanted to be an anthropologist, too. What to do? Ethnobotany was the perfect intersection of plants and culture. Indigenous people passed down generations of knowledge on medicinal plants. I felt certain our greatest advances in medicine would come from investigating that ancient wisdom. And so I set out, after a double course of botany and anthropology at Bryn Mawr, to pursue my doctoral degree in the new field of ethnobotany at Harvard.

My doctoral fieldwork in the Amazon rainforest earned me some recognition and a position at Cornell. I was glad to be back home in Ithaca with Mother, Dad, and my sister. My mother was pleased to have me home as well. She had not been very enthusiastic about my career choice. She was much happier when my younger sister Amaryllis became a librarian, a much more suitable profession for a young woman, as it generally involves fewer poisonous snakes, exotic diseases, and hostile conditions than my work.

The classroom had finally emptied of students. I walked to the open window and leaned out. My pupils had one week to study before their final exam. Then I would have one week to grade them. Then freedom. For three months, anyway.

I walked up and down the aisles of the classroom, pushing in chairs, straightening desks, and retrieving stray bits of paper distractedly. My thoughts were never far from my upcoming fieldwork, and now I could focus on the expedition I had been planning for months. My departure date finally imminent, I could hardly contain my excitement. And this time I had planned out every detail in advance. Last summer's expedition to Africa had not gone according to plan. Dad's old agriculture student, Elspeth Grant, now Mrs. Huxley, had welcomed me warmly. I appreciated her offering me her camp in Kenya as my home base. I remembered her well from her year at Cornell. She was just as charming and vivacious – and good with a rifle – as when she was a student here ten years ago. But Elspeth seemed to attract adventure, and the trip had proven less conducive to botanical research than I anticipated. I didn't regret the experience, but this summer would be different. To the outside observer, it sounded much more sedate an endeavor, but that suited me fine. I was looking for a tree. Not just any tree, of course, but the world's rarest tree. It was purported to be in the Three Kings Islands just north of New Zealand, and there was only one of its kind left. My goal was to be the first botanist to find it and describe it scientifically. I planned to propagate it so the species would not die out. And who could guess what useful properties the bark, leaves, or fruit of this tree might hold? I smiled, confident that by the end of the summer, I would know the secrets of this tree.

Later that afternoon, I sat at my desk reading. My office door was closed, hopefully a sign for inquisitive students to stay away. But the windows were open, and I could hear an occasional birdcall. The sunlight streaming in made me lethargic, and I wanted to take a nap. Instead I was reading journal articles to prepare for my expedition, and I willed my eyelids open whenever I felt them grow heavy. A forceful knock on the door startled me, and my heart sank.

"Come in," I called, expecting to see a young face or two peep in filled with questions about the final examination. Instead, the door swung open fully to reveal two dapper men wearing natty gray suits and even fedoras. They were overdressed for the weather and the location; they didn't look like other professors, even from the law school.

"Professor Linden?" the taller of the two men asked.

"Yes?" I said with hesitation as I rose from my desk chair. "How may I help you?"

"I'm Mr. Johnson, and this is Mr. Smith," he said, gesturing to the other man. My first thought was that those had to be phony names. My second thought was of the Johnson Smith Company, which sold novelties in an entertaining catalog and on the back pages of comic books. Perhaps they were traveling salesmen with whoopee cushions and magic tricks in their briefcases. That thought amused me, and I smiled.

"We're from the United States Department of Agriculture," he continued.

"Oh, pleased to meet you," I said, my smile fading as I tried to look more professorial. I offered them handshakes and gestured toward the two empty chairs in front of my desk. The men took off their hats and sat down. I sat back down, too.

"What brings you to Cornell today?" I enquired. I knew other researchers from the Department of Agriculture, but these men were not familiar to me.

"We came to discuss your upcoming fieldwork," Mr. Smith explained.

"Oh, yes. Of course. I leave for Three Kings Islands at the end of the month." The agency was providing most of the funding for the expedition, so it was not surprising they were interested, but Messrs. Johnson and Smith had not been among the USDA staff with whom I had dealt before.

"Yes, well, there's been a change of plans," Mr. Smith continued. "While we understand the importance of your expedition, something more pressing has come up. We need you to do some fieldwork in a different location."

"What?" I said sharply. My smile had disappeared completely now. My plans . . .

"We need an experienced ethnobotanist for a vital expedition to Malaya, and we understand you are the most qualified in the field. It really can't be anyone else," Mr. Johnson added in an ingratiating tone. Ah, flattery.

An old trick, and I wouldn't abandon my plans to fall for it.

"No, I'm sorry, but I really can't go. My plans for fieldwork are all set. Maybe I could swing by Malaya if I have time after I've completed my work, but I don't think that would be likely. I have to be back in time for classes again, of course. Besides, I'm not an expert on the plant life of Malaya or the culture, so I don't see how I could possibly be the best person for the work."

"Professor Linden, let me be more clear. We need you in Malaya, and that is where the agency will be funding you to do fieldwork. We've withdrawn the funds for Three Kings. That can wait. This can't. As far as your qualifications, we have no doubt of your ability to perform the necessary botanical and cultural work. We heard very complimentary things about you from the field station in Kenya."

"So you're saying I don't have a choice in the matter?"

"That's correct. Not if you want to have an expedition this summer," Johnson said with finality.

"Oh, I see," I said. But I did not see. They surely couldn't force me to go. But going nowhere was out of the question. Dreaming about the summer expedition was what got me through the harsh Ithaca winters. The new plants, the new people, the adventure of it all. I'd never been to Malaya, but it had always intrigued me. And it would be warmer than Three Kings. Those islands were south of the tropics, and it would be winter there. Not like an Ithaca winter, but still a bit cool.

"Well then, I guess you'd better tell me what sort of research and collecting you need done in Malaya," I said with a sigh of resignation.

"Very good. We need you to go to Tioman Island, off the eastern coast of the Malay Peninsula. We have a report of a plant there with antimalarial properties, and we need you to investigate. Find out from the locals what the plant is and how to grow it, and bring some back so we can begin propagating it here," Smith explained.

"What plant? I don't recall reading about a recent discovery. What journal is the plant described in? Why not send back the botanist who discovered it? Surely he is more suited for the job."

"The information has not been published, and we can't reveal our source. We don't know the name of the plant, only that Tioman is where to find it."

"You can't tell me where you got this information? But you're willing to send me halfway around the world on a wild goose chase?"

"Yes, that about sums it up," said Johnson.

"But why? What's wrong with quinine as an antimalarial? Surely there is plenty of *Cinchona* growing on Java. You can try cultivating some of that."

"We are attempting that, but it's crucial we have an alternative source of antimalarial medication should we lose access to the *Cinchona* production on Java."

"I don't see why that would be the case," I said. It seemed ridiculous. I knew the current production there could easily meet the demand.

"Professor Linden, please understand we cannot share all the details with you, but we have ample reason to suspect it may become scarce in the future and would like to have other treatment options available. Now we've taken the liberty of adjusting your flights already. You'll be leaving on the Pan American Clipper as planned, but you'll be going to Singapore, not New Zealand. Our contact at the Raffles Museum will be available to help you once you arrive. Of course, you'll stay at the Raffles Hotel. It's all taken care of. You just have to go, talk to the people, get the plants, and come back. It'll be a piece of cake for you," said Johnson.

"A piece of cake? I appreciate your confidence in me, but I'm not so sure. I don't speak Malay. I don't know anything about Tioman. The only thing I even recall about the place is a special tree there. A strangler fig they revere that someone named 'Mother Willow,' if I'm not mistaken."

"Well, that's already more than we know. Strangler fig, eh? That sounds like it could be useful. Bring some of that back, too," Smith said. Johnson nodded in agreement.

"You know it doesn't actually strangle *people*," I explained. I was beginning to think Johnson and Smith knew nothing about plants and weren't even from the Department of Agriculture.

"No, no, of course not," Smith said, laughing hollowly. "But bring some back just the same." The two men rose simultaneously and put their fedoras back on. I stood up, too.

"Professor Linden, we appreciate you taking on this mission. The Department of Agriculture appreciates it, too. Heck, even FDR appreciates it. We'll wire you more details and your tickets. Good day," Johnson said, and the two men tipped their hats to me as they retreated from my office.

I slumped back down in my chair. What had just happened? All my careful plans had now gone out the window. I had less than three weeks to prepare for an expedition to a place I knew next to nothing about. To find a plant I knew nothing about. But FDR would appreciate it? I seriously doubted President Roosevelt would care so much about my summer research as to send me five thousand miles from my original destination.

I no longer wanted to take a catnap in the warmth of my office. Now there was too much to do. I would have to go tell my father first and see what he made of the whole business. And then I'd go to the library. I needed to read up on the flora and culture of Malaya. At least Amaryllis would help make quick work of finding all the relevant books. She knew the stacks of the Agriculture Library like the back of her hand.

Chapter 2

The staccato clacking of my heels on the tile floor reverberated through the deserted hallway as I walked to my father's office on the first floor. His door was open, and I peeked in. He was writing at his desk. Looking up, he put down the pen and sat back in his chair.

"Ivy, come in. How was your final lecture today?" he asked with a grin.

"Hi, Dad. It was fine," I said as I sank into the worn burgundy leather chair opposite his desk. "You won't believe what just happened."

"Let me guess. Two men just told you you're going to Malaya!"

"You know about it?"

"Yes, they came to see me first. Wanted to know if I thought you'd be up for the trip. I assured them you would be."

"You did *what?* Oh, Dad, I can't believe my plans are ruined. And you could have stopped it? Why did you tell them I'd go?" I asked with frustration.

"I knew it was too good an opportunity to miss, Ivy. I'd go myself if I could. That expedition to Malaya and the Dutch East Indies in 1906 was one of the highlights of my career. You won't regret going. That tree you're so keen to find will wait another year, I'm sure."

"Well, why don't you come, too? At least you've been there before."

"Oh no, I couldn't possibly join you. I promised your mother we would go to Chautauqua this summer. We already have tickets to several concerts, lectures, and the opera. They're doing *Madame Butterfly*. We can't miss it. Besides, I'd only slow you down. You'll be fine on your own. I'm just writing to my friend Chasen at the Raffles Museum now. He'll take good care of you and get you all set up to go to Pulau Tioman. I've never been *there*. I do envy you," he said with a wistful sigh.

"Thanks, Dad. I appreciate your help. I'm going to need it. I don't even really know what I'm looking for. Those two men didn't tell me very much. Do you know them?"

"No, not at all. I don't think they usually work for the Department of Agriculture. I bet those weren't even their real names," he said, grinning. It was obvious the situation amused him.

"Why are you so excited? My meticulous plans are ruined."

"Honestly, Ivy, I didn't think that tree was so very interesting. No one else is going to look for that. But this . . . This is something else. This could be very important."

"I don't see why. There's plenty of quinine available from the *Cinchona* plantations on Java."

My father unfolded the copy of today's *Ithaca Journal* lying on his desk. There was a photo of three U.S. Army bombers flying over the skyscrapers of Manhattan on the front page. "'Chinese Regain Half of Lost Territory. Japanese Bombers Busy,'" he read. "'Duce Parades Gas Forces, Cannon for Fuehrer.' I know you prefer to read about the natives of the Amazon and Africa, but sometimes we have to pay attention to what the real savages are doing. I don't think we'll always be able to ignore what's going on in Europe and Asia."

"No, I suppose you're right. But I don't see what it's all got to do with me."

"I think we've all got a part to play, and this mission, I mean expedition, has got your name written all over it. After last summer in Africa, I know you'll be fine," he said, beaming with pride. The flattery of Johnson and Smith had not swayed me, but seeing my father's delight had begun to change my perspective. Maybe this was important.

"Fine. You've convinced me. I'll go, not that I seem to have much say in the matter, anyway. I guess I'll be studying as hard as my students next week."

Standing up, my father walked to one of his bookshelves and pulled a small brown hardcover book off the shelf and handed it to me. It was a Malay phrasebook.

"This will get you started. I'm sure Chasen will send someone with you as a translator, but best to know a few words."

"Thanks, Dad," I said as I took the little volume and riffled through the pages.

"No, no. Let's start now. Say 'terima kasih,'" he instructed, slipping into professor mode. I repeated the phrase.

"I'm going to the library now before Amaryllis goes

home. I hope she'll help me find some useful books and journal articles."

"Good idea. Tell her not to be late for dinner tonight. Her mother was most displeased last night. Off you go," he said as he ushered me out of his office.

After retrieving my satchel from my office, I locked the door behind me and walked over to the library, hopeful it would be empty and I could have Amaryllis to myself. The weather was so pleasant that it seemed a shame to enter the hushed dimness of the library, but I had no choice. I found Amaryllis alone at the reference desk. As my shadow fell across her open book, she looked up warily, but smiled when she saw me.

"Hi, Ivy! Boy, am I glad it's you! I was afraid it was a student coming for some last minute help finding books," Amaryllis said with relief. "Just an hour left today," she added, glancing at her wristwatch.

"Sis, it's worse than a student coming for some last minute help – it's a professor," I said, shrugging apologetically.

"What? Why? Your classes ended today. What could you possibly need now?"

"I hate to say it, but I need all the books on Malayan plant life that you have. And on the culture of Malaya. And on malaria and its treatment and prevention."

"That might be a lot of books," Amaryllis replied, narrowing her eyes. "Why?"

I started to explain about Johnson and Smith as we walked toward the massive oak card catalogs. Before I got very far, she interrupted.

"Remember when we ordered the magic tricks from Johnson Smith? And the ventriloquist's dummy? I never did learn how to not move my lips," she said with a sigh. I was gratified we'd had the same thought, but there was no time for reminiscing now.

"Yes, well this pair was from the Department of Agriculture, not the Department of Novelties, and they brought me the most distressing news. They cancelled my expedition and are sending me to Malaya instead of the Three Kings Islands. To look for some antimalarial plant they seem to have heard a rumor about. That's all I know."

"How dreadful! I know you were looking forward to that trip, though I can't quite fathom why. Still, Malaya seems like it's right up your alley. Full of poisonous snakes, man-eating tigers, headhunters, and the like," she teased.

"Yes, it does have all those attractions, and I'd want to go there someday, of course. But only after I've had a proper amount of time to prepare." We'd opened up a few long, narrow drawers. Conveniently, 'Malaria' was right before 'Malaya.' We both used stubby pencils to jot down titles and call numbers on scratch paper and headed off into the stacks in opposite directions.

After a few minutes, we met back at the reference desk with armloads of books. I selected the most promising titles, and Amaryllis checked them out. She stacked the rest of the books behind the counter with a note reserving them for me, not that anyone else was likely to come looking for these particular volumes.

"I'll help you find some journal articles on Monday," Amaryllis offered. "They'll have the latest research."

"Thanks, Amaryllis. You're a lifesaver. What would I do without you? Say, maybe you want to come with me?

It would be fun!"

"Come with you? And miss having the house to myself while Mother and Dad are in Chautauqua? Not on your life!"

"Oh, that reminds me. Dad said not to be late for dinner tonight."

"See, that's just what I mean. I'm looking forward to some independence while they're gone. Do you want to go to the movies tonight? There's a new Dorothy Lamour picture at the Strand. *Her Jungle Love.* Sounds like it's made for you!" Amaryllis said with a giggle.

"Ugh, no thanks! You know how I feel about those movies. They're silly at best, and at worst depict Indigenous people as savages, not as members of cultures filled with eons of natural wisdom. We could learn a lot from them. And don't even get me started on that Dorothy Lamour. She's not some exotic siren. She's from New Orleans, and she worked as a secretary."

"Well, it's just for fun. I'm going. It's in Technicolor. And it's got Ray Milland."

"I'll pass on Ray Milland, too. Besides, I've got too much to do now. I have to get started on this reading before I have my final exams to grade." I glanced at my watch; it was almost five. "I'll help you close up."

Once we had made sure there were no students hiding in the stacks, I gathered up my heavy leather satchel and headed to the exit as Amaryllis took a final look around inside, turned off the lights, and locked the doors behind us.

We chatted as we walked through the campus until we got to the point where we had to go in opposite directions, Amaryllis to our family home on Fall Creek

Drive and me to my rented house on Forest Home Drive. I walked along shifting the heavy bag of books from shoulder to shoulder. I didn't mind the exertion, but I knew I'd drive back to the library for the rest of the volumes. Soon I came to the little white bungalow I called home.

When I'd been offered the teaching position at Cornell, my mother was ecstatic. She assumed I would move back home and assured me she had kept my bedroom just as I'd left it. But I had to disappoint her. I couldn't live there and feel independent. At first I thought I'd just rent a room somewhere, but when I heard that the chapel was looking for a tenant for the parsonage next door, I jumped at the chance. I remembered visiting the little cottage back when Pearl Buck and her husband had lived there while she worked on her master's degree. I was entranced by her stories of China and further encouraged that I, too, could travel the world, despite being female. This was before she became a famous author, of course. A few years ago, she'd bought a farm outside of Philadelphia, and once on a trip back to Bryn Mawr, I had stopped to visit. I wasn't sure she'd remember me at all, but she had welcomed me so warmly. So I felt like her former abode was just the right location to start my professional life.

As I walked up to the front porch, a sleek form darted out from a bush and made a beeline for me. I paused and stooped to pet Osiris as he wound around my legs. It was hard to believe the tawny ball of fluff that Elspeth Huxley had given me when I departed Kenya last year had matured into this muscular, svelte creature. It was also surprising that the name that Elspeth had so grandly bestowed upon the Abyssinian kitten was now fitting. His bright green eyes and oversized ears gave him an exotic, wild appearance, but he had not looked like he could ever reign over the kingdom of the dead. However, in the last year he'd almost grown into his ears and had perfected his hunting skills, bringing me daily offerings of mice and, regrettably, the occasional chipmunk and songbird, the latter giving me pangs of guilt lest my friends at the Laboratory of Ornithology find out. I picked some burrs from his smooth coat and pet him for a few moments while he purred contentedly. He followed me inside eagerly. While he liked to hunt, he didn't seem to consider his prey to be food and was happy to see me each day for his dinner.

Inside, Rama sat regally on the back of the green velvet sofa, his eyes closed and his feet tucked under him. I suspected he was meditating on the path to nirvana and had lived many previous lives, not just the usual nine of felines. As Osiris and I disturbed his solitude, Rama opened his blue eyes, stretched, and jumped down to greet us. The two cats sniffed each other, and then Rama rubbed against me, as if to remind Osiris that I belonged to him first. The Siamese had been surprisingly patient with the new kitten and only occasionally swatted him away when he didn't feel like playing.

I dumped the weighty satchel of books on the floor, kicked off my shoes, and collapsed onto the sofa. Both cats began meowing in protest. I got back up, went to the kitchen, and opened a can of Puss 'n Boots. Their clamoring did not stop until they were both greedily lapping at saucers of the pungent food.

I sat back down on the sofa, watching the cats lick the

plates, and then themselves, clean and wished someone would put my dinner down in front of me. But that was not to be. I could have gone to my parents' house for dinner and then to the movies with Amaryllis for a distraction, but there was too much to do now. After a few minutes, I switched on the radio, and dance music drifted into the living room. I went back to the tidy, white kitchen to heat up some leftovers.

After dinner, I settled down on the couch with a monograph on the flora of the Malay Peninsula written more than forty years ago. From the cloud of dust and musty smell that greeted me when I opened it, I suspected I was the first person to take the book out of the library. I spent an hour absorbing different plant species and then picked up the Malay language book my father had given me. I tentatively repeated a few phrases, and Rama's ears perked up while he lay beside me with closed eyes. I wouldn't have been surprised if he understood.

I reflected on the unexpected events of the day. If my father hadn't been so excited at the prospect of me going to Singapore and Malaya, I would have been much more upset by the disruption of my methodical plans. Better to think of it as a challenge than a disappointment. Maybe this expedition *would* prove more interesting. Still, there was another regret I hadn't allowed myself to consider before. I had plans to meet a colleague in New Zealand. We had corresponded by mail for months now. He was a professor of botany at the University of Otago. Like me, he'd only had the position a couple years, so I figured he was about my own age. We'd had a very congenial correspondence about the plant life of Three Kings

Islands, and the topics had become more personal as the exchange of letters went on. We shared similar worldviews and tastes in books and art. I was looking forward to meeting him. To discuss plants, of course. But maybe . . . Well, that was foolish. I didn't even know what he looked like, anyway. I had pictured him with sandy hair and wire-rimmed eyeglasses, wearing a tweed jacket with suede elbow patches, maybe smoking a pipe, but as equally at home in the forest as in the library. He probably wouldn't have lived up to my expectations, so perhaps this was for the best. I'd have to write him a letter to explain I wouldn't be visiting after all. Maybe he'd be disappointed, too. The thought cheered me slightly.

Later I went upstairs, the cats trailing behind me, and got into bed. Spring nights were still cool in Ithaca, and snow was not unheard of in early May, so I was glad for the warmth of the chenille bedspread, covered with a fuzzy design of two showy peacocks and a border of pink and yellow flowers. The cats nestling against me provided additional warmth, although I knew they would each depart during the night to make their nocturnal rounds. I read for a while, a new book by Isak Dinesen called *Out of Africa*. Dinesen was a pseudonym for Baroness Karen Blixen, and I wondered if Elspeth knew her. I'd have to remember to ask in my next letter and enclose a photo of Osiris so she could see what a regal feline he had become.

CHAPTER 3

Normally I would have spent Saturday putting the finishing touches on my preparations for the trip to Three Kings, but now I felt like I was practically back at the very beginning. The botanical equipment I was taking to press specimens and bring back cuttings and seeds to propagate wouldn't change. Neither would the field journals, camera, film, and binoculars. My leather hiking boots with the sturdy rubber soles could stay, too. But now I needed to pack clothing for a hotter, wetter environment. I pulled out the heavier slacks, blouses, and jackets from my trunk and replaced them with the lightweight cotton and linen clothes I had acquired for the trips to the Amazon and Africa. The problem with traveling by Clipper was that I needed to look presentable for the journey. That meant a smart traveling suit, some stylish, feminine skirts and blouses, and a few simple day dresses. I recalled that the Raffles Hotel was known for being quite swanky. The men might be able to show up at the Long Bar wearing the same outfit they had just shot a tiger in, but it wouldn't do for me. I chose two additional dresses, including a formal evening gown, hopeful that was enough variety to get me through any social engagements. I added mosquito netting and my pith helmet to the top of the pile.

For several hours I occupied myself with reading my new books, jotting down notes and sketches of promising plants. Maybe one of these plants was the species I was supposed to find. Maybe it would be as easy as asking the islanders which one was useful against malaria. Maybe no one had ever thought to ask them before. I was beginning to build up enthusiasm for this mysterious quest. And just maybe it would go so smoothly that I would still have time to visit Three Kings afterward.

When I felt I could absorb no more, I picked up the day's copy of the *Ithaca Journal* from the bottom step of the porch where the paperboy had thrown it hours before. Unrolling it and opening it up, a little advertisement reminded me to "Wear a Rose for MOTHER on Mother's Day Tomorrow." Oh, it had slipped my mind with all the excitement. We were taking Mother to dinner at the Monarch Restaurant on Sunday. Amaryllis and I had chipped in to buy her a new Smith-Corona typewriter from Rothschild's Department Store. Then I noticed the small ad from the Strand Theatre. "Last Times Today." Maybe I *would* go see *Her Jungle Love* tonight. It did seem a shame to miss a movie in Technicolor.

I took the bus downtown and grabbed a bite to eat at the Normandie. I sat at the counter of the luncheonette and ordered a chicken salad sandwich, a cup of tomato soup, and a root beer. I was happy to see no one I knew and pulled the little Malay phrasebook from my handbag to study while I ate, silently repeating the words to myself.

To pass a few minutes before the show, I admired the chic new summer dresses in the windows of Holley's and Crawford's Department Store. Rudolph's had a display of new radios in streamlined wooden cabinets. I briefly wondered if one of them would have been a better Mother's Day gift than the typewriter. No, Mother would like the typewriter. It was useful and a beautiful emerald green enamel. And quiet. The salesman had let us try the floor model, and the keys made a gentle swishing sound. That would make Dad happy as well. Mother wrote a gardening column for the newspaper. At first it had just been for the local paper, but then other newspapers had taken note, and it had been syndicated. Would-be gardeners across the country now read Mrs. Iris Linden's "Garden Spot" each week, hoping they would learn to grow the dahlias, cacti, orchids, and prizewinning tomatoes she made look so easy. Of course she had the full resources of Cornell's College of Agriculture at her disposal, experts in botany, plant breeding, ornamental horticulture, and plant pathology. Yet she possessed the one skill that could not be taught in the classroom or acquired through books: the proverbial 'green thumb.' She could coax any seed to sprout or flower to bloom. Even the most learned professors sometimes asked their colleague Dr. Linden if his wife might just come and have a look at a plant that was giving them problems. Amaryllis had inherited this trait, yet I was not so fortunate. I'd have to ask Barbara to explain that to me someday. She was one of Dad's botany students back in the twenties, but now she was Professor McClintock at the University of Missouri. Her work in maize genetics was becoming very well known, and she was even awarded a Guggenheim Fellowship to study in Berlin a few years ago. But she had said in her last letter that she didn't particularly like Missouri. Her colleagues weren't so accepting of her. I understood, and I sometimes wondered if the other professors here treated me better than they would have because of my father.

I glanced at my wristwatch. Time for the show. I walked over to the Strand Theatre, hoping I wouldn't bump into any of my students. Or worse, another professor. The marquee of the Tudor-style building announced *Her Jungle Love* was on the bill for tonight. It was a far cry from the traveling Shakespeare productions that had sometimes played here before the talkies had taken center stage. I pulled the little brim of my hat down as far as I could and walked up to the window to buy a ticket. Inside, I bought a small glassine bag of popcorn and climbed the stairs to the balcony. There was less of a chance of being seen up here. Most other patrons would be too preoccupied with each other in the dark and relative privacy afforded by the balcony to notice a Cornell professor watching such lowbrow entertainment.

The lights dimmed, and the red velvet curtain parted to reveal the movie screen. A newsreel and a couple cartoon shorts played before the main feature started. Then the music swelled, and the credits rolled over a lush tropical isle background of mountains and palm trees. Two flyers were looking for a fellow aviator lost during a typhoon. Flying for Indo-Malayan Transport. Well, that was a coincidence. There were plenty of other jungles for Dorothy Lamour to find love in, but it seemed she was on an island near Malaya. Maybe she would mention what plants are good for malaria and save me a trip.

Naturally the flyers found sarong-wearing Tura alone on the island with just her pet lion cub and chimpanzee for company. I groaned audibly at the sight of them. How did two species that live in Africa end up in Malaya? I didn't dare to look closely at the foliage in each scene, or I'm sure I would have felt even more outrage. At least the plants were green thanks to the Technicolor.

The plot was laughable and predictable, but I found myself being drawn in and less critical about halfway through. By the end, I was rooting for the hapless flyers as they were threatened by crocodiles, unfriendly islanders, and crumbling caverns. I even hoped Ray Milland would pick Tura over his whiny high society fiancée. Of course he did, and it was "all's well that ends well," except for the pilot they had originally sought out to rescue; he'd made a tasty snack for a hungry crocodile. While I had to admit the story was entertaining, it was completely ridiculous; I knew my jungle expedition would not contain the sort of adventure that makes for a good movie. And my only jungle love would be the new species of plants I was sure to see.

When the final credits stopped rolling, the theater lights came on, and the crowd clapped enthusiastically. They had not been as critical an audience as I and were satisfied by the scantily-clad Lamour and her assortment of incongruous animal companions. Perhaps they had the right idea, I reflected, as I crumpled the empty bag of popcorn and departed the theater unobserved.

The next day, I affixed a bow of yellow ribbon to the new typewriter and carefully placed it in the back of our motorcar, cushioning it with a blanket on all sides to keep it secure. The Stout Scarab was not mine, but really belonged to my father. He had wanted us to share it, though, and I had the driveway to accommodate it, while he had a less conspicuous Chrysler in his own driveway. He said we could use it for fieldwork and take our students out on local botanizing trips. But I suspected that was just an excuse to acquire the unique automobile. It was sort of a miniature bus, streamlined and named for the beetle it resembled. It had proven useful for both of us over the past two years, and the students did enjoy piling in to visit different locations. We would take it to dinner today, although my father would inevitably insist on driving, relegating Amaryllis and me to the back. I gave 'Tut,' as I called the car, a fond pat on its sleek, glossy teal green hood.

I pulled up to the curb in front of my parents' house and waved. My mother and Amaryllis were already sitting on the porch. Mother was smiling and wearing a gardenia corsage. Amaryllis dashed over and opened the rear door to help with the typewriter. I carried it up the walkway while she stood in front, shielding the gift with a flowered shawl.

"Happy Mother's Day!" I said, while Amaryllis drew the shawl away with a flourish.

"Ohhhh," Mother gasped with delight. "It's beautiful! It's just the model I wanted! Thank you, girls. You really shouldn't have," she said, beaming. I knew we'd chosen the right present and placed it on the table inside the door.

I kissed Mother on the cheek and inhaled the heady scent of the gardenia.

"I've been growing the gardenia in one of the

greenhouses near the library all year, and lucky for me it bloomed just in time for Mother's Day," Amaryllis said with pride.

"And lucky for all of us that it was the gardenia, not the titan arum, that bloomed," Dad said, chuckling as he came outside. He could never resist making a joke about that most unusual specimen, with its practically obscene giant inflorescence reeking of rotting flesh.

"Perhaps you should have left that one in Sumatra where it came from, Reed," Mother said. "And those durian trees, too," she added, wrinkling her nose. "Ivy, I do hope whatever you're supposed to find does not smell so dreadful."

Dad began ushering us to the car, opening the back door for Amaryllis and me as if we were still children. He settled Mother in the front and sat in the driver's seat beside her. Amaryllis sprawled out on the back seat, and I sat in the middle seat. It was turned around to face the little table that pulled out from the side of the car. As we began to crawl down the steep streets of Ithaca like the beetle for which the car was named, I wished I had turned the seat around to face forward and see the road ahead of us. But the ride was short, and we soon arrived at the Monarch for supper.

We had a superb meal of steaks and fresh asparagus, followed by Peach Melba and tiny cups of strong coffee. Dad had already informed Mother about my change of travel plans, and she was not nearly as enthusiastic.

"Ivy, why don't you just tell those men no? In fact, you should just come to Chautauqua with us instead. Wouldn't that be lovely, dear?" she suggested.

"Mother, I can't say no. I have to do fieldwork. I can't

waste the summer at Chautauqua, as pleasant as that would be. There's nothing for me to discover there," I retorted.

"Oh, I'm not so sure about that, Ivy. Professor Oakley's daughter discovered a very eligible bachelor there, and now they're married," she said smugly.

"Well, I'm not just Professor Linden's daughter. *I'm* Professor Linden, too. And if I want keep on being a professor here, I've got to make a name for myself."

"Yes, I suppose so. But you know how I worry. Especially about you flying. We lost too many friends last year. And I have a feeling you didn't even tell me everything about your trip to Kenya last summer."

She was right; we had lost several friends in airplane accidents, but I wasn't worried about that. The Clipper was known for its safety. And she was right about last summer. I'd left out plenty of details about that trip. Why worry her needlessly? Besides, nothing like that would happen again.

"Don't worry, Mother. It'll be perfectly safe, and Dad even has friends at the Raffles Museum. They'll look out for me," I reassured her. I didn't need anyone to look out for me, but there was no convincing her of that.

After supper, we took a scenic drive along Cayuga Lake. We passed the airport with the new hangar as we headed north, and I thought back to our earlier conversation. None of us spoke, and I wondered if everyone was thinking back to that day in 1932 when we'd all gotten to fly at the airport. Not just fly in the airplane, but actually take the controls. It was exhilarating, but now the memory was tinged with sadness.

"What's your next column on, Mother?" Amaryllis asked, as if to change the subject no one was talking about.

"It's on different varieties of lilacs," Mother said, brightening. "They should be in bloom in Rochester any day now, and of course Memorial Day is coming up. I do wish the photographs could be in color, though. I certainly do look forward to writing the next column using my Mother's Day present."

The rest of the ride was pleasant, and I was sure to steer the conversation away from my trip. My mother would have been doubly disappointed about the change in destination if she had known I had plans to meet Professor Bracken at the University of Otago. I had confessed my correspondence with him had extended beyond the botanical to Amaryllis. She had let it slip, and our mother would periodically ask me how that "nice young man in New Zealand" was doing with a feigned nonchalance to hide her hopefulness that a suitor had met my exacting specifications.

The sun was low in the sky when we arrived back at my parents' home. I came inside for a few minutes to see the latest orchids blooming in their greenhouse. As I left to go home, my father pressed a large book into my hands.

"Here, Ivy, I thought you could use this. For your trip."

I looked at the title. It was a plant physiology textbook I already had.

"Oh, thanks, Dad, but I have this book already," I said as I started to hand it back to him.

"This is a new edition. I think it might be useful," he

said, pushing it back toward me. I appraised the cover skeptically; it looked older than the one I had. But I could see there was no arguing, and I shrugged, giving him a kiss on the cheek. I did the same to Mother and Amaryllis and walked out to Tut, reclaiming the driver's seat.

When I got back home, I parked Tut carefully in the narrow driveway and traced my finger around the scarab design on the hood. Osiris appeared out of nowhere and followed me inside. I put the heavy book down on the table. I was sure I had a newer version. When I opened the cover to check the publication date, I did not see the title page I expected. Instead, a compartment had been cut out from the pages of the book. Concealed in a hollow inside the thick book, where facts of plant physiology should have been, was a small Colt vest pocket pistol. I closed the cover.

CHAPTER 4

After I had loaded up the motorcar with my books from the library and additional journals with articles that might be relevant to the expedition, I drove over to my building and began to bring everything up to my office. Once it was all inside, I got to work reading. Every now and then, one of my students would stop in to ask a question about the final exam. At noon I walked downstairs to my father's office for lunch. Mother had sent sandwiches for both of us.

"You didn't already have that edition of the plant physiology book, did you?" Dad asked as he unwrapped the wax paper covering his sandwich.

"No, I certainly did not."

"Well, it's good to have. Just in case. You'll take it with you, won't you? You never know when you might need it."

"Sure, Dad. I'll take it with me," I promised. I didn't see what good it would do, though. I doubted the little pistol could stop a charging tiger or a determined crocodile. He handed me an extra magazine filled with bullets.

"Take this, too. I picked out the mother-of-pearl

grips just for you. Don't mention it to your mother, though."

"That goes without saying," I said, laughing. We didn't speak of it again.

In the afternoon I penned a letter to Heath, as I now called Professor Bracken of Otago, telling him of my change of plans. I would post it via airmail, but I knew he wouldn't get it in time for me to receive his reply before I left.

Before I knew it, a week had passed. It was Monday again, and my students were back to take their final exams. I handed out copies of the questions and sat down to read while they began furiously scribbling out the answers. I didn't look forward to deciphering their handwriting, but I knew I would get it all done by the end of the week, and then the semester would really be over for me.

By noon almost all the students had handed in their papers. I told the remaining stragglers that their time was up, and they reluctantly put down their pens. After depositing their efforts in my office, I met Amaryllis at our father's office. Mother had sent a picnic lunch for us, and we walked outside to find a spot to spread a blanket. The trees were now fully leafed. While the chance of snow had finally passed, the temperature could still dip enough for frost at night.

"Have you heard more details about your trip?" Dad asked.

"Yes, the tickets arrived today. They're flying me to San Francisco. Faster than the train I was supposed to take. And they changed my reservations aboard the

Clipper for Auckland to Manila, instead. Then a steamer to Singapore. Someone there will fly me to Tioman."

"Oh, I do envy you," he said wistfully.

"I don't know, Dad. The more I read, the less I know what I'm even looking for."

"I'm sure you'll find whatever you're meant to find," he said cryptically as he munched on an egg salad sandwich.

I shrugged, and the topic turned to the new varieties of daylilies that Mother and Amaryllis had planted. We lingered over the pleasant conversation and Mother's oatmeal cookies until I couldn't put off the inevitable. I stood up to brush the crumbs off my skirt and headed back inside to begin grading the final exams.

The newly sharpened red pencils lined up in a row cheered me slightly as I sat down at my desk with the stack of blue composition books in front of me. Perhaps my students had learned the material so well that my crimson points would not be dulled.

I gave up after a few hours and sharpened all the pencils again. I knew it would take me a few days to get through all the exams and then tally the grades for each student. This was my least favorite part of being a professor, and the mounting excitement for the upcoming expedition only made the task more unbearable.

After several days of work punctuated by breaks to practice Malay, the exams were finally graded. I submitted the grades and posted the scores for the students to see. Most could be proud of their efforts, and I was gratified to know a new crop of students had gained some knowledge and appreciation of botany.

Now I could turn my full attention to last-minute

preparations for my trip. I had received nothing more from Johnson and Smith in the way of instructions. I decided to adopt my father's attitude and embrace the unknown that this journey held, a departure from my usual desire to plan out every detail.

At last it was the eve of my flight. I had dinner with my parents and Amaryllis at their home. My mother assured me I was still welcome in Chautauqua if I changed my mind, but there was no turning back now. I gave Amaryllis the instructions for feeding Rama and Osiris while I was gone and knew she would spoil them with homegrown catnip and extra saucers of milk.

The next morning, I went over my checklist one last time. I tried to close my trunk, but the latches wouldn't fasten. I took out the bulky pith helmet and replaced it with a wide-brimmed felt bush hat that Osa and Martin Johnson had given me when they came back from Borneo. I caught myself wondering if it might be bad luck for a moment, but immediately banished the thought. I locked the trunk and carried it outside to Tut. The automobile was packed with my collecting equipment and other gear. Soon Mother, Dad, and Amaryllis rolled up in their Chrysler.

"Are you all set, Ivy?" Dad asked. "You did pack the plant physiology book, right?"

"Yes, Dad, it's right here," I said, patting my leather shoulder bag.

"Good, keep it close by just in case there are any plant physiology issues you need to deal with." Fortunately, my mother and Amaryllis had ignored this odd exchange and were occupied with pulling a few errant weeds in the flowerbed and fawning over the cats, respectively. I knew I was leaving things in good hands and would probably return to a tidier garden and plumper cats.

We piled into the Scarab with Dad at the wheel and drove downtown toward the airport. Once again, a hush fell over us as our conversations drifted away. Finally, Mother broke the silence when we arrived at the airport.

"Are you sure you wouldn't rather stay here for the summer?" she asked. "You can still change your mind."

"No, Mother, I have to go. It's a commercial flight. It's perfectly safe. Don't worry."

"How can I not worry? After what happened to Osa and Martin last year? They were on a commercial flight. And then Amelia."

It was true we had lost friends last year. Osa and Martin Johnson were on a commercial flight to California. The weather had turned ominous, and the pilot hadn't seen the mountainside looming in front of them. Martin had died in the crash, and Osa was still recovering from her injuries. It seemed cruelly ironic after all the dangerous flying they had done in their own airplanes throughout Africa and Borneo that they should experience this tragedy on a routine commercial flight at home. Of course, Amelia Earhart's tragedy was not so routine, as she was on the final leg of her attempt to fly around the world. Although almost a year had passed, we still held out hope that she and her navigator, Fred Noonan, might be found alive somewhere.

I tried to reassure my mother as best I could. Meanwhile, some porters had come over to us to help with the luggage and equipment. They began to stow my trunks in the cargo hold of the waiting aircraft. I hoped my mother didn't realize the silver Ithaca Airways airplane was a Lockheed Electra, not too different from Amelia's plane. But we were only flying the well-traveled route to Chicago, not over the vast Pacific.

Once all the trunks were safely aboard, one of the men even offered to take my shoulder bag, but I didn't want to let it out of my sight. Not only did it have the little pistol, but also my Malay phrasebook and trip journal, which would keep me occupied for the cross-country journey.

A few other passengers had begun milling around the aircraft. Soon a steward came out to examine tickets and began ushering the travelers aboard.

"Goodbye, Ivy. Have a safe trip. Send us a telegram when you arrive in San Francisco," my mother said stoically. I could tell it was an effort for her not to shed a tear.

"I know you'll find what you're looking for. We're proud of you," Dad added.

"Good luck, Ivy! Have fun and watch out for those tigers and crocodiles!" said Amaryllis, throwing her arms around me.

A steward helped me through the cabin door, and I found my seat. I looked out the window and watched Mother, Dad, and Amaryllis retreat a safe distance to the Scarab. As the other nine passengers and I settled in for the flight, we heard the sound of the engines starting. We began to taxi to the runway. I waved at my family until I could no longer see them. The engines hummed, and we started to race down the runway, picking up speed until we were airborne. As the plane banked to turn toward Chicago, I watched Tut and the three waving figures grow smaller and smaller. There was no turning back now, so I gazed out the window on the greenery below and wondered what I might discover on this journey.

The flight was pleasant enough with just a little turbulence. Whenever the plane shook or dropped a bit, I remembered Amelia telling me it was just like driving over a bumpy road and not to worry. Soon we were landing in Chicago, and I had a few hours to stretch my legs before the next flight. I wanted to wait on the runway to watch my equipment being unloaded, but I was shepherded inside and assured it would all be transferred to the next aircraft.

I found a corner table in the United Air Lines lounge and sat down to catch up on correspondence. I wrote a long letter to Elspeth Huxley first, then a short one to Osa Johnson, telling her of my expedition and that I was taking the bush hat she and Martin had given me along on the adventure. The hours passed, and then it was time to embark on the next leg of the journey aboard a United Air Lines Mainliner. The trip from Chicago to San Francisco would take just about eleven hours with a stop in Cheyenne, Wyoming for fuel.

United's Mainliner was the most luxurious version of the Douglas DC-3 aircraft. The original twenty-one-passenger configuration would have been plenty plush enough for me, but Johnson and Smith had booked me on the 'Skylounge' model. There were seats for just fourteen passengers, seven on each side of the aircraft. The seats, well-padded lounge chairs that could swivel and recline, were even more comfortable than those found in most homes.

I climbed the metal staircase that had been rolled up

to the side of the plane, and a stewardess dressed in a smart sage green suit and matching pillbox hat escorted me to the seat I'd occupy for the flight. Moments later, another stewardess came by to offer me hot coffee and tea. I accepted a cup of tea and watched with interest as the other passengers embarked. They were mostly men in business suits and a few couples. I speculated about why each person was making the trip. Probably for business, I guessed, but one young couple was clearly on their honeymoon.

I noticed the seat in front of me start to swivel slowly, then suddenly turn to fully face me. "Hello, sweetheart," said the man occupying the seat as he eyed me. "I'm Bob Lloyd. What's your name?"

"Hello, Mr. Lloyd. I'm Ivy Linden."

"Is it Miss or Mrs. Linden?" he asked, his gaze falling on my left hand.

"It's Dr. Linden, although my students call me Professor Linden."

"Professor? What do you teach? English? Home Economics?"

"No, I'm an ethnobotanist. Sometimes I teach botany, sometimes plant physiology."

"Oh, you must be smart," he said, looking chagrined. "I don't like smart women," he added. This was not the first time I'd heard such a comment and had been on the verge of a sharp retort when the stewardess announced all seats needed to face forward in preparation for takeoff. Mr. Lloyd readily complied, and I was glad to see only the back of him for the remainder of the journey.

Soon the aircraft was ready to depart, and the twin engines came to life. We were airborne and heading west in no time, the lights of Chicago disappearing behind us. After about an hour in the air, the stewardess came through the cabin to announce that dinner would be served shortly. She set up a small table in front of each passenger, complete with white tablecloth, china, and silverware. She served each of us a hot chicken dinner, accompanied by mixed vegetables, mashed potatoes, and a warm roll. I looked at the tiny porcelain salt and pepper shakers with the United Air Lines logo on my table and briefly considered keeping them as a souvenir of this luxurious flight. But I reminded myself that would be stealing, and I'd be stuck carrying them around for the next two months. Besides, I could always swipe them on the way home.

After some tapioca pudding for dessert, the stewardess cleared away the dishes and then the little tables. She returned to the cabin to offer magazines and decks of cards to the passengers. A woman behind me tapped my shoulder and asked if I'd like to join her and her husband in a game of Hearts. I readily agreed, relieved the unpleasant man in front of me had not turned his seat to face mine again. I swiveled around, and the stewardess placed a card table in the aisle for us. The man across the aisle from me consented to play as well, and the four of us occupied the next few hours amiably.

After dozing off in the plush recliner for a while, I felt the plane begin to descend. We had passed over the dry, flat land of the Midwest, and as we approached Cheyenne, the Rocky Mountains were now barely visible in the distance. After a smooth landing, all the passengers disembarked from the aircraft. As comfortable as the seats were, it was good to be up and walking again. We filed into the brick terminal and milled around for a bit. I stopped at the lunch counter to get a little paper cup of coffee and went outside to admire a fountain near the terminal. Made of terracotta tiles, a tower a bit reminiscent of the Empire State Building was set in the middle of a round fountain decorated with bas-relief clouds and aircraft very similar to the one that had brought me to Cheyenne. I sat on the edge of the fountain, watching the water dancing around the tower and marveling at the expanse of open sky with a view for miles.

Once again, it was time to depart. All of us returned to the Mainliner, which had been fueled and was ready to take us on the final leg of our journey to San Francisco. The stewardess, who could not possibly have slept, looked just as bright and fresh as when we left Chicago. She served us a breakfast of eggs, bacon, and grapefruit halves once we were airborne again. As we flew over mountains and lakes, I thought about the plant life far below and wondered what might be left to discover right here in our own vast country. The view from the window was so mesmerizing that I didn't open the Malay phrasebook once.

Some hours later, I felt the aircraft begin to dip as we made our approach to San Francisco. Once we had rolled to a stop at the airport, I gathered up my belongings. Only then did it occur to me I didn't know what to do next. My flight on the Pan American China Clipper did not depart until the following morning. I began to chastise myself for not planning lodging and transportation, but as I disembarked I caught sight of a man in a dark suit at the end of the ramp. As I got closer,

I realized his suit was the uniform of a chauffeur, and he was holding a small placard with my name. I needn't have worried. He insisted on taking my bag, which I reluctantly gave up, and led me to a waiting car, explaining that he was taking me to the Mark Hopkins Hotel downtown. My gear would be transported to the Pan American terminal in Alameda. I would have liked to oversee this process myself, but decided to trust that it would be taken care of properly and instead enjoyed the scenery as we drove into the city.

The chauffeur accompanied me into the hotel, ensured that I was checked in and would be taken care of by the concierge, and told me he would collect me at eight the following morning to drive me to Alameda for my flight. Finally alone in my room on the fifteenth floor, I admired the view of the city, then freshened up and changed my clothes. Back in the lobby, I asked the solicitous concierge to send a telegram to my parents announcing I had arrived safely, and then I strode down the street toward Union Square. There I caught a streetcar to take me to Golden Gate Park.

I was tempted to visit the aquarium or the African Hall at the California Academy of Sciences, but instead I slipped upstairs to a part of the building not open to the public. I walked past cabinets filled with pressed plant specimens until I reached the office of the herbarium curator. I rapped softly on the doorframe. The white-haired botanist bent over a pressed sample looked up at me.

"Ivy Linden!" she exclaimed. "What a surprise! Come in, come in," the curator said as she rose to greet me. We embraced, and she gestured to a chair in front of her desk.

"Hello, Alice! I'm sorry to drop in without warning, but I only just found myself with some time to spare in San Francisco, and of course I wanted to see you." Alice Eastwood was a botanical legend, and I was still humbled to think of her as a colleague. She was almost eighty years old now, but she was still going strong. Alice had saved the Academy's herbarium collections from destruction in the 1906 earthquake and had been their guardian ever since. Not only did she tend to the samples in the laboratory, but she collected them herself in the field, too. Although it was still rare, it was practically unheard of for a woman to do fieldwork when Alice started in the previous century.

We spent the rest of the afternoon chatting about my family, her recent field trips in the United States, and my upcoming expedition. I promised to collect duplicate samples to deposit in the Academy's herbarium on my way back home.

I walked part of the way back to the hotel and then took a cable car to Chinatown, as I didn't feel like having dinner in the swanky hotel restaurant. I strolled along Grant Avenue and chose one of the many chop suey houses marked with a gaudy neon sign. I ordered the standard fare, knowing the dish was not authentic at all, but it seemed like a fitting choice for my last night in the States. I was tempted to take in a floorshow at one of the neighborhood's famed nightclubs afterward, but I knew it would be unseemly for a woman alone, and more importantly, I had to turn in early to be rested for tomorrow's journey. I walked back to the Mark Hopkins. From my perch above the city I watched twilight turn into night as the automobile headlights, streetlights, and neon signs twinkled below.

CHAPTER 5

The black sedan pulled up to the curb in front of the Mark Hopkins at precisely eight the next morning. The same chauffeur emerged from the automobile, took my bag, and opened the door for me. As he closed the door, it occurred to me that I didn't even know whom he worked for or how this had all been arranged. I felt vaguely uneasy, but before I could ask any questions, he was behind the wheel again, and we were motoring toward Alameda. There was little traffic as we cruised along the Bay Bridge, and soon we reached Oakland. In a few more minutes, we were at the Pan American terminal at the Alameda Airport. Beyond us, the China Clipper, a big Martin M-130 four-engine flying boat, lay at anchor in the Pan American Lagoon.

A porter met the car, and the chauffeur entrusted me to his care. He was expecting me, he explained, and all my gear had already been loaded aboard the Clipper. I wanted to see it for myself, but decided not to make a fuss. The porter also mentioned that there was another woman traveling to Manila alone, and they had taken the liberty of putting us in the same sleeping compartment. There was some time before the flight, so I sat inside the air terminal, a large but rather utilitarian structure which belied the luxury of the Pan American aircraft and the glamour of the exotic destinations it would visit.

Finally, boarding was announced, and a small group of us made our way down a long ramp into the lagoon where the China Clipper awaited us. There were to be just eight passengers on this leg of the trip to Hawaii, the porter explained as he helped each of us aboard. We were shown to comfortable chairs in a central lounge area. I sat down on what resembled a plush sofa that would be found in a living room. Small rectangular windows on both sides of the fuselage gave us a view of San Francisco across the bay.

The aircraft swayed gently as the crew moved about in final preparations for the flight. There were no pontoons attached to the wings like on other flying boats, but seawings called sponsons projecting from the base of the fuselage. The whole crew introduced themselves to us as they went back and forth through the cabin to prepare for departure. The other passengers consisted of four businessmen, a married couple, and the other woman traveling alone.

"I'm Helen," said the pretty blonde with carefully curled hair and a smart peaked hat. "Are you by yourself, too?"

"Yes, I'm Ivy. I think we're going to be sharing a sleeping cabin."

"I'm so happy there's another girl aboard. I've never been to the Orient before. Or on a flying boat. I'm going to Manila. To get married," she added with a gleaming smile. "My sweetheart Harry is there, and we just couldn't wait until he came home, so I decided to join him. It's loads more exciting than New Jersey, anyway. Are you meeting a sweetheart, too?"

"No, I'm a professor of botany. I'm going to look for a plant," I said, my voice trailing off as I realized how odd it sounded. Helen looked at me with wide eyes.

"A professor? A plant? By yourself? What an adventure! Have you been there before?"

"No," I confessed. "I've been to South America and Africa to look for plants, but this will be my first trip to Asia."

"And you're really going by yourself? Won't someone be meeting you?"

"Yes, I think so. In Singapore, anyway. Someone from the museum there." I was about to start telling her of the search for the plant with antimalarial properties, but it occurred to me she might not be that interested, and maybe I wasn't supposed to tell anyone, anyway. The whole trip seemed more secretive than a typical botany collecting expedition.

I needn't have worried about making small talk, as Helen began a lengthy discourse on how she'd met Harry, their courtship, and wedding plans. As she grew more and more animated, I realized she would be my constant companion for the entire trip across the Pacific. I began to suspect she would have no trouble talking for the whole journey, and my Malay phrasebook would be neglected for this stage of the trip, as well. But I didn't mind her cheerful chatter yet, and I was happy for the companionship.

Finally, it was time to depart; the steward asked us to fasten our seatbelts until we were airborne. I turned toward the window as the four engines whirred to life.

We taxied away from the pier slowly while the small crowd gathered there waved farewell. Picking up speed, we headed out of the lagoon toward open water. Now the hull of the flying boat cut through the waves as we accelerated, and the shore became a blur. I was engrossed in the process of taking off until I felt a sudden pain. Helen, now silent, had grabbed my arm with a vise-like grip, surprising for such a delicate woman. I patted her hand, and she loosened her hold.

"Don't worry, Helen. We're almost in the air, and it's going to be a perfectly safe trip. Let's look out the window now." She obeyed, and the Clipper broke free of the water. We gained altitude and circled back over Alameda and Oakland before flying over the Bay Bridge and then the spectacular orange of the Golden Gate Bridge. I marveled at the feats of modern engineering that led to the construction of both bridges, made even more amazing by viewing them from above in this streamlined flying boat that would carry us across the Pacific in just a few short days. Such marvelous advances were barely believable, and yet I couldn't help wondering what older wisdom and knowledge was being brushed aside in the name of progress. It made my task all the more urgent. I might have continued in my reverie, gazing out at the blue of the Pacific, had Helen not regained her composure and enthusiasm for telling me of her domestic plans.

I listened politely with little interest until she started to talk about her garden.

"I am going to miss the garden at my family's home in New Jersey, though. They don't call it the 'Garden State' for nothing. You should see the tomatoes we grow.

And all the flowers. My mother would pick a fresh bouquet every day in the summer. But we can't take all the credit. Our secret is a newspaper column that we read every week. We always follow the hints in the 'Garden Spot.'"

"Yes, I read that one, too," I said, chuckling.

"That Iris Linden is so full of knowledge. She must have the best garden. I'd sure like to meet her someday."

"She would love to meet you, too. So would Amaryllis, I'm sure. You and Harry should come for a visit when you return from the Philippines."

Helen looked at me blankly, speechless for a moment.

"Iris Linden is my mother," I explained. "Amaryllis is my sister, and she's got a green thumb, too. I don't, so I just stick to teaching about plants. And looking for new ones and the uses that people in other cultures have for them."

"I can't believe it!" Helen said with a squeal. "Wait until I tell my mother about this! What are the chances of traveling with Iris Linden's daughter for five days? We *will* come visit, and maybe I can bring my mother, too."

"Of course, we'd love to have her. Will you start a garden in your new home in the Philippines?"

"Gee, I don't know. I haven't thought about it. Maybe there already is one at Harry's bungalow. I guess I should learn about the plants that grow there."

"I have an idea. How would you like to be a special correspondent for the 'Garden Spot?' You can write a column about what you are growing and send some photos. I know my mother would like that."

"You mean it? Gosh, that would be swell. My mother would be so proud of me," Helen said, beaming.

"And could you talk to the local people about the plants they grow that you've never seen before and write down how they use them? And save some seeds for me?"

"Oh, yes, that would be wonderful! I didn't know how I could occupy my time when Harry's not at home, but this will give me a purpose! I'll learn everything I can to report back to you and your mother. Now I'm even more excited than before!"

Helen's anxiety about the flight had completely dissipated, and we settled into easy conversation, interrupted only by the steward serving us a hot lunch and, later, dinner. Afterward, he announced that our sleeping chambers had been made up and showed us to a small, curtained area with an upper and lower berth. I offered to take the top bunk, and Helen seemed relieved. Once we were both changed into our sleeping attire with the curtains secured around us, we bid each other goodnight and let the soft and steady hum of the four engines lull us to sleep.

CHAPTER 6

Only the smell of coffee was enough to entice me from the comfort of the plush mattress. I peeked through the curtains and saw that Helen was just waking up, too. We dressed and went back to the lounge to have a light breakfast of pastries and fruit. The sun was rising, and we were nearly at our destination. As I looked out at the expanse of blue below, I spotted a shape emerging on the horizon. It came into focus, and the steward announced we would be landing shortly.

Safely buckled in again, we flew over Oahu, and I recognized the profile of Diamond Head from photos I'd seen. Then we saw a cluster of buildings close to the beach and a larger city I knew must be Honolulu. Passing it, we descended as we reached Pearl Harbor, the U.S. Navy's base with battleships lined up in a row. The captain made a smooth landing in the water, more gentle than on land, and we skimmed along until we came to a stop at the dock of the Pan American terminal.

The crew helped us ashore where a small group of Hawaiian men dressed in flowered shirts played ukuleles, and women in grass skirts welcomed us with flower leis. A double rainbow extended over Pearl Harbor, seemingly also to welcome us. Looking toward the center of the island, a forested ridge rose up beyond the inhabited regions. The steep terrain looked untouched, and I wondered what plants might grow there and nowhere else in the world. Looking back to the water, the row of warships was unsettling and seemed out of place in such a serene locale.

The Pan American representatives gathered us together and ushered us onto a small bus to take us on a short sightseeing tour of Honolulu and deposit us at the Royal Hawaiian Hotel where we would stay overnight. We passed the Aloha Tower and the opulent Iolani Palace before entering the resort area of Waikiki Beach where the massive, pink Moorish-style hotel waited for us.

A small army of porters from the Royal Hawaiian solicitously took our luggage and led us to our rooms.

"Ivy, what are you going to do for the day?" Helen asked.

"I haven't decided yet, but I suppose I'll go to the Bishop Museum and the Foster Botanical Garden. I have a few colleagues I could visit."

"Oh, don't you want to go to the beach? That's what I'm going to do."

"I hadn't thought about it, but I guess that would be nice. I didn't bring a bathing suit, though," I said, certain that would put an end to the matter.

"No bathing suit?" Helen exclaimed. "You're traveling across the Pacific to all these tropical isles, and you didn't pack a bathing suit?"

I shrugged and realized Helen was leading me by the hand back toward the lobby.

"There's a lovely boutique right here. I'm sure they have something that would suit you," suggested Helen.

"Well, I guess it couldn't hurt to have a bathing suit. A day at the beach might be nice," I said reluctantly. Then again, no one even knew I was here, and I could always visit the botanists at the gardens and museum on the way back. Before I knew it, I was carrying a parcel containing a new swimsuit, a skirted princess-style in a print of diagonal green palm trees on a white background. Within an hour we were lounging at the Royal Hawaiian's private beach and watching bronzed young men surfing. My Malay phrasebook languished untouched.

After lunch, a ride in an outrigger canoe, and several exotic cocktails with pineapple juice, it was time for dinner and then a hula show. There was dancing on the lanai in the evening, but our flight was departing very early the next morning, so we decided to turn in right after dinner, the distant melody of the orchestra a lullaby as we drifted off to sleep.

The sun had barely risen when we were back at Pearl Harbor waiting to board the Clipper for the next leg of the journey. The composition of our group had changed slightly. Two of the businessmen on the first flight were staying in Hawaii, and two other men had taken their places. One was an affable Midwesterner who began to talk nonstop about his cornfields to anyone who seemed vaguely interested. The other man said nothing, but nodded politely when he sat down and immediately opened a newspaper. I noticed he kept his brown leather briefcase close by, and I could just read the name "K.

Ohrwürmer" embossed in gold lettering on the top.

Once again we were skimming along the waves and lifted into the air, the row of battleships transforming into bathtub toys. After about six hours of flying over an unbroken expanse of blue, an improbably small land mass came into view. How the crew of the Clipper had found Midway Atoll was beyond my knowledge of navigation, but I was grateful for their expertise. We set down in the lagoon at Sand Island, and the crew moored the aircraft to a landing barge. Soon a small launch came out to retrieve us. We arrived at the Pan American dock, surrounded by clear water and brilliant white sand.

In contrast to the volcanic islands of Hawaii, this flat coral atoll had almost no vegetation. There were a few small trees and scrubby bushes and a vegetable garden to provide food for the Clipper guests and the small number of permanent residents. What the island lacked in flora it made up for in fauna, of one variety anyway. Everywhere we looked were albatrosses, which the Pan American crew affectionately called gooney birds.

We were shown to our rooms at the Pan American Hotel and given a light lunch on a verandah overlooking the water. Helen and I changed into our swimsuits and went to explore the beach. Since the island was so small, we decided to walk around the entire perimeter, marveling at how the albatrosses paid us no attention. Almost-grown chicks still sporting some of their fluffy juvenile feathers entertained us with their first attempts to fly.

Back at the hotel for supper, Helen and I were relieved to be served a tasty fish dinner rather than one of the new friends we'd made earlier. The chef laughed when a fellow traveler asked about eating the birds.

"Goodness, no! That would be bad luck! We can't send you off across the Pacific with one of those gooney birds around your neck, now could we?"

The next morning found us in the air again, heading further west to another speck of land called Wake Island. A couple hours into the flight, the steward instructed everyone to gather in the lounge, and we observed that a white ribbon had been placed on the floor of the cabin. The pilot turned over control of the aircraft to the co-pilot and came to join us. The crew gazed at their watches intently and then announced that we had just crossed the International Date Line, escorting us one at a time across the ribbon. I had given up readjusting my watch as the time changed during our trip, but now the whole day had changed! We had 'lost' a day, but the steward assured us we would get it back when we returned home.

Landing on the water had now become routine for us, though I still felt a thrill as the big plane swooped gracefully down to meet the sea. We taxied up to the pier at Wake and walked a short distance to the Pan American Hotel. Like Midway, Wake was a coral atoll composed of small islets with little vegetation due to the lack of soil. The Clipper base was actually on Peale Islet. Beside the beach there were some tennis courts to occupy the visitors, but I had other plans. Once we settled in, Helen and I went to the hotel restaurant, and I requested to meet the chef.

Mrs. Jenkins, the wife of the hotel manager, greeted us warmly, and I asked if she would give us a tour of the gardens. I had read about the success of Pan American's experimental hydroponic vegetable gardens and was excited to see them in person. She was happy to oblige and proudly showed us the soilless gardens that she called a 'hydroponicum.' All types of vegetables including lettuce, radishes, cucumber, string beans, and tomatoes were growing in fluid-filled vats in a greenhouse. Agricultural scientists had worked out the precise amounts of nutrients to dissolve in water to provide the optimal growing environment for the crops. I was impressed by the high yields of pest-free crops and felt sure the technique would be widely adopted in the future.

Helen and I spent the rest of the afternoon at the beach, watching the bright fish flit about the reef and tiny hermit crabs navigate over seashells, coral, and bits of driftwood. At dinner we enjoyed some of the fine produce of the hydroponicum, then retired for the evening.

The next day's travel brought us to a very different island, Guam. It was not a flat atoll, but a large volcanic island with rugged, foliage-covered terrain, much like the Hawaiian Islands. It also had an Indigenous population, known as the Chamorros, who had settled on the island thousands of years ago. I longed to talk to the local people and ask them about their traditional uses for plants, but there was no time. It could be the focus of an entire expedition of its own. Instead, Helen persuaded me to don our swimsuits once again, and we explored the beach, finding all sorts of seashells and shady areas in the rocks along the shore where butterflies and hermit crabs as large as baseballs cooled themselves from the tropical sun.

After a pleasant evening at the Pan American Hotel, we were on our way to Manila, where Helen and I would disembark. The Clipper would go on to Hong Kong without us after that. As we took off, I noticed that our group was smaller; the man with the briefcase had departed at Guam. I couldn't help feeling relieved. Though he had said little during the days of the trip, I frequently felt his gaze upon me. But whenever I looked up, his face was buried in a book or newspaper. I asked Helen if she had noticed it, too.

"Ivy, you're an attractive young woman. Men are supposed to stare at you. He was probably too shy to talk to you, but I'm sure he wanted to."

"I don't know, Helen. Well, I'm glad he was too shy. He didn't seem like my type, anyway." I thought about the few times my glance had accidentally met his cold gray eyes and shivered.

"Your type? It seems to me if they don't have leaves and roots then they're not your type!"

I laughed and shrugged. Then I finally confided in Helen about my non-botanical interest in Professor Bracken.

"My mother always says if it's meant to be, it will be," she said, patting my hand. "Maybe you'll get to see him yet on this trip."

"I suppose anything's possible," I said, though I harbored strong doubts.

Our last leg of the flight across the Pacific was calm and pleasant, but I was happy to finally see the verdant islands of the Philippines below. We circled over the large island of Luzon and approached the bustling city of Manila from the west, making a smooth landing on

Manila Bay and taxiing to the Pan American base at Cavite, near the U.S. naval base.

Helen had somehow managed to change into fresh clothes and do her hair and makeup. She looked stunning. I felt bedraggled in my rumpled linen traveling suit, but then I remembered she would be seeing her fiancé soon, and the effort was no doubt expected.

We disembarked from the aircraft, our faithful steed for so many days. I patted her flank as we thanked the crew for our safe and comfortable flights. We started walking up the ramp to the terminal when Helen broke into a run. A young man in a white suit was waving and coming our way. Harry, I surmised. My suspicion was confirmed as they locked into a tight embrace, and he swung Helen around in a full circle. By the time I had reached the couple, Harry had put her down, and Helen grabbed my hand.

"Harry, this is my new friend, Ivy! We had a swell time together all the way from San Francisco. You won't believe it, but her mother is Iris Linden, the woman who writes those gardening columns I devour each week!"

"Nice to meet you, Ivy," Harry said, clasping my hand. "Thanks for looking out for Helen for all that way. Won't you join us for dinner tonight?"

"Oh, thank you Harry, but I couldn't. You and Helen must have so much to catch up on. I'll leave you two alone tonight, but maybe another time. I'm in Manila for four days until my ship departs."

"Nonsense," said Helen. "You'll come tonight. Harry and I have our whole lives together," she said, gazing into his eyes.

"We'll pick you up at the Manila Hotel at eight,"

Harry added.

"Okay, well, thank you. I appreciate it. It's so nice to meet you, Harry." Helen and I embraced, and the couple walked off arm-in-arm toward Harry's waiting sedan. I followed the rest of our group into the terminal. I spoke with one of the porters who assured me my equipment would be safely stored in the Pan American hangar until my ship was ready to be loaded with cargo.

Taxis were arranged to take us to the hotel, and we sped from Cavite to the center of Manila. I could see why it was called 'The Pearl of the Orient.' The magnificent architecture ranged from the old Spanish Colonial style to new buildings in a streamlined modern design. And the population was just as diverse, with peoples from all over Asia and the West. It was a grand city, and I knew I would enjoy exploring it for a few days.

We pulled up to the Manila Hotel, a colossal structure in the Spanish Mission style common in the American Southwest. I mentioned looking forward to visiting the famed rooftop garden, but another passenger in the cab told me it had been enclosed to create a top floor penthouse for some American army general named MacArthur. It seemed like a shame. I'd have to be content exploring the lush tropical gardens surrounding the building.

Porters carried our bags into the palatial lobby and led us to the reception desk. Soon it was my turn to check in, and the young man at the desk gave me a key. I thanked him and started to walk away.

"Miss, oh, Miss Linden there is a telegram for you," he called after me.

I came back, a bit surprised, but I figured it was from

my parents sending me good luck for the expedition. I'd have to let them know I'd made it this far already.

I tore open the thin envelope and pulled out the typewritten sheet to read:

PROFESSOR LINDEN= STEAMER TO SINGAPORE SUNK STOP PROCEED THERE IMMEDIATELY BY ALTERNATE MEANS STOP GOOD LUCK STOP JOHNSON AND SMITH USDA

CHAPTER 7

"Miss Linden, are you unwell?" the polite young man asked. I realized I had been standing immobile for some time, reading the telegram over and over, as my mind reeled. I was blocking the reception desk for other guests.

"I'm fine, thank you. I'm terribly sorry. I've had a change of plans, it seems," I said as I wandered away. I noticed there was a Pan American desk in the lobby, so I went up to it and rang the little bell to get someone's attention. An agent came out of the office to help me. I explained that I would not be taking the expected ship to Singapore, and the agent assured me my gear would be safely stored until I made other arrangements.

"Pan American doesn't happen to fly to Singapore, does it?" I figured I would have been booked on the flight already if they did, but it was worth asking.

"No, we don't, but if you can get to Bangkok, you can take Imperial Airways to Singapore," he explained. "But we don't fly to Bangkok. If you come back tomorrow, the daytime Pan American agent will be here, and he might have some other ideas."

I thanked the man and proceeded up to my room. It was a lovely suite with rattan furniture and a white canopy of fine mesh hanging over the bed. It looked fit for a princess, but I knew the netting was there to keep out the mosquitoes, not evoke a fairytale.

I sank down on the bed, realizing I was completely alone for the first time in days. And it was quiet. No hum of airplane engines or Helen's convivial, yet constant, conversation. I would have relished the solitude if it were not for the uncertainty weighing on me. How would I get to Singapore now? Why had I even agreed to come? I should have told Johnson and Smith no. I would have been better off in Chautauqua, I thought dismally. There was nothing to do about it tonight, though, so I decided to try to put it out of my mind. I stepped into the white tiled bathroom and drew a bath.

Somewhat revived and wearing a fresh dress, I returned to the lobby to wait for Helen and Harry to pick me up for dinner. I wished I'd evaded their polite invitation and could have had dinner in my room, but I didn't want to be rude.

Harry's cream-colored sedan pulled up at eight on the dot. He got out and opened the door for Helen, who ran over to me and led me to the car. We sat together in the back seat while Harry gave us a brief tour of the city before we pulled up at his bungalow.

Helen showed me around what was to be her home. She was delighted, but already planning to put her own touch on the place once she and Harry were married. It was dark now, so a tour of the garden behind the house would have to wait for another day. We sat down at a fine teakwood dining table, and Harry's cook served us a traditional meal of chicken adobo, rice cooked in coconut milk, plantains, and cassava cake for dessert. The Spanish influence was obvious, and I hoped to visit some smaller villages to discover more traditional foods using indigenous ingredients that were common before the Spanish arrived.

"Ivy, Helen tells me you're headed to Singapore in a few days to study some plants. That sounds very interesting," Harry said.

"Thank you, Harry. Yes, that was my plan. But when I got to the hotel, there was a telegram informing me the ship I was to take had been sunk."

Harry's handsome brow furrowed as he replied, "Yes, there's been an increase in ships sinking under dubious circumstances for the past year or so. I have my suspicions about who's responsible. Maybe it's better to fly there."

"I would rather fly, but it seems there's no direct way to get there on the airlines. It's up to me to make other arrangements, so I'll have to figure out another way."

"Say, Ivy, I have an idea. My company has a cargo plane going to Singapore tomorrow. I might be able to get you aboard. There would be enough space for your equipment, but there are no seats in the back. It's a long flight, and it wouldn't be the level of comfort you're used to, of course. I wouldn't normally suggest it for a woman, but Helen tells me you've traveled all over to out-of-the-way places."

"Harry, I can't believe it! You're a lifesaver! I can pay your company whatever the fare is. I won't mind how uncomfortable it is at all. I can be ready to leave anytime, although I'll be sorry not to see more of Manila and you and Helen."

"You'll visit us on your way back home," Helen said,

beaming with pride that her fiancé had saved the day.

Harry excused himself from the table to call his company and tell them to transfer my equipment from the Pan American hangar to their aircraft in the morning and expect a passenger.

My spirits lifted at the unexpected stroke of luck, and I enjoyed the rest of the evening chatting with Helen and Harry. Helen was delighted to tell him about being appointed a special correspondent to the "Garden Spot" and her plans to document all the local plants and their uses for me.

Later, back at the hotel, I told the night desk clerk that I would be checking out the next morning and asked him to send a telegram to Johnson and Smith, as well as to my parents.

Harry and Helen insisted on picking me up the next morning to drive me to Nielson Field just south of the city, where the plane was being loaded. When we arrived, I saw it was not a flying boat, but a DC-3 in a cargo configuration without passenger seats in the back. The pilot and co-pilot were overseeing the loading of the cargo when we approached.

"Hello there, Harry. I hear we're taking a passenger with us to Singapore. I hope he gets here soon," the pilot said, glancing at his watch.

"The passenger is right here, Pete," Harry replied. Pete looked at the three of us blankly.

"Oh, is he the invisible man? I was told he's a professor. We don't have time to wait around for some absent-minded know-it-all with his nose in a book."

"That would be me," I interjected. "I'm Professor Ivy

Linden, but you can just call me Ivy. I really appreciate you fitting me and my equipment aboard on such short notice."

Pete was dumbstruck, but the co-pilot managed a whistle. "This is the best cargo we've ever flown," he said, looking me up and down. I began to think this was a mistake.

"Knock it off, you two. Professor Linden is a dear friend of my fiancée Helen, soon to be Mrs. Hartman, and you'll make sure she gets to Singapore safely and is treated with all the respect you'd give a Sunday school teacher or your maiden aunt."

The two men looked abashed and muttered apologies. I didn't appreciate being likened to a Sunday school teacher or a maiden aunt, as I was a long way from either one, but if it got me to Singapore I couldn't complain. Then I saw my equipment being loaded and breathed a sigh of relief. Somehow everything had worked out.

Helen got a blanket and pillows out of the trunk of the car, and she and Harry came aboard the plane with me. Helen tried to fashion a seat for me with the cushions, and I settled down on the floor outside of the cockpit. The cabin was filled with wooden crates strapped to the floor. Everything seemed secure, but I couldn't help wondering what would happen if one came loose during the flight. As if reading my mind, Harry went around to each crate and surreptitiously gave it a shove to make sure it was fixed in place. My own pile of trunks was stowed near the rear of the aircraft.

Pete came in and handed me a bulky parachute. "Here. Just in case. Never had to use one yet." I didn't know how to use it, and he didn't seem to be offering to explain it to me, so it became another cushion to lean against.

Pete took his place in the cockpit. Helen and Harry bid me a safe trip and descended from the plane. Tom, the co-pilot, closed the cabin door and joined Pete in the cockpit. One by one, the engines started up. It was louder than I was expecting. After a few minutes of examining gauges, Tom turned around toward me and gave me a thumbs-up gesture. I replied with the same and felt the aircraft begin to move. We taxied down the runway, picking up speed until I felt us climb into the air. I wanted to look out one of the small rectangular windows to see the city from above, but I decided to wait until we leveled out. Soon enough we were stable, and I clambered over to a window to gaze down at the scenery. Dozens of islands were scattered in the sea below, some tiny and some long and mountainous. I was transfixed by the shades of blues and greens and watched the panorama below for some time. Eventually I sat down again and pulled out the Malay phrasebook to practice. Helen had also given me a paper bag with some sandwiches. I went to the cockpit to offer some to Pete and Tom, and they happily accepted. After I ate my sandwich, I wrapped myself in the blanket and curled up for a nap. Although it was a far cry from the Mainliner, I had no trouble dozing off. I was awakened when the plane hit a patch of turbulent air. Nothing to worry about, I thought. Tom turned to check on me, and I gave him a grin and a thumbs-up. He seemed relieved that I wasn't afraid and turned his attention back to the instruments.

The rough air didn't last long, and I fell asleep again.

When I woke up, I went back to the window. We were skirting along the coast of a large landmass, which I figured had to be Borneo. We finally left it behind and were over open water again. This had to be the last stretch of the trip. I sat back down and wrote in my journal for a while. I felt the plane gradually begin to decrease in altitude. Now I stood between Pete and Tom as Singapore materialized before us.

"We'll be landing at Kallang Aerodrome in a few minutes," Pete shouted to me. We circled over the island city at the tip of the Malay Peninsula. I could see an expansive harbor filled with ships, large modern buildings, ornate temples of all kinds, and bustling streets, some broad and tree-lined, others narrow and clogged with all manner of vehicles. The airport appeared below, and we made a circle before Tom told me to sit down for the landing. The terminal building with its circular control tower was a modern masterpiece, all glass and streamlined curves.

Pete expertly set the heavy aircraft down, although not as smoothly as the Clipper's water landings had been. Once we had rolled to a stop, I scrambled out the door and onto the tarmac for a view of the breathtaking pink and orange sunset. We were only about eighty-five miles north of the equator, and the air was still steamy.

"Where are you staying, Professor Linden?" Pete asked.

"Uh, the Raffles," I said, more as a question. It hadn't occurred to me that the hotel wasn't expecting me for over a week and might not have a room available. "Is that where you and Tom are staying?"

"No," Pete said, laughing. "We'll stay with the plane

and fly back tomorrow. We'll store your equipment in the hangar and get you a cab. Anything you need to take with you?"

"There's one trunk that I'll take now, and the rest can stay here. Thank you very much for the flight and everything. How can I repay you?"

Pete smiled slyly and seemed to be considering his words carefully, then just replied, "No need, Professor. It's an honor to transport such special cargo. I'll let Mr. Hartman know we delivered you safely."

"Well, at least let me treat you and Tom to dinner," I said, pressing some money into his hand and hoping he wouldn't be offended.

"Thank you, we'll drink to your health and the success of your expedition. It would be our pleasure to fly you again someday."

A taxicab rolled up, and the driver put my steamer trunk into the automobile. I said goodbye to Pete and Tom, and the driver closed the door for me. We headed into the heart of the city, passing grand colonial edifices, modern structures, and charming older two-story buildings with terracotta-shingled roofs housing shops and cafes on the ground floor. The streets were filled with automobiles, streetcars, bicycles, pedestrians, and even rickshaws, which seemed to be a popular mode of transportation. The cabdriver, a Chinese man who spoke impeccable English, pointed out the sights.

Soon I recognized a famous sight myself: the world-renowned Raffles Hotel. A line of majestic traveler's palms flanked both sides of the hotel's spectacular white façade. The driver stopped the car under the broad awning covering the entrance. A bellhop appeared to take my trunk, and an imposing bearded doorman in a turban and some type of a white military uniform opened the door for me. He appeared to be a Sikh from India and greeted me with a proper British accent.

Inside, I was overwhelmed by the grandeur of the lobby. A soaring expanse, balconies from the two floors above overlooked the white marble lobby decorated with potted palms, ornate chandeliers, and plush upholstered easy chairs. I followed the white-suited bellhop to the registration desk, instantly aware of how out of place I looked. My pale green linen traveling suit was in need of pressing before today's flight, but now I was positively disheveled. And here I was just showing up without a reservation, more than a week early. Now I was less worried about if they had a room for me and more concerned about if I could afford one. Or if they would turn me away on sight as unsuitable for such high-class accommodations. It was bad enough to be an American, but an unkempt American at that. I reflexively smoothed my hair in an attempt to appear more presentable. It might have been my imagination, but the man at the desk seemed to be eyeing me warily, as if I were one of those wild animals that reputedly wandered into the hotel on occasion.

"Hello, I hope you can help me," I said, forcing a smile and a bright tone of voice. "I was supposed to arrive nine days from now, but my plans changed and I'm early. You don't happen to have a room available, do you?"

"I'm sorry, miss, we are quite full at the moment. I doubt we can accommodate you. You say you have an upcoming reservation?" he asked skeptically.

"Yes, I'm Dr. Ivy Linden. From Cornell University." I

felt foolish as soon as I said it; I suspected the clientele of this place typically hailed from Cambridge and Oxford, not some upstart school founded a mere seventy-three years ago.

"Just one moment and I'll check your reservation," he said, turning some pages in a leather-bound ledger. I began to prepare to return to the airport and ask to sleep in the plane until the clerk looked up at me with an ingratiating smile.

"It seems we do have a room for you after all, Dr. Linden," he said, handing me a key. "Your account has been prepaid, and you can stay as long as you like."

I was stunned and thanked the clerk profusely. "It is our pleasure, Dr. Linden. We hope you enjoy your stay with us," he said with a slight bow and told the porter to show me to room 315.

In short order, I was settled into my room on the top floor. Johnson and Smith had apparently spared no expense. It was a large suite with a sitting area and writing desk, spacious bathroom, four-poster bed, and a second door leading to the balcony overlooking the Palm Court. After unpacking my trunk, I decided to place an order for room service. I didn't feel like making myself presentable enough to eat in one of the restaurants or begin exploring the city. The menu had a lot of options with French names, but I chose the "Chicken a la King, American Style." After a few minutes, another porter arrived with my dinner. It looked quite a bit fancier than the same dish I enjoyed at the State Diner in Ithaca, but it was a comforting reminder of home.

Afterward, I sat in a wicker chair on the balcony, watching the palms of the Palm Court sway gently in the moonlight and wondering what to do next. I decided to visit the Raffles Museum in the morning and hoped my unexpected arrival would not be problematic for my hosts there. It was still early when I climbed into the big four-poster bed and arranged the mosquito netting around me. The swish of the ceiling fan provided a gentle breeze and soothing sound that lulled me to sleep in no time.

CHAPTER 8

It felt good to be clean, properly groomed, and dressed in clothes that were not rumpled from days of traveling. Looking thoroughly presentable again, I emerged from my suite in search of coffee and breakfast. The hotel café did not disappoint, and then I set off to find the Raffles Museum. It seemed everything in Singapore was named after Sir Thomas Stamford Raffles, who had founded the city of Singapore in 1818. I knew him less for his colonial administration achievements and more for his contributions to botany and zoology. A member of the Linnean Society and founder of the Zoological Society of London, he had described multiple previously unknown plants and animals, and several species were named in his honor.

After a fifteen-minute walk, I came to the impressive domed museum building with arched windows and classical columns decorating its façade. Inside the rotunda, I asked for Mr. Chasen, the director of the museum, and the clerk at the reception desk suggested I look around while he fetched him. I spied a whale skeleton suspended from the ceiling of the gallery to my right and went to investigate.

The massive skeleton was the focal point of the room, which was lined with glass display cases filled with preserved animal specimens. Beyond that, another gallery was visible with the skeleton of an elephant in the center. Around it stood smaller taxidermy elephants and hoofed mammals. Horned heads were mounted on the walls above cases filled with small mammals, reptiles, and birds. A larger case held a young male orangutan from Borneo. Permanently clinging to a tree branch, he stared out at me with kind eyes, and I wanted to reach out and pat his orange-red fur. While I appreciated the value of such specimens to science, I couldn't help wondering how anyone who was fascinated by these creatures could 'collect' them and deprive them of their natural life in the wild. I knew my collecting could never go beyond plants, and even then I sometimes felt a twinge of guilt when I cut off a stem or branch to take back to the herbarium.

I was pondering what the orangutan's life on Borneo had been like when footsteps on the marble floor broke my train of thought.

"Ivy, what a pleasure to meet you," a fair-haired man with a British accent said with a smile while extending his hand to me.

"Mr. Chasen, it's my pleasure. I'm sorry to arrive unexpectedly."

"Call me Fred, my dear. It's no problem, although I didn't expect you for another week or so. But that will just give us a bit more time to prepare for the expedition. I do wish I were going with you, but I'm tied up. Tweedie will go with you to Pulau Tioman. He's the curator here, but he's a zoologist like me, so he'll just be along to guide you and translate. He always employs the local peoples on an expedition, so he'll get the people who know best to lead the way. You can tell him about exactly what you're looking for."

"Oh, that's a bit of a problem. I don't know exactly what I'm looking for. I wasn't even supposed to be coming here."

"Ah, well, someone wants to make sure you find it, whatever it is. I was told by the American consulate to provide you with whatever assistance you require. But, of course, I'd do whatever I could to help Reed's daughter, even without the insistence of the American government. Too bad he didn't make the trip with you."

"Yes, I would have liked for him to come, too. He was very enthusiastic about the expedition and remembered his time here fondly."

"Why don't you look around the galleries while I attend to some business? Then we can meet Tweedie for lunch. We can show you the vast collections that are not on public display, and I'm sure you'll want to see the herbarium."

Fred left me, and I wandered around the museum for the next few hours, looking at exhibits of animals, seashells, minerals, fossils, and anthropological artifacts. It was a world-class collection, although plant life was underrepresented, as usual. The public would rarely get to see the extensive collections of pressed plants stored away from view in so many museums.

I was in the last hall of exhibits when Fred reappeared with another man, dressed like him in a white tropical-weight suit.

"Ivy, I trust you've been enjoying the museum. This is Michael Tweedie, our curator." The man looked to be a bit younger than Fred and closer to my age. He stuck out his hand.

"Pleasure to meet you, Ivy. My friends call me Tweedie. Fred has told me all about your father, and I'm excited to come along on your expedition. I've been to Tioman before, but focused on crustaceans. Didn't pay much attention to the plants, I'm afraid. But I'm sure my friends there will remember me and help us find what you're seeking. Must be rather important to have the consulate involved. The British government doesn't share my enthusiasm for crabs, I'm afraid."

"The American government doesn't usually pay much attention to what I'm doing," I said with a laugh. "I appreciate you helping me, especially on such short notice."

"Let's go have lunch," Fred suggested. "There's a noodle place close by that we like. We can talk about the expedition, and you can tell us your plans."

Soon the three of us were seated around a small table in a cozy restaurant. A ceiling fan spun lazily overhead, but did little to help the equatorial heat. I explained what I knew about my mission, observing Fred and Tweedie exchange a glance when I recounted the visit from Johnson and Smith.

"And my ship from Manila was sunk, but I lucked into a flight here on a cargo plane, and that's why I'm early," I concluded.

"I had arranged for a chartered flight to Tioman for us, but I don't suppose I can change it to leave sooner. You could use the extra days to study our herbarium collection. In fact, we could use your help to mount and identify some of the newest specimens," Tweedie suggested. I readily agreed, and we enjoyed a pleasant lunch.

In the afternoon, Fred and Tweedie gave me a tour of the diverse collections housed on the upper floors of the museum, hidden from public view. I could have spent days poring over trays of jewel-like beetles, dragonflies, and butterflies pinned in precise rows. The herbarium collection was impressive, though smaller than that of Cornell. Indeed, there were stacks of pressed specimens waiting to be mounted on the special heavyweight paper used as a backing in all herbaria, labeled, and then filed away in the cabinets housing similar species. It would be a welcome way to fill my days until our flight to Tioman. Mounting the specimens was as much artistic as scientific, and I liked arranging them on the paper and wondering who might look at the sample years in the future.

It turned out both Fred and Tweedie were newlyweds, a second marriage for Fred who had two young daughters with his first wife. They both insisted that their wives wanted to have me over for dinner. I rather doubted that, but politely accepted the invitations. Although I knew I should avail myself of their hospitality, I really just wanted to explore the city myself. So I was glad to have no commitments for the evening and planned to return to the museum the next day to get to work.

I walked back to the hotel by a different route to see some new sights. After freshening up in my room, I ventured back out and wandered through the maze of streets in Chinatown. There were all kinds of small shops selling fruits and vegetables, traditional medicinal herbs, silk goods, and ceramics. Watching the other pedestrians was just as interesting as the shops' wares; some were dressed in traditional Chinese clothing, while others wore Western attire or Indian saris, and Muslim women had scarf-covered heads. After eating dumplings from a vendor's cart, I made my way back to the hotel. I didn't feel like retiring to my room so early, so I stopped in the bar for a drink.

The Long Bar was, indeed, long. A dark wooden bar with a row of green leather stools stretched from one end of the room to the other. A few patrons sat at the bar, singly or in small groups. I chose one of the little glass-topped tables and sank into a cushioned wicker chair. A waiter appeared and greeted me warmly.

"Good evening, miss. May I suggest our famous Gin Sling? It's very refreshing and most suitable for the ladies."

I agreed to the drink, and soon he returned with a frothy, pink concoction. The oversized glass had a pineapple and cherry garnish. I felt conspicuous with the flashy cocktail, but it seemed to be the expected drink for a woman, so I sipped it slowly and took out my journal to record the day's events.

I returned to the museum the next day and got to work on the stack of pressed plant samples to mount. Some were unfamiliar species to me, but I was able to identify many of them. There was no permanent curator of the botany collections, but botanists from around the world would periodically stop here while on expeditions and lend their expertise.

That evening I returned to the Long Bar for a drink.

I ordered a Pimm's, which was less garish than the Gin Sling, and wrote in my journal while watching the other patrons come and go. I had scarcely finished my drink when the waiter brought a second one.

"Thank you, but I didn't order this."

"It is compliments of the gentleman at the bar," he explained and left before I could ask who had sent the drink. I scanned the row of patrons, wondering who it could have been, and looked around at the other tables. No one appeared to be paying any attention to me, and most people seemed to be there with a group or at least another person. I shrugged, sipped the new drink, and started writing again.

The next day, Tweedie insisted I have dinner at his home and meet his new bride, Elvira. We passed a delightful evening, and Elvira shared stories of growing up in Hobart on the island of Tasmania. I wasn't tired when I got back to the hotel, so I stopped at the Long Bar to write in my journal again. I ordered a gimlet and observed the well-heeled clientele when I looked up between sentences. People nodded or smiled politely when they passed my table. No one seemed interested enough to be my benefactor from the previous evening. And yet, when the gimlet glass was empty, another appeared unbidden.

I looked at each person at the tables around me and then went down the line at the bar. On the last stool, a dark-haired man swiveled around and gave me a wink. He turned back before I could even get a good look at him.

I studied his form, trying to decide what to do. His white linen trousers and shirt were in need of pressing.

Part of me wanted to go up to my room and ignore him, but curiosity got the better of me. I smoothed my skirt and blouse and walked toward the bar, new gimlet in hand.

"Excuse me," I began. The man turned to face me. He looked to be no more than thirty with dark, wavy hair, a thin mustache, and deep brown eyes. The unbuttoned collar of his wrinkled shirt revealed a fine silver chain with a cross around his neck above a patch of dark curls. He did not look like a proper British gentleman, I concluded.

The man stood up and flashed a movie-star smile at me. It seemed the room had gotten much warmer, and I could only dimly recall what I had intended to say.

"Hello," I said. "Thank you for the drink tonight and last night. Was that you?"

"I would be foolish to say no, if it were not," he replied. His accent revealed he was definitely not one of the King's subjects.

"Would you care to join me?" I asked, motioning to my table while realizing that was not at all what I had meant to say.

"With pleasure, miss," he said, following me back with his drink.

"I'm Ivy," I said, needlessly adding, "I'm from America."

"It is a pleasure to meet you, Miss Ivy," he said, taking my hand and raising it to his lips. "And so nice to meet someone from so close to home. My name is Jacinto Diente de León. But please call me Jay. All my friends do."

"Pleased to meet you, Jay. *Jacinto*, hyacinth, is one of

my favorite spring flowers."

"*Usted habla español. Muy bien.* Not many people here speak Spanish, so it is easier if I am Jay."

"I learned to speak Spanish because I've spent some time in South America."

"I've never been to South America. I am from México. Ciudad de México," Jay explained.

"How did you end up here?"

"It is a very long story," he said as the waiter approached.

"Another Coca-Cola, Mr. Jay?" the waiter asked.

"Sure, Henry. Thank you."

I glanced at the empty glass.

"I never drink alcohol when I'm flying in the morning," Jay explained.

"Oh, where are you flying to?"

"I'm never quite sure until the morning. I show up and see where I'm supposed to go. Every day is a surprise, usually. Only sometimes do I know in advance where I'm going."

"You mean you're flying the plane?"

"Yes, that's right. I am a pilot," he said, and I could see he was sitting up just a bit straighter.

"What kind of aircraft do you fly?"

"Whatever the company wants me to. Whatever is right for the job. It depends if it's a cargo flight or passengers."

"Well, what do you like best?"

"I would prefer just the cargo. The passengers can be very demanding. They forget where we are and think we should have all the amenities of a big airline. For instance, next week I have a chartered flight. I've been told it's some very special clients. Some kind of a professor, apparently. I have to fly him and his group to an island off Malaya, and I have to wait around for him. They are paying me to stay, but I have to be at his beck and call. I would rather be flying than waiting on some snooty professor."

"How do you know he's snooty? Or even a he?"

Jay laughed, and I felt myself growing indignant.

"I suppose you're right. But a *she*? That would be even worse, to have a female to take care of, who would be afraid of the snakes and insects and bats."

"Not all *shes* are afraid of snakes and insects and bats."

"Again, I suppose you are right, Miss Ivy. But the debate is purely theoretical."

"Is it? As a matter of fact, I'm not Miss Ivy, but Professor Linden. And I'm here to go to an island off Malaya. And I'm not afraid of any snakes or other animals. At least not any I'd find in the wild."

Jay looked at me wide-eyed. "Forgive me, Professor Linden. Yes, you do not seem like the type of she who would be afraid of some animals or need much taking care of. I am sure you will be no trouble at all. I will fly you there, wait obediently with the plane, and fly you back to Singapore."

"Thank you," I said, aware that I had somehow gotten off on the wrong foot with the pilot. "Thank you for the drinks, Jay. That was kind of you. I hardly know anyone in Singapore. It's nice to meet you." I glanced at my watch. "I should be going. Have a safe flight tomorrow."

"*Buenas noches, Profesora* Linden."

CHAPTER 9

The days passed pleasantly in Singapore as I migrated between the Raffles Hotel and the Raffles Museum. I didn't mention the encounter with the pilot to Fred and Tweedie. I hadn't seen him at the bar again, and maybe he wasn't even the pilot who would be flying us to Tioman. Surely there were multiple pilots in Singapore.

Finally, it was the eve of our departure. Tweedie had amassed his own equipment for collecting crustaceans, and I had a list of botanical specimens to obtain for the museum's collections. At least the trip would not be wasted if I didn't find the original quarry.

Tweedie and I agreed to meet at the airport at the Qantas Empire Airways terminal at nine o'clock the next morning. After packing up what I would need for the trip, I left my comfortable Raffles suite. The concierge summoned a cab for me and assured me that my room would be undisturbed for however long I'd be gone.

The taxi took me back to Kallang Aerodrome, and I found the Qantas desk. The clerk instructed me to wait while they finished transferring my equipment from the hangar to the aircraft. The minutes ticked by slowly as I repeatedly glanced at my watch. It was now five minutes past nine. After five more minutes, I went back to the desk and asked if they had a message from Tweedie, but they did not. I was surprised he was late, but at least we had a chartered flight so the plane wouldn't leave without us.

Five more minutes went by, and I began to wonder how I could contact Tweedie. As I got up to see if I could find a telephone, Elvira walked into the terminal. Alone.

"Elvira, am I glad to see you. I was getting worried. Is Tweedie on his way?" I said, trying to look past her.

"Ivy, no, I'm afraid he's not. That's why I came. He's had a relapse of malaria. It started in the middle of the night. He insisted he'd be fine by this morning. But he's still got a high fever and chills. I wouldn't let him get out of bed."

"Oh, I'm so sorry Elvira. I hope he'll be okay."

"Thank you, Ivy. He'll be right as rain in a few days, but there's no way he can travel now. Would you like a ride back to Raffles?"

I was about to agree, when the Qantas clerk interrupted.

"Professor Linden, the aircraft is fully loaded and ready for you and Mr. Tweedie to board."

"I'm afraid Mr. Tweedie has fallen ill. Malaria. I guess I'll have to postpone the flight."

"Oh dear, rescheduling might be a bit of a problem," the clerk said. "We'd assigned you our best pilot for such an excursion, but he might not be available later. I can check the schedule." The clerk walked back to the desk and started paging through a ledger.

The terminal door opened again.

"*Buenos días, Profesora. Está lista?*"

"Good morning, Jay. How nice to see you again," I said as he walked toward me and bowed slightly. He was wearing a smartly tailored khaki Qantas uniform with a military-style jacket.

"Is this our other passenger? Another beautiful lady professor? This must be my lucky day," Jay said, winking at me and taking Elvira's hand.

"This is Mrs. Tweedie. Her husband was our other passenger, but he's been taken ill. I'm afraid I'll have to postpone the trip now."

"Señora Tweedie, what a fortunate man your husband is to have such a lovely wife to nurse him back to health."

Elvira was blushing and speechless as she stared at Jay.

After a moment, I cleared my throat. "Yes, Mr. Tweedie is, indeed, lucky in that regard. Perhaps you'd better return to him, Elvira."

"Oh, yes, Ivy. Of course. We'd best be going, I suppose."

"Please take good care of Tweedie, and tell him I'll miss him," I found myself saying as I gave her a hug. "I'm going to go to Pulau Tioman anyway." The thought had suddenly occurred to me, and it seemed like a good idea until I heard the words come out of my mouth. Jay grinned a self-satisfied smile. I started walking Elvira back to her waiting automobile.

"My goodness, Ivy. Do you think that's wise? To go by yourself?" Elvira said.

"I'm hardly going by myself. Mr. Diente de León had mentioned he's being paid to be at my beck and call, and he was sure I'd be no trouble at all."

"Yes, I'm sure. But what kind of trouble is he?"

"Nothing I can't handle," I said, unconsciously patting my shoulder bag with the little pistol safely tucked inside.

"Do be careful, Ivy. Michael will be furious with me when I tell him I let you go without him."

"It's not your fault. Just tell him how headstrong and independent American women are. I'll look out for interesting crabs for him," I said, giving her another embrace. "Go take care of Tweedie, and I'll be fine."

"Good luck, Ivy. I hope you find what you're looking for."

I went back inside the terminal and told the Qantas clerk that I'd be taking the flight anyway.

"Very well, miss. The steward will escort you to the aircraft."

The steward took my other bag and led me to the plane, but I soon realized we were not going to where I had landed before in the DC-3. We were going away from the tarmac and toward the water. On one side of the airport was a harbor at the mouth of the Kallang River. It dawned on me that the flight had to be aboard another seaplane.

I spied a white twin-engine biplane on floats. Two thin red stripes ran down each side of the fuselage from the nose to the tail. On the nose beneath the stripes was lettered "Qantas Empire Airways Ltd." And above the stripes, in red script, was painted "*Libélula.*" Jay sat on one lower wing, near the fuselage, dangling his legs above the water.

"Profesora Linden, we are ready for you. Are you certain you want to go without your colleague?"

"Yes, Jay. I'm sure," I said, although I was not. "And

please call me Ivy."

The porter handed my luggage to Jay, who stowed it in the plane. He took my satchel and placed it in the cabin, as well. I used a little ramp to step from the dock onto one pontoon. Then I climbed up onto the lower wing and into the cabin by way of a small door behind the cockpit. There were two seats in the cockpit, plus a single seat behind the co-pilot's seat and a bench seat behind that which could seat two. The configuration was similar to the interior of Tut, but not quite as spacious. The rear of the plane held all the cargo.

"You can sit wherever you'd like, Ivy," Jay said, motioning to the rear seats.

"I'd rather sit in the cockpit, if that's all right with you."

"Of course, Ivy. You will be my co-pilot," he said, winking again.

I climbed into the right seat up front. The cockpit was cramped, with a dual-control stick between the seats in front of the instrument panel. There was a bowtie-shaped extension for the pilot branching off of the stick to the left and a small handle branching to the right for the co-pilot, in the event he, or in this case she, needed to take control.

Jay squeezed into the left seat and helped secure my safety belt. Once he was settled, he did a check of all the instruments. A mechanic standing on the floats spun the propellers by hand a few turns and returned to the dock. Jay made a few more adjustments to the controls, and the left engine came to life. A moment later, he started the right one. He and the mechanic exchanged a thumbs-up, and we began to taxi away from the dock. The aircraft picked up speed as we cut through the water, and soon we were airborne. The panoramic view from the cockpit was spectacular, and I was enthralled as we circled above the city.

We leveled out, and the plane felt very stable. But it was clear that we were flying, not just sitting in a lounge, like the Clipper and Mainliner flights had seemed. Still, it was much more comfortable than my last flight in the cargo hold. We finally left Singapore and turned north to fly along the eastern coast of Malaya. The scenery below switched quickly from the bustling city to dense jungle. I peered down just as eagerly, wondering about all the undiscovered plant life below. I was so absorbed in the view that I had practically forgotten about Jay until his arm brushed against mine. I looked up at him and grinned.

"Beautiful scenery," I said.

"Yes," he agreed, looking at me. It felt warmer in the cockpit. "Do you want to fly her?"

"Oh, yes, please!"

"Go ahead, take the controls," Jay said, nodding at the small stick in front of me.

I gingerly grasped the stick, while Jay still held onto the yoke on his side. He took his hands off the controls.

"There, now you are flying the airplane. Just keep her steady for a while. I'll take a siesta," he joked, closing his eyes.

I was tempted to bank the plane hard, but decided against it. It had been a long time since my first and only lesson. The controls felt familiar, but this was a larger plane with two engines, and maybe there were finer points I did not know.

"Very good, Ivy. Now we will try some turns." Jay told me what to do, and I followed his instructions. "You are a good student, not just a professor. You are doing very well for your first time flying an airplane."

"Oh, but it's not my first time. I flew once before. Back in 1932. A friend of mine took me flying and let me fly the plane."

"Ah well, he was a good instructor then."

"It wasn't a he."

"Of course, I should have known better with you. Let me guess, it was Amelia Earhart," Jay said, laughing.

My hand shook on the stick, the nose of the aircraft dropped, and Jay took hold of his yoke again. I looked away, feeling a lump in my throat but determined not to shed a tear.

"Ivy? Have I said something wrong?"

I looked at Jay, forcing a smile, and said, "As a matter of fact, my instructor *was* Amelia Earhart. She took me up for my first airplane ride. I never dreamed she'd let me take the controls. She took my parents and my sister for flights, too. We were devastated last year. She was so close to finishing her flight around the world."

"I am sorry, Ivy. I never met her, but I know some of the pilots who met her when she passed through Singapore last year, and they all respected her. It was a loss for the whole world, but especially those who knew her."

"Thanks, Jay. I'll just look at the view for a while and leave the flying to you."

"Certainly. It is a short flight. Not much more than an hour, so we will be landing soon enough."

I gazed down at the scenery below. A narrow strip of

white beach separated the deep green foliage from the turquoise of the water. Some islands took shape ahead of us, and we turned toward them, away from the coast of Malaya. We passed over several small, jungle-covered islands until we reached a larger one, Pulau Tioman. A ring of white sand circled the rugged green interior of the island. We flew along the western coast, and a cluster of small buildings appeared near a jetty that stuck out into the water. Jay passed over the area once and circled back around.

"We'll land here," he said as he pulled back on the throttles. We came in parallel to the beach, skimming along the water. Jay steered us toward the jetty and cut the engines.

"Stay here," he said as he went to the back cabin and opened the door. Once the propellers had come to a stop, he took one end of a heavy rope that had been coiled under a seat and climbed out onto the wing. He tied one end of the rope to a strut beneath the wing above the float. He grabbed the other end of the rope, jumped onto the jetty, and secured the rope to a metal cleat so the aircraft was fixed in place. He stepped back onto the float, ducked under the lower wing, and stood up at the nose of the plane. I watched him pat the nose gently, and it seemed like he was saying something. I looked away, sensing I was intruding on a private moment. A minute later, his head popped up at the open door.

"Coming now, Profesora Ivy?"

I scrambled out of the cockpit, retrieved my satchel, and slid onto the wing. Jay took my hand, and I stepped onto the float and then the dock. Not surprisingly, our arrival had attracted some attention. A small group had formed at the end of the jetty to greet us.

"How's your Malay?" I whispered to Jay.

"Not as good as my Spanish, English, French, Italian, and Portuguese. But I can order a drink."

My heart sank, and I cursed my lack of preparation and the mosquito that had felled Tweedie. I glanced back at the plane, thinking we could just leave now. But the small group had expanded to include some children who were running toward us eagerly, pointing at the plane. I'd have to try to explain who we were and why we were there.

"Hello," I said slowly in Malay. "My name is Professor Ivy Linden. I am here to study plants. Michael Tweedie from the Raffles Museum is my friend."

"Tweedie, Tweedie!" several people exclaimed in recognition. A man came forward.

"Welcome to Pulau Tioman," he said in English. I breathed a sigh of relief. "I am Johari. I speak English and can translate for you. Where is Tweedie?"

"Tweedie has malaria and couldn't come with us. This is our pilot, Jacinto Diente de León."

"Please call me Jay. It is a pleasure to meet you. Thank you for welcoming us to your beautiful home," Jay said in perfect Malay as the two men shook hands. I looked at him in astonishment as they continued to converse in Malay at a level beyond my comprehension. Next the children were jumping up and down with great excitement. I surmised he had offered to give them rides in the plane.

"Miss Ivy," Johari said in English again, "we are honored to have you visit us from America. We are at your disposal during your stay. We all remember Mr.

Tweedie so fondly and hope he makes a fast recovery. He is welcome to visit Tioman anytime, and you are, too, as his friend. Come now and have some refreshments with us," he said, leading us toward the cluster of buildings.

"This is Kampung Tekek," Johari explained. "There are a few other *kampungs*, or villages as you would say, on the island. There are about eight hundred of us living on Tioman now. Most of us are fishermen. Some of us were born here, and some of us came from the mainland. We stopped here one day and never left. And now we have brought our wives and had families."

By now, about twenty villagers of all ages had gathered around us. I was happy to see some older women, as I figured they would be most knowledgeable about the traditional uses of plants. Johari led us to a garden area with some sturdy logs for seating. Jay and I sat down and each accepted a young coconut to drink. The villagers were clustered around us, and it was clear they didn't receive visitors too often, at least not by airplane.

"Miss Ivy, please tell me of the studies you wish to make on Tioman, and I will translate for the others," said Johari.

"I am here to learn about the plants on the island and make some collections to take back to Singapore and America. I especially want to know about how you use plants as medicine. I am looking for plants that you use to treat malaria, but I am interested in anything you would like to tell me.

"I would like to talk to different people, both men and women, and younger and older people, and ask them about the plants they use. I will write down notes, and then I would like to see the plants and collect a sample with your permission."

Johari summarized my plan for the villagers in Malay. They discussed it among themselves for a few minutes.

"Miss Ivy, we are happy to host you as our guest in Tekek. Please stay with us in the village. When you are ready to collect plants, you can stay at the camp that Tweedie and his colleagues made when they stayed here. It is in the jungle in the interior of the island, at Sedagong, about halfway between here and Kampung Juara on the east coast of the island. There is a path that connects the two villages, and the camp is not far off the path."

"Thank you, Johari. Please thank everyone for me. That would be ideal. Of course I will pay everyone for their time, and I'd like to hire a few young men as guides."

Johari translated this, and everyone seemed agreeable. He said something to Jay, who replied in the affirmative. I gave him a questioning look.

"And I will give everyone who wants to fly a ride in the airplane," he said, beaming. The children squealed with delight, and the adults began talking excitedly among themselves.

I felt my tension ease. Perhaps forging ahead without Tweedie had not been a mistake. After we finished drinking the refreshing coconut water, I asked if we could unload the cargo from the plane. Several young men volunteered to help us. Everyone was amused that I insisted on carrying some crates up from the beach myself. I presented two older women with a sack of rice, and they seemed pleased.

Once the cargo hold was cleared and the equipment stored ashore in a communal building, we sat down to rest again.

"It appears you can do more than order a drink," I said to Jay.

"I guess I've picked up more Malay than I realized in eight months," he said with a shrug.

"Eight months? You came to Singapore eight months ago from Mexico?"

"Eight months, but from Spain, not México. I have not been home for several years."

"Oh, I'm sorry. That must be difficult. You told me it was a long story, but maybe you'll have time to tell me."

"Maybe," he said, and I pried no further.

CHAPTER 10

By the evening, we'd settled in to our accommodations in the village. A family with two young girls had offered me a spot in their simple home, which I gratefully accepted. Jay had announced he would sleep in the plane, but Johari would have none of it, giving Jay a place of honor in his home.

I had organized my equipment and set up a small work area for pressing and drying specimens in a structure with open walls and a tin roof. The children took some interest in my activities, though it could not compete with the airplane. I showed them how I could take a flower or leaves and put them in the plant press between sheets of paper to flatten them out. Then they would be placed over a small camp stove for twelve hours to dry. The process was difficult in the heat and humidity of the tropics, but Dr. MacDaniels had devised a portable drying apparatus for just such use. He had received his doctoral degree in botany from Cornell in 1917 and returned as a professor in 1920. His specialty was pomology, the study of fruits, and he had studied bananas in Polynesia, so his invention was born of necessity, and many of us had adopted his design in the field. I was lucky enough to be able to talk to him anytime about the finer points of sample collection, pressing, and drying. Although he asked me to call him Larry, as my parents addressed him, I couldn't quite do it, and he was always Dr. MacDaniels to me.

I felt the same way about Ethel Bailey's father. He was a renowned botanist and had been at Cornell since 1888, the year before Ethel was born. She, too, became a botanist and was now the curator of the herbarium there that bore her father's name, the Liberty Hyde Bailey Hortorium. Ethel had traveled all over the world with her father collecting plant samples from China, Japan, Latin America, and the West Indies. She was even the first woman in Ithaca to obtain a driver's license and served as her father's chauffeur on top of all her botanical duties. She would have been a welcome companion on this expedition. I hoped the collections I made would live up to her high standards and looked forward to delivering the samples I collected on Pulau Tioman to her capable hands for posterity.

Once I was satisfied with my makeshift laboratory, I wandered outside to see what had become of Jay. I found him fishing with some of the men of the village, thoroughly at home. He'd jettisoned his uniform jacket and wore only the khaki trousers and shirt with the sleeves rolled up. I realized the flight was so short back to Singapore that he could have easily flown home after depositing me on Tioman. I felt more comfortable now that we had been welcomed into the village and I was set up for the collecting phase of the expedition. He really didn't need to stay, and yet I didn't suggest he leave.

Jay and the other men brought their catches back to

the village where women prepared the fish, along with an assortment of vegetables and fruits which grew in small patches around the houses. The area of flat land between the sandy beach and the point when dense vegetation took over was not wide enough for extensive cultivation. The elevation increased sharply in the jungle, making clearing more land for farming impossible. But the villagers seemed to subsist quite well on what they were able to catch at sea or grow in that limited area. Combined with trade from the mainland, they had a varied and nutritious diet. And a delicious one, as the talented women soon proved to us with their dinner.

Our meal of fish and rice was accompanied by cooked young leaves they called *sayor salang*. I asked to see the plant that the leaves came from, and one woman showed me a small tree growing at the edge of the jungle. She explained they used the bark to treat toothaches. I knew there would be much to learn on Pulau Tioman.

We walked back to the rest of the group, and my nose detected a distinct smell. Distinctly unpleasant. And yet I knew that meant it was time for dessert. To my delight, another woman brought over a basket full of brilliant green, round fruit covered in spikes. Each fruit was about five inches in diameter and emitted a pungent, yet indescribable, aroma. I recognized it at once as durian, but these fruits were smaller, rounder, and a brighter green, clearly a species I had not seen before. The villagers explained it was *durian duan*, and I knew I had another specimen to collect.

The durians were cut in half and distributed to the group. Jay wrinkled his nose, but accepted it politely. The flavor of the creamy yellow flesh of the fruit was as sublimely delectable as the smell was repulsive. I could not think of another food where the smell and taste were so at odds and wondered how anyone had decided to try eating one in the first place, between the odor and spikes. I asked about the uses for durian, besides as a delicious treat. The villagers talked about it amongst themselves for a few minutes, laughing.

"*Durian duan* does have certain uses. The leaves and roots can be used to reduce fevers. But the way we like to use it best is to increase desire," Johari explained.

"We call that an aphrodisiac," I said, glancing at Jay. He hadn't touched his durian. Now he looked at it even more skeptically.

"Aren't you going to eat it?" I asked.

He looked around, realizing he was the only one who hadn't touched his dessert. He scooped out a bit of the yellow flesh.

"*Salud*," he said, raising the fruit toward me and quickly popping it in his mouth. His expression changed from repulsion to curiosity. He finished the rest of the fruit, and some children collected the empty rinds from us and took them away. "Not bad, but I will stick to oysters, like Casanova."

"Oh, I thought we'd take a crate of durians back with us to Singapore," I teased.

"*Dios mío*, I could never do that to my sweet Lula."

"Lula? Who is she?" I asked, not really wanting to know the answer. This Don Juan probably had a girl in every airport.

"Lula is my best girl," he said, gesturing toward the airplane gently bobbing next to the jetty. "*Libélula*. Dragonfly."

"Oh, of course," I said, feeling a tiny ripple of relief. "I should have asked you to introduce me properly."

"She is a de Havilland DH.90 Dragonfly. She is a special model on floats instead of wheels. We came to Singapore at the same time. I've never let anyone else fly her before," he added.

"Thank you, Jay. I'm honored. Don't worry, I'd never ask her to carry a smelly crate of durians for me. Even if I do find them very exciting. Botanically speaking, of course."

"Of course, Profesora. It's been a long day, and I think I will retire for the evening. *Buenas noches.*"

"Good night, Jay. *Dulces sueños.*"

Most of the villagers had gone back to their houses already. Jay followed Johari and his family in one direction, and I followed my hosts in the opposite direction. Soon I was reclining on a woven mat beneath a mosquito netting, listening to the night sounds of frogs and insects calling to their mates.

In the morning, I arose with the first light and crept out of the house to watch the sunrise. The little girls, Mawar and Melati, soon found me. Their mother, Kasih, brought me some sweet ripe papaya, which they called *betik*, and some small bananas, or *pisang*. I was picking up new words, and we managed to make ourselves understood with a combination of Malay, some English, and hand gestures. I gathered that her husband, Kiambang, had already left in his fishing boat for the day. I followed Kasih and her daughters around for the morning, helping with their chores and noting which plants they used.

Later in the day, I asked some of the older women to take me around their gardens and tell me how they used each plant. Johari came along as an interpreter, and I made notes about each species in my field journal. Aside from the durians, no one showed me a plant that reduced fevers or prevented malaria, but it was all useful information. I collected some samples of their cultivated plants and put them in the press. Later, I asked to see the plants growing wild on the outskirts of the village and noted more species that they used to treat different medical conditions.

I hadn't seen Jay all day, and Johari explained that he'd left early on a fishing boat with some of the men. It seemed this was turning into a nice vacation for him. They returned in the late afternoon, in time to deliver a new batch of fish to the women for dinner. Jay proudly displayed a large golden fish he'd caught called a dorado, but I knew by its Hawaiian name, mahi-mahi. I tried to help with the preparation, but the women wouldn't let me, and so I stuck to making note of the herbs and vegetables they used for flavoring.

To Jay's relief, no durians were offered to us after dinner.

"Do you want to go back to Singapore, Jay?" I finally asked. "I'll be fine here until you come back for me."

"Of course not, Ivy. I'm here to help you for as long as you need me."

"Help me? You were out fishing all day."

"That is true, but I have been getting to know the men of the village. Johari's two nephews have offered to come with us to the camp at Sedagong. They will be our guides and help with the equipment. They are serious young men, strong and knowledgeable about the island. We will be in good hands with them."

"We? You're coming to the camp with me?"

"Yes, Profesora. I think that would be best. Do you not agree?"

"Yes, I suppose so, Jay. Thank you for engaging Johari's nephews for me. I will pay them, of course, and I have more goods to give to the villagers, too. Are you going fishing again tomorrow?"

"No, I have other plans. Good night, Profesora Ivy."

The next day I began to systematically interview small groups of villagers, starting with the oldest residents. I asked them about the plants they cultivated and collected from the wild. Everyone was eager to share his or her knowledge with me. Most people mentioned the same plants, but once in a while someone told me of a unique plant and its use.

By mid-morning I still had not seen Jay, but then I heard the engines. The Dragonfly purred briefly, and for a moment I worried he was, indeed, departing. Then I remembered his promise to give rides in the airplane. I suspended my questioning, and we all walked down to the jetty. A small group of children waited to board the plane. Mawar and Melati were first in line. Jay lifted them into the cabin and then helped three little boys aboard. The boys were small enough to all fit on the bench seat in back. Jay unfastened the rope holding the plane in place, closed the door, and started up the engines again. He taxied away from the jetty and turned to take off. Kasih looked stricken and grabbed my hand. I tried to reassure her that it would be fine as the plane picked up speed and broke free from the water.

We waved at the Dragonfly as it climbed over us, tiny faces visible at the windows. Jay flew the children around the island for about five minutes and then landed at the jetty. The children scrambled out, running to their families and laughing, trying to convey the magic of the flight. Jay asked for more passengers, and slowly some adults came forward. He helped four men board the aircraft and took off again. When the men landed, they were not as ebullient as the children had been, but seemed impressed by the experience. Jay flew several more loads of passengers, until everyone who wanted a ride got to fly.

I continued my interviews the next day, this time asking about plants that grew wild in the jungle. While the villagers told me of many interesting plants collected occasionally to treat particular ills, no one mentioned anything like what I'd supposedly been sent to find. I didn't want to ask leading questions, but I finally resorted to asking about wild plants that were used to prevent or treat malaria. Johari translated the question, and there was a good deal of discussion in Malay that I could not follow. Finally, the group seemed to come to a consensus, and Johari spoke.

"Yes," he said, "There is such a plant. But it is rare and valuable. And difficult to obtain. We only collect it to use in very special cases, as a last resort, because it is very powerful in many ways. We do not tell outsiders about it, but we have decided to make an exception for you. Your Mr. Jay has shared his magic of the air with us, so we will share ours with you. My nephews will take you to the camp at Sedagong, and from there they can lead you to the only place where the plant grows on the island."

I was overwhelmed by the trust the villagers were placing in me. I assured them that I would only take a small sample and would try to help them propagate the plant more easily. They seemed satisfied, and we agreed to set out for Sedagong the following morning.

CHAPTER 11

I arose early again, eager to get started on our excursion into the jungle of Tioman. I packed up some bundles of supplies to take with us so I could collect seeds, cuttings, and specimens to dry. Johari explained that his nephews, Wira and Jasmi, would lead us along the path between Tekek and Juara, the village on the opposite side of the island. Sedagong was about halfway between the two villages, a distance of only two miles, but it would be slow going with the terrain.

We set out by ten o'clock. Several more boys tagged along, helping to carry the supplies and food for a few days. The path into the jungle was easy enough to follow, worn bare by many feet. The elevation increased along with the density of plants. Our progress was especially protracted because I stopped often to scrutinize a particular tree, shrub, or vine. I decided not to make any collections along the way, but noted what to sample on the return trip.

After about an hour of walking, we rested near a waterfall cascading over boulders slick and green with moss and algae. We arrived at Sedagong after another hour's walk. The camp itself was a few hundred feet from the path in the bush. The boys who had come along for the trek set down the packs of supplies. I found some rolls of Life Savers candy to give them, a meager reward for their services, but all I could offer at the time.

Swinging machetes to clear the way, Wira and Jasmi led Jay and me away from the well-traveled path and into the thick brush. Soon a small structure with a thatched roof came into sight, the base camp Tweedie and his colleagues had constructed on an expedition a few years prior. There was just one large room. I expected to spend some time patching the roof and clearing away spider webs, bats, and all manner of wildlife that had made their home there in the intervening years, but the hut was in surprisingly good repair. The floor was clean, almost as if it had been recently swept. I asked Wira and Jasmi if they had come to the camp in advance to prepare it for us, but they denied performing such a service. We set up our sleeping mats, and I arranged my supplies. Behind the shack, an area free of vegetation made an ideal spot for a fire. In fact, a circle of rocks held the charred remains of a campfire. I looked at it closely. Someone had been to the camp very recently. Wira and Jasmi said no one from Tekek had been there, but maybe someone had come from Juara. That seemed like a reasonable conclusion.

We agreed to visit the spot with the special plant the following day, as it was some distance from the camp. I spent the rest of the day describing nearby plants in my journal and collecting some interesting samples. We went back to the hut, and I asked Jay to open one of the parcels for me. He undid the wrapping on the bundle.

"*Dios mío, Profesora*. This is what we have carried into the middle of the jungle for you?" Jay said, holding up a stack of newspapers. "You need to read *The Ithaca Journal* now?"

"No, Jay, the newspapers are important scientific supplies, not for reading. Although if things get too boring, they can come in handy for that, too." I took a pile of newspapers and showed him how I pressed the plants between the pages, numbering them and noting in my journal what number had been collected where, along with my suspected identification. I carefully bound up the completed collection in the plant press. The bundle would be dried when we got back to Tekek.

Jay initially watched me, but soon he was reading the newspaper. Wira and Jasmi had gone off to gather firewood and ripe fruits to eat. When they returned, Jay went out back to help them make the fire. He took some sheets of *The Ithaca Journal* to use as kindling. In a few moments, he was back inside holding out something toward me.

"Ivy, we started to make the new campfire in the circle of rocks. When we cleared out the old ashes, I found this." I took the charred scrap of paper he held out and peered at it. It was a bit of newspaper. The edges crumbled in my hand. Just a tiny section remained. In the waning light I could just see some writing. It wasn't in English. Or Malay. Or Chinese.

"*Triumph des Willens*," I read. "By Leni Riefenstahl, it says. It's an ad for a movie. 'Now playing,' I think it says. I know some German."

"Yes, I do, too. And that is also what I read. What do you make of that, Profesora?"

"I don't know. Someone used an old German newspaper for kindling, I guess," I said with a shrug. Jay went back to start the new fire, but he seemed preoccupied.

When the campfire was ready, we cooked fish marinated in lime juice that we'd brought from Tekek wrapped in banana leaves. By then it was dark, but too early to go to bed. Wira and Jasmi entertained us with traditional songs, but soon went inside. Jay and I sat together as the fire dwindled.

"Ithaca. Is that where you're from? Like Odysseus."

"Yes, that's right," I said with a laugh. "But my Ithaca is very different. It's not an island in Greece, but a town in the middle of the state of New York. Surrounded by woods and lakes and deep gorges formed by glaciers. But I guess I'll always go home to Ithaca, just like Odysseus."

"It sounds idyllic."

"I guess it is. I suppose one always has to leave home to appreciate just how nice it is to come back. What about you? Will you go home someday?" Jay looked away, and I instantly regretted the prying question.

"I would like to go home someday. I didn't want to leave it to begin with."

"What happened?"

"My father decided I should attend university in Spain, like him. He decided that I should be an architect, like him. And so I went to Barcelona to study. I did well in my classes, completed the assignments on time and adequately. I knew I could graduate and find work as an architect. And yet, something was missing. One day I was walking to class with a friend. He was telling me about the design for a building that had come to him that morning while taking a bath. Instead of marveling at his unique idea, I was astounded by the fact that he thought of architecture while in the bath. And then I realized what I was missing: the passion to be an architect."

"What did you think about in the bath, instead?" I asked.

"I asked myself that, too. And the answer surprised me. Flying. I wanted to fly. On the days I spent looking up at the magnificent architecture of Barcelona, it was only when an airplane flew overhead that I felt my heart take wing."

"So you learned to fly?"

"I quit the university. My father was furious. And I enlisted in the Spanish Air Force. My mother was devastated. But I wanted to learn to fly, and that seemed like the best way. I had no thoughts of a civil war coming to Spain and happily progressed through the training program. The day I made my first solo flight was my proudest moment, better than any university diploma."

I waited for Jay to continue, but he was silent. After a few moments I said, "I can tell you're a natural pilot. Being grounded as an architect wouldn't have suited you. Surely your parents aren't still angry with you, are they?"

"Thank you, Ivy. Angry? No, I suppose not. My father is just disappointed now. Maybe that's worse."

"I'm sure that's not true, Jay. I'm sure they're proud of you," I said, although I had no way of knowing. Not only was I spoiled by growing up in my idyllic home of Ithaca, but also by having parents who supported my choice of unusual career. I couldn't imagine having my future prescribed by my family's desires.

"Don't you think we should be well-rested for tomorrow's expedition, Profesora?" Jay asked, changing the subject.

"Yes, I suppose it's time to turn in, Jay." We crept quietly inside the shack so as not to wake Wira and Jasmi, settled onto our sleeping mats, and drew our mosquito nets around ourselves.

When I awoke the next morning, I found Jay, Wira, and Jasmi already eating breakfast and drinking a tea they had brewed from the leaves of a nearby plant. I made note of it, collected a sample, and enjoyed the warm beverage while the air was still cool. We made our plans for the day and departed along a disused path leading into the bush. Wira and Jasmi led the way, their machetes clearing an opening for us to pass through the dense foliage.

Eventually the brush thinned out, and we could hear the sound of water. We came to a small stream with a huge boulder on its bank. The rock was partly obscured by a massive ficus tree with a vast array of small aerial roots that had grown down to the ground and joined together to form an immense trunk. The canopy of the tree had to be a hundred feet in the air, and vines streamed down from the upper branches. Such a colossal tree must have been centuries old.

Wira and Jasmi led us to the side of the tree opposite the boulder. There was a narrow opening between some sections of trunk that revealed a hollow interior. The ficus tree had grown over an existing mature tree, which had died and rotted away, leaving an empty cavity where the original tree had been. This was why it was called a strangler fig.

This must have been the tree I'd heard described as 'Mother Willow.' Whoever had called it a willow knew no botany, but the moniker of 'Mother' was apt. This tree clearly sustained more life, both vegetable and animal, than she had taken away. Her canopy was filled with birds, and I could spot multiple types of plants growing amidst her upper branches.

Wira slipped inside the tree and gestured for us to follow. The four of us squeezed inside together. I peered up at the top of the tree, wondering why we'd been brought here. The Buddha had sat beneath a fig tree and attained enlightenment. But Wira and Jasmi explained that the plant I was seeking was at the top, not the bottom. We would have to climb heavenward to get it.

Wira went first, with me following close behind. I noted each handhold and foothold he used and tried to do the same. Jay followed me, and Jasmi brought up the rear. The climbing was not too difficult thanks to the latticework formed by the aerial roots. I willed myself not to think about the height or the descent later. The close-up view of many insects, spiders, and small reptiles took my mind off the rapidly disappearing ground far below.

Eventually we neared the canopy of the tree, her own branches festooned with vines of many kinds. I gradually became aware of an unpleasant odor. It was not the smell of a durian, but more like rotting flesh. I looked back at Jay, and he was attempting to bury his face in his outstretched arm, so I guessed he smelled it, too.

Wira motioned for me to stop climbing. Jasmi advanced past me to join Wira at a cluster of leaves. They spoke too quickly for me to understand for a few minutes, but they seemed agitated. Then they turned and gestured for us to ascend to their level. Jay and I scrambled up the last few feet to join them, the smell growing more pungent.

The two men parted to reveal an astonishing sight: a massive flower whose appearance could only be described as fleshy, with an aroma to match.

"*Bunga pakma*," Wira said, pointing at the enormous bloom.

"A *Rafflesia!*" I cried with delight. Like the hotel and museum, this unusual type of flower was named after Sir Stamford Raffles.

"*Dios mío, Profesora.* Surely this is not what we've climbed up here to see? An ugly, stinking flower?" Jay said with disgust.

"Ugly? I think it's quite beautiful. And the smell is an ingenious way to attract flies to pollinate the flower." The bloom was almost two feet across. Five huge, reddish petals mottled with lighter colored warts surrounded a central bowl with a flat, pale protuberance in the middle.

I explained that the flower was a parasite and had no leaves or roots of its own. It could only grow on a particular species of vine in the grape family called *Tetrastigma*. I pointed out the host plant and noted just one bulbous bud forming on a nearby vine. Eventually it would become a massive flower, but there was only this one in bloom now and no way to know how many would develop later.

I looked at the flower closely. The interior had a smooth central disk lacking the spikes I recalled seeing in drawings and in a preserved specimen. I began to suspect it was a unique species not observed before. I asked Wira and Jasmi where else the flower could be found. They both agreed that it only grew here, in the canopy of Mother Fig, as I'd renamed her, and nowhere else on the island. They didn't know of this type growing on the mainland anywhere, either. But they said there were usually many flowers and many developing buds, not just one, and it was forbidden to leave so few. They didn't understand who would have taken so many. Looking at the host vine, I could see cuts where other flowers had been excised. The knife marks in the woody vine looked recent.

It was clear I could not collect a sample of so rare a flower. It was impossible to know how many *Rafflesia* buds were waiting to erupt from the vine, but I couldn't take the chance of collecting the last of the population, or maybe even the species. I explained this to Wira and Jasmi. Jay sighed with relief that the stinking flower would not be coming with us.

I collected a cutting from the *Tetrastigma* vine, which was plentiful, and we descended from Mother Fig, carefully backing down. I managed to forget about the great height by convincing myself it was just like climbing down from my childhood tree house perched in the big, old apple tree in my parents' backyard.

Safely on the ground again, we rested for a while in the shade of the great fig tree. I half-heartedly collected some other plants growing in the area. Returning empty-handed would be disappointing, not so much for failing to bring back the antimalarial plant I'd been sent to retrieve, but for missing the opportunity to describe a new species of *Rafflesia*.

We headed back to camp at a leisurely pace. I pressed the new specimens and detailed the day's disappointment in my journal. But I formulated a plan: I had brought a small camera along, so I would go back up the tree to take some photos. I had a sketchbook and colored pencils to makes some drawings, as well. If I couldn't collect a sample of the new *Rafflesia*, at least I could document its existence.

At dinner, I asked Wira and Jasmi about who could have collected the *Rafflesia*. They didn't know, but were sure it was no one from Tekek. And people from the other villages would never have left just one in bloom.

Chapter 12

I followed Wira up the great fig tree again the next morning while Jay and Jasmi waited below. The ascent was familiar now, and we reached the canopy of leaves faster than the previous day. The single fetid bloom was still there in all its glory, some flies happily buzzing about in search of the rotting flesh they had detected.

I braced myself between three intersecting branches to be stable enough to take a few photographs and make a drawing. While not as good as a sample, the images might be enough to determine if it was an undiscovered species.

I sketched the flower and colored in the drawing. Then I snapped some photos at different angles. Trying not to breathe, I leaned in for a close-up shot of the bowl-shaped interior. It was then that I saw it. I took the photo, then let the camera fall around my neck. I held my nose with one hand and reached into the center of the flower. From the surface of the light peach-colored flesh, I carefully retrieved a strand of hair.

A strand of blond hair. A long blond hair. I showed it to Wira who looked at it blankly. I pulled out a small glass vial from my pocket and placed the hair inside. We descended from the tree, and I called Jay over to see my discovery.

"I found something you should see," I said.

"Another flower? A new plant? I hope this one does not smell," Jay said. I held out the little glass vial for him to inspect.

"A bit of spider's silk?" he asked.

"No, Jay. It's a strand of hair. Human hair. From a blond woman."

"That seems unlikely, Profesora. What would a woman be doing in that tree?"

"She might have been doing exactly what I was doing. But she got there first. And took all the flowers but one."

"Maybe a bird dropped it there on its way to make a nest," Jay suggested. "Are you sure it's a hair? I think I would have noticed a woman with long blond hair in the village, anyway."

I glared at Jay. "Yes, it's a hair. We can look at it with a magnifying glass at camp. And it obviously didn't come from someone in the village. Or me." I tried to explain to Wira and Jasmi that it was a hair. They had never seen a fair-haired woman on the island.

Back at camp, Jay conceded it appeared to be a human hair after peering at it through the magnifying glass.

"But Profesora, it cannot be that another woman went up that same tree."

"It can be, Jay. I'm not the only woman who collects plants in the field. There are others. And I even know one who has such long blond hair."

"Would your friend come here without you knowing it?"

"I didn't say she was my friend. Far from it. Besides, she's German, so I wouldn't know if she were coming here."

"German," Jay repeated in a flat tone.

"Yes, from the University of Göttingen. Her name is Emerald Asche-Böhrer." Despite the heat, I shivered.

"Could she have been here?"

"I suppose so," I said as memories of last summer in Africa came flooding back. I had hoped I'd never run into her again.

"Remember that scrap of newspaper, Ivy?"

"I remember it," I said glumly. That explained why the camp was so tidy. And why the flowers were gone. I was surprised she had even left one. If something were of value to her, she would take it. She had no concern about protecting a species or preserving it for the use of the local people.

I suggested we spend one more night at the camp and return to Tekek in the morning. We were a subdued group as we sat around the fire that evening. Wira and Jasmi seemed preoccupied, perhaps worried they would be blamed for the disappearance of the flowers. Jay seemed needlessly troubled, too. All he had to do was fly me back to Singapore, and his job was done. Whether or not I brought back the antimalarial plant was of no consequence to him.

Wira and Jasmi excused themselves, leaving me with Jay by the dwindling flames. I involuntarily shivered again as I wondered if Emerald Asche-Böhrer had sat in this very spot.

"Are you cold, Ivy?" Jay asked.

"No, just thinking."

"I'm sorry you will return without your special plant."

"It's okay, Jay. I don't care about bringing the plant back." That was true. But to be bested by Emerald Asche-Böhrer was another matter entirely. I could not help caring about that. "Well, look on the bright side. At least we won't have to bring back that smelly flower in Lula."

Jay smiled tautly. "Yes, there is that. But I would have let you bring it back. Especially now that I know who else wants it."

"What do you mean?"

"The Germans. I thought I escaped them, but the Nazis have found me even here in this remote place."

"The Nazis? I said she was German, not a Nazi."

"Is there a difference now?"

"I don't know. But they weren't looking for you, I'm sure. They wanted the same plant. I don't know why. I don't even know why I was sent to get that plant, really. There have to be other more promising replacements for quinine than a rare parasitic plant that's hard to propagate."

Jay was poking at the dying embers of the campfire with a stick. I suddenly wished I were back home, sitting around a campfire toasting marshmallows with my parents at Chautauqua.

"What do you mean you escaped the Nazis?" I finally asked. Jay put down the stick and looked at me.

"When I joined the Air Force in Spain, I was naïve. I simply wanted to fly. But then the coup came, and we were at war. But we weren't just fighting amongst ourselves. No, all the governments sent their airplanes and pilots to one side or the other. The Germans and the

Italians sent theirs to help Franco and the Nationalists. Finally the Soviets came to help us. And so I was flying a *Mosca.*"

"A *Mosca?*"

"Yes, a fly. That's what we called the Soviet's Polikarpov I-16 fighter. At first I was eager to fly the little plane. Even then I did not think ahead. But I found out soon enough that I liked to fly, not to shoot. Or to be shot at. And then the Nazis came in their Messerschmitts." Jay grew silent and prodded the embers again.

"What happened?"

"On the last mission I flew, we were overrun by the Messerschmitts. They hit the plane of my comrade, and he parachuted out as his *Mosca* went down. But the Nazis in the Messerschmitts were not satisfied to destroy the aircraft. They killed my friend with their machine guns as he floated down to earth."

"I'm sorry, Jay," I said, placing my hand on his arm in a lame attempt to console him. I wanted to comfort him, but there was nothing I could do to ease the pain that was palpable in his voice.

"I was luckier," he continued. "My airplane was badly damaged, too. But I did not dare bail out. I knew I could not make it back to our base, but I was near the French border. I flew into France and managed to put the plane down in a field near a small town. I had some slight injuries, and the villagers cared for me until I recovered. But I didn't go back to Spain. My enlistment had expired while I was recuperating. And I am not Spanish. It wasn't my fight. So when I was strong enough, I went to Marseille. I took passage on the first ship I found that was not bound for Spain. The ship was heading east. Eventually I found myself in Singapore and decided to stay. I was happy to fly again and happy to trade the ugly *mosca* for the lovely *libélula*."

"You're right, Jay. It's not your war. I'm glad you didn't go back."

"Thank you, Ivy. But I wonder if fate has other ideas," Jay said with a shrug. He excused himself, leaving me to ponder his story and the day's unwelcome surprise as the last of the embers died.

CHAPTER 13

Late the next afternoon, we emerged from the bush at Tekek's familiar cluster of buildings. The trip back along the trail was slow as I stopped to collect plants and note them in my log. Even though I would be returning empty-handed with respect to my original quest, at least the herbaria at the Raffles Museum, Cornell, and California Academy of Sciences would benefit from the expedition.

Everyone from the village came to greet us, and Wira and Jasmi began hurriedly talking to the elders. I slipped away to my workspace to set up the earlier samples in the dryer and press the newer samples. When I'd taken care of them, I rejoined the group.

"Wira and Jasmi have told us about the theft of the *bunga pakma*," said Johari. "No one on the island would do such a thing. And yet no one who does not live on Tioman could know of the flower and its properties."

I showed him the strand of blond hair. "Someone from another village must have taken the owner of this hair up the tree."

"Yes, it must be so. But they would not have let someone take all but one of the flowers. We all know it is necessary to leave many to grow and gain their powers."

"Maybe they had no choice. Maybe they were threatened."

"Threatened? I cannot imagine such a thing. Tomorrow we will walk to Juara, the village on the other side of the island, and ask what has happened. Perhaps they will have a good explanation."

The evening meal was subdued as each of us contemplated the loss of the flowers. For me it was purely scientific, but for the people of Tekek it presaged a loss of their culture and innate knowledge of the natural world as other people with other priorities intruded.

Nearly the whole village accompanied us on the walk from Tekek to Juara the next day. Since we stayed on the path and I didn't stop to collect any samples, the trip took us less than two hours. Johari led the way with groups of children occasionally running ahead. We emerged from the jungle to find a small village similar in size and style to Tekek, situated on a protected cove on the eastern side of Tioman. Children from Juara ran out to meet us, happy to have some new playmates. An older man and several elderly women soon joined us. Johari greeted them animatedly, and we were led to a covered pavilion area and given coconuts to drink.

Johari introduced Jay and me to the elders. It seemed the younger men were out fishing. Gradually a few more women joined us, abandoning their gardens and other tasks. I gathered that once the pleasantries were concluded, Johari began to tell them of the loss of the flowers. The villagers reacted with distress. The news was obviously a surprise to them.

"Johari, please ask them if someone was here. A

woman with fair hair," I said, handing him the vial with the single blond strand. He spoke quickly as they passed the vial around.

"Yes," he said. "They tell me a man and a woman came on a small boat. They spoke some Malay. They said they had just gotten married and were on what you call a 'honeymoon.'"

"Did they ask about the flower or other plants?"

Johari consulted with the villagers for a moment. "No, they asked about a place where they could be alone together. They seemed to already know about the camp at Sedagong. The villagers sent some boys with them to show them the camp, but then they were alone. The couple stayed there several days and came back to the village. Then they left in their boat."

"What did they look like? Where were they going?" I asked.

Johari translated my questions and received an answer. "They say the woman was very beautiful, but pale as a ghost. The children were afraid of her light hair and white skin when they first saw her. And her eyes were green, like a jewel. But the man was ugly, no match for such a woman, with eyes the color of a steel knife blade and a hard face that didn't smile. They didn't say where they were going."

"And no one saw them with the flowers?"

The group of villagers agreed that no one had mentioned the flower to them, and the pair didn't seem interested in such things. I began to think Jay had been right. Maybe the hair had gotten dropped on the flower by some other means. But that didn't explain the fresh cuts where other flowers and buds had been excised.

"Isn't there anything else they remember about the couple?" I asked. "Did they give anything to anyone?"

The villagers were answering no, when a small girl, who had slipped away a few minutes before, returned to the group. She tugged at Johari's arm and opened her closed fist. We all leaned in for a look.

On her little palm was a gold ring with a green stone carved into the shape of a beetle. A ring I had seen before. On the hand of Emerald Asche-Böhrer. My heart sank.

Johari asked her where she had gotten the ring. The girl explained that the woman had not given it to her. She had seen her wearing it, though. On the day after their boat left, the girl found it in the sand. It must have slipped off the woman's finger without her noticing.

The girl held the ring out to me, prepared to give up her secret treasure, but I folded her fingers around it again. It was of no use to me, and she might as well keep it.

The group discussed the loss of the flowers and agreed no one would harvest any until more had grown back. The villages would take turns visiting the vine in the Mother tree to make sure the flowers were safe.

The women of Juara showed me around their tidy village and gardens. The little girl who had found the ring brought me to a spot on the beach and told that was where the sea turtles came to lay their eggs. She and the other girls would protect the nests from lizards and crabs who would try to eat the eggs and young hatchlings.

We departed from Juara and made our way back across the island to arrive at Tekek before dark. As we ate our evening meal, I pondered what to do next. There seemed to be little to help with the *Rafflesia* situation. Either the population would grow back and survive, or it was too late. The flowers would be difficult or even impossible to propagate away from their natural environment. I wondered why Emerald had even bothered to come for the plant. Or why I had, for that matter.

"Is the flower really so important to treat malaria?" I asked Johari.

"We do use it in dire cases, but it is not the main use," he replied.

"Please tell me what other uses you have for it. I have to know why the couple took the flowers." Johari spoke to the others for a few minutes. Initially there was some laughter, but then the tone turned serious.

"The flowers have other uses. Like the durian, they increase desire."

Jay snorted.

Ignoring him, Johari continued, "But the most important use is in childbirth. The women make a special extract from the flowers and buds. It makes the birth easier and the mother recovers more quickly, so she can have another baby sooner. Maybe that is why the woman wanted the flowers."

"Maybe," I said skeptically. I doubted Emerald wanted those flowers for personal use or that the man she was with was actually her husband. It seemed unlikely to me that she had developed a maternal streak since I last saw her.

I spent the next day packing up all my dried specimens while Jay went fishing with the men of the village. They returned with a bountiful catch that the women prepared for us in the evening as a farewell feast. We would return to Singapore the following morning.

Before departing, I presented our hosts at Tekek with the remainder of the food and medical supplies I had brought with us, paid Wira and Jasmi for their guide services, and sat down with the women to make a list of things they wanted from the mainland. I figured I'd send Jay back with a planeload of items for them, although it could not repay them for their hospitality and sharing their wisdom and knowledge with me. And I felt oddly responsible for the loss of their precious *Rafflesia*. Even if I somehow found Emerald Asche-Böhrer and recovered the flowers and buds, they could not have been replanted on their host vine in Mother Fig. Only time would tell if enough *Rafflesia* were hidden in the vines to emerge and ensure the continuity of the population.

The pressed samples and equipment were stowed in the rear hold of Lula. As I said farewell to the people of Tekek, I noticed Jay at the nose of the aircraft once more, stroking it gently. He joined me after a moment, helping me into the cabin. While I settled into the cramped cockpit, he retrieved the rope that anchored us to the jetty, closed the door, and took his place to my left. Jasmi turned the propellers a few revolutions, then backed away as Jay had taught him to do. The engines roared to life.

I waved energetically as we began to taxi away from the dock. Jay pushed the throttles forward, and we picked up speed. As we broke from the water, the people of Tekek waved, and children jumped up and down. Jay turned and made a pass over the beach, dipped the wings back and forth, and set us on course for Singapore.

CHAPTER 14

Back at Kallang Aerodrome, Jay arranged for my supplies and some of the samples to be stored at the Qantas hangar, while the specimens destined for the Raffles Museum came with me in a taxi back to the hotel, as did Jay.

"Profesora Ivy, I'm sorry you did not find what you set out to discover," he said as we rode back to the Raffles. "Will you go back to America now?"

"Thank you, Jay. It's all right. I suppose I'll go back home after I've deposited all the samples in the museum. I had originally hoped to go to New Zealand, but I doubt I'll have time now."

We pulled up to the hotel, and a porter arrived to help me. I expected Jay to remain in the cab, but he exited, too.

"I also live here, Profesora," he explained. "The airline keeps a small room for me when I am not flying."

We stopped at the reception desk to retrieve our keys. The opulence of the lobby was a striking contrast to the accommodations on Tioman, and yet it felt bland and lifeless by comparison. But I supposed a bath would remind me of the pleasure of modern conveniences. I was even more dirty and disheveled than the first time I'd arrived in this grand hotel. The well-trained clerk pretended not to notice as he handed us our room keys.

"A telegram for you, as well, Miss Linden," he said, handing me a thin paper envelope. I thanked him, shoved it in my bag, and proceeded to my room along with the porter.

Jay indicated his room was on the second floor. "I trust I will see you again before your departure, Profesora?" he said as we parted company.

"Yes, of course, Jay. Thank you for everything. I appreciate all your help. And Lula's, too."

"*Hasta luego*, then, Ivy."

I continued up to the third floor and found my room just as I'd left it. After tipping the porter who had carried my bag and the bundle of plant specimens, I closed the door behind him and reveled in the silence. It was the first time I'd been completely alone for days. I kicked off my shoes, began to draw a bath, and undressed. I was about to immerse myself in the deep, white porcelain claw-foot tub and wash away the grime of days in the bush when I remembered the telegram in my bag. Maybe it was from my parents. It could wait. But then curiosity got the better of me. I retrieved the envelope, hastily tore it open, and pulled out a sheet to read:

PROFESSOR LINDEN= CHANGE OF PLANS STOP PROCEED TO VANIKORO SOLOMONS AT EARLIEST CONVENIENCE STOP FURTHER INSTRUCTIONS AWAIT FROM RO BOYE STOP JOHNSON AND SMITH USDA

I crumpled up the sheet in disgust and threw it into the wastepaper basket. A languid soak in the tub was no longer possible. I washed mechanically, my mind preoccupied with the unwelcome message. What did it even mean? Who were they to send me on this fool's errand? I had fulfilled my end of the bargain already. I would just come home and salvage what I could of the summer before I had to prepare for classes again. I could even take in a few concerts at Chautauqua if I left right away.

I was so irate that I could not even enjoy feeling clean for the first time in recent memory. I put on a fern green day dress and fixed my hair. I sat down with my journal at the writing desk and added some details to each day's entry. But my irritation only grew when I came to the passage about the little girl showing us the ring she had found in the sand. I took the vial containing the single hair from my bag and held it up to the light. I put it in the desk drawer. I unwrapped the little pistol, which had been so unnecessary, and turned it this way and that to catch the light, just like the blond strand had done. I wrapped it back up in a handkerchief and placed it in the drawer as well. Then I retrieved the telegram from the wastebasket, smoothed the paper as best I could, and put it back into the envelope. I tucked it in my purse and went down to the lobby.

First I looked in the Long Bar and then the dining rooms. Then I went to the front desk and asked for the room number of Mr. Diente de León. 214. Back upstairs I went and knocked lightly on the door. After a moment, the door opened slowly.

"Profesora, what a surprise. I had not expected to see

you again so soon," Jay said with a broad grin. "Please come in." He opened the door wide, and I saw he was freshly shaved, his dark hair still damp. His white linen shirt was half unbuttoned. I involuntarily glanced at the dark curls visible there. He followed my gaze, but made no effort to cover himself. I felt my cheeks redden as he closed the door behind me.

"Have a seat, Ivy," Jay said, gesturing to two rattan chairs with a small table between them. His room was perhaps a quarter of the size of mine with no sitting area or desk. But he had a fully stocked bamboo liquor cart and, without asking, poured me a gin and tonic. I didn't protest, remembering the few mosquito bites I'd gotten on Tioman. A little quinine was a good idea. Jay poured himself one, too, and sat down in the other chair. He smiled at me expectantly.

"I read my telegram," I said, holding the wrinkled sheet out to him. He took it and read the message.

"What does it mean, Ivy?"

"I don't know."

"I think it means you need a pilot." Jay grinned, and I knew I was going to Vanikoro, wherever that was.

"Surely you're otherwise engaged, Jay. Qantas doesn't just let you fly anyone anywhere, do they?"

"There are other pilots, but only I fly Lula, and she is who you need to take you. A ship would take too long. And there are no scheduled flights. The Solomon Islands are remote. And I have always wanted to go there. You know, it was a Spaniard, Alvaro de Mendaña, who discovered them. He thought they held the gold of King Solomon's mines."

I laughed, but saw he seemed serious.

"I don't expect King Solomon's gold is there, Jay. But I know what is: malaria. Surely that's why I'm being sent there. Mendaña didn't really discover the islands. People were living there thousands of years before he sailed there. And so they will have a vast knowledge of the plants that can be used to treat all sorts of diseases," I explained.

"That sounds less interesting than a gold mine, Profesora. But I will arrange the trip. When shall we go?"

"I have to go to the Raffles Museum and deposit all my new samples from Tioman there," I said. I would have liked a week to read up on the flora and culture of the Solomons, but that was a luxury I didn't have.

"Let's go the day after tomorrow, then. You can visit the museum tomorrow, and I will stock up on provisions for the trip and make sure Lula is in top form for such a journey. Do we need to take one of your colleagues from the museum with us?"

"That sounds like a good plan, Jay. I don't think we need anyone from the museum, even if they could accompany us on such short notice. It seems like Mr. Boye on Vanikoro will know what to do once we get there." With that we agreed to meet for dinner the next evening, and I left for the museum with a satchel filled with my pressed samples.

Chasen and Tweedie greeted me with much enthusiasm. Tweedie had recovered from his bout of malaria and was disappointed to have missed the trip.

"Don't worry, Tweedie, you didn't miss too much, although everyone remembers you and sends their regards. Johari and the other people of Tekek took good care of us. Me and Jay, the Qantas pilot, I mean. It proved useful to have him along. He charmed everyone with rides in his airplane. We went to Sedagong with two of Johari's nephews. They took us to see a *Rafflesia* at the top of that huge fig tree, but there was just one flower blooming. I think it was a new species. I took photos and drew pictures, so I'll have to compare them to the samples and drawings here."

"That sounds like an interesting discovery," Tweedie said ruefully.

"That's not the interesting part. Someone else got there first, not too long before us. They collected many flowers and buds. I'm afraid the population won't recover."

"Who could have done such a thing? I'm sure any expedition would have come through Singapore, and we've met no one with such an interest other than you," Chasen said.

"I think I know who it was. They left some clues behind. It's a German botanist named Emerald Asche-Böhrer." Tweedie and Chasen exchanged a glance. "I've met her before, unfortunately," I continued. "She's a ruthless collector with little regard for the local peoples and environment."

"No one came through here, Ivy. It seems hard to believe someone, even a German, would not visit us," Tweedie said. "Will you go back to the United States now?"

"That was my plan, but my sponsors at the U.S. Department of Agriculture wired me to go to a place called Vanikoro in the Solomon Islands. I'm going the day after tomorrow."

Chasen got a huge leather-bound atlas down from a

bookshelf and found a map of the Solomon Islands. Just east of New Guinea, the group contained hundreds of islands with the largest ones forming two parallel chains with a passage between them. Vanikoro was not part of the main grouping of islands, but a bit south, closer to the New Hebrides in a small cluster known as the Santa Cruz Islands.

"I seem to recall a timber company based there," Tweedie said.

"I'm to report to a Mr. R. O. Boye, apparently. I suppose he has information on another antimalarial plant. I'll come back here tomorrow and mount some of the samples from Tioman." I gave Tweedie the film from my camera and asked him to develop the photos. I figured they would be ready by the time I returned from Vanikoro, and we could determine if the *Rafflesia* looked like a new species then.

I spent the next day immersed in the herbarium, mounting my new samples and looking at ones previously collected in the Solomon Islands. I made lists of promising plants to collect. At least the herbaria would benefit from this unexpected expedition. The spontaneity of it bothered me less than usual, as I felt I could trust Jay to organize the supplies and plan the route. If I hadn't met Jay, I'm not sure how I would have arranged the trip.

That evening, I had dinner with Jay in the Tiffin Room at the Raffles. Over dishes of aromatic curries, he told me the route he had mapped out for the trip. We would fly east along the coasts of Sumatra and Java in the Dutch East Indies, then to Darwin in Australia, Port Moresby in Papua New Guinea, and finally Tulagi in the British Solomon Islands Protectorate, before we reached the remote island of Vanikoro.

"We'll make it to Surabaya by tomorrow night," Jay said, his eyes gleaming. "We'll be on Vanikoro in four day's time. But we could get there sooner if we flew at night, too."

"No, let's stick with daylight," I said, thinking of that impossibly small dot surrounded by water on Chasen's map. No need to take any extra risks.

We agreed to meet at six the next morning in the lobby for an early start. I went back to my room to pack up again. Enjoying the comfort of the Raffles had been short-lived.

CHAPTER 15

"*Buenos días, Profesora,*" Jay said with a grin and a slight bow. He was more chipper at six in the morning than anyone should be; the prospect of flying to new places obviously delighted him.

"Good morning, Jay," I said as I handed over my room key to the clerk. Once again, he promised my room would remain just as I'd left it until my return, whenever that would be. A porter helped us carry our luggage to a waiting cab. Jay had a small satchel, but I was more encumbered.

"Profesora, you do not travel lightly," Jay said as he hefted one of my bags into the trunk. He peeked inside and saw the bag was filled with newspaper. I shrugged apologetically. I had surreptitiously gathered all the old copies of the *Straits Times* that I could find lying around the hotel to use for pressing samples.

The taxi dropped us off at the Qantas hangar at Kallang Aerodrome. Jay had arranged for Lula to be loaded up with my gear, plus a small extra fuel tank that would allow us to go a bit farther each day. We stowed our bags in the rear cabin, and I climbed aboard the aircraft while Jay consulted with his mechanic and reviewed the flight plan. Finally, we shoved off from the dock as the propellers started to whir. Jay pushed the throttles forward, and the Dragonfly rose into the air.

We hugged the coastline of Sumatra, the rugged hills of the vast island to our right with smaller islands spilled out like drops of absinthe to our left.

"Take the controls, Ivy," Jay said after a while. I gently took the stick, flattered he trusted me with his precious Lula. She purred away, as contented as Rama and Osiris back home.

After some time, Jay said he'd take the yoke again. I peered out the window, taking in each clump of land surrounded by turquoise and wondering what natural treasures lived on each one. Eventually, I sensed the aircraft losing altitude. Jay announced we would soon land in Batavia.

A bustling port city appeared on the western end of Java. We skimmed along the bay, coming to a stop at the Qantas dock. While Jay saw to refueling the aircraft, I stretched my legs. Soon enough we were back in the cramped cockpit heading further east over Java. After several hours of following the coastline, another larger city came into view. Jay set the Dragonfly down at the dock at Surabaya. We had company. A large flying boat was already moored near there.

"Jay, does Qantas normally operate a route here?"

"Yes, from Singapore to Sydney. It's a partnership with Imperial Airways. That's a Short Empire," he said, gesturing at the four-engine flying boat dwarfing Lula.

"It looks like a tall empire to me. So I could have just taken this luxury flying boat all the way to Australia?"

"Well, yes, technically, Profesora, you could have

done that. But then how would you get to Vanikoro? You need Lula for that. And me. And you wouldn't have gotten to fly *that* airplane. Isn't this better?" he said with an ingratiating smile.

"I guess so," I said, remembering the comfort of the Clipper. Surely the British version was every bit as sumptuous and more. Perhaps I should not have relinquished the trip planning to Jay after all.

"Come, Ivy," Jay said, reaching out his hand to help me to the dock. "We'll go to the hotel now." Jay went back to the nose of the aircraft, patted Lula, and retrieved our small overnight bags. We left Lula in the capable hands of some Qantas mechanics who would refuel her and check to make sure everything was tiptop.

Jay led me to the terminal, and I waited a few minutes while he spoke to some of the other staff. Then we met a waiting taxi to take us to the hotel. I was surprised to find Surabaya as modern as Singapore and even more surprised when we pulled up to the Hotel Oranje. It could have been Raffles' sister.

"It was built by the same family as Raffles," Jay explained as he paid the taxi driver and led the way to the entrance. The lobby was part of an addition to the original structure, in the latest *moderne* style with Art Deco friezes and stained glass that would have looked at home in the Empire State Building. Once again, I felt shabby in the swanky hotel where smartly dressed men and women sat around in club chairs, speaking Dutch or English in British and Australian accents. I guessed some of them were the passengers from the moored flying boat, on their way to or from Sydney.

"It's been a long time since we've seen you, Mr. Jay,"

the front desk clerk said, smiling officiously as he handed Jay a key. "And your room is right next door, Miss Linden." We had too little luggage to require the assistance of a porter, so Jay took the lead to our rooms.

"I've stayed here a few times before. Sometimes I fly as co-pilot on the Short Empire," he explained. "Shall we have dinner? We could walk around the city and find a little place. It is too stuffy here for my taste."

I readily agreed, knowing the stares I'd get in the hotel restaurant. I was wearing slacks and had no skirt or dress to change into for dinner. We freshened up for a few minutes, then met in the lobby again and walked out into the humid air, a blaze of pink and orange coloring the twilight sky.

The city reminded me of Singapore, with broad, tree-lined streets and colonial buildings. We turned down an alley off a larger street and found a small restaurant on the first floor of a low white building with a terracotta-tiled roof. There were no other foreigners inside, only local people, a good sign. We ordered two specialties, fried duck and vegetables in a peanut sauce. By the time we finished dinner, it was dark with a huge orange full moon hanging like a lantern to guide us back to the hotel. It would have been nice to enjoy a longer walk in the night air, but Jay reminded me we had to leave early the next morning. The trip to Darwin would be even longer than today's flight.

The Qantas mechanics had Lula serviced and fueled for us the next morning. The sun was barely up when we began to taxi out of the bay. Soon we left Java behind, first flying over Bali then Lombok, according to Jay's charts. After flying over several more islands, we made a stop at Kupang on the western side of the island of Timor to refuel.

As I walked around to stretch my legs, I recalled another visitor to this Dutch colony, the infamous Captain Bligh. After surviving the mutiny, he and a few other sailors traveled thousands of miles in a small open boat to reach this place. It was certainly a feat of navigation, but I was chiefly interested in his ill-fated voyage because he was to collect breadfruit from the islands of French Polynesia. It never did become the staple crop they had expected. I would have liked to explore Kupang, but Jay had us on a schedule as strict as the standard Qantas timetable, and we took off again within an hour.

We flew southeast, away from Timor and over open water. Jay suggested I take the controls. There was little to see below us now, so I was happy to concentrate on piloting the aircraft. Jay made sure we were on course, telling me to correct our heading periodically. Eventually, he took the controls back as we approached Australia. I admired his competent hands on the yoke, strong but with a delicate touch, as he expertly guided us to Darwin's harbor.

Compared to the lush, mountainous islands we had just left, the Australian terrain was flat with scrubby foliage. The town looked much smaller than I expected. Unlike the grand cities of Singapore, Batavia, and Surabaya, Darwin had mainly low, simple wooden buildings. Aside from the palm trees, it could have been a sleepy town in the American West.

Jay secured Lula at the jetty in the harbor. This was also a stop on the Empire flying boat route. We walked to the Qantas hangar at the main airfield, and Jay consulted with the mechanics to ensure the aircraft would be ready in the morning. When he'd finished giving them his instructions, one of the men walked away, revealing a photograph on the wall behind him. I started at the sight of a familiar face smiling back at me: Amelia Earhart with her impish grin and tousled hair. She had signed it: "To My Mates in Darwin, Adventure is worthwhile in itself - Amelia Earhart - June 29, 1937." For some reason, it had not occurred to me that our route so far had closely followed her final journey. She had left Darwin for New Guinea, and we would, too. Jay turned toward me and saw my distress.

"Oh, Profesora, your friend. I am sorry," he said, taking my arm and leading me out of the hangar. We had a short walk into town to the Victorian Hotel, a two-story stone structure that looked like it belonged in England, not just south of the equator on the other side of the world. "This is where all the aviators stay when they come to Darwin," Jay explained.

"Even Amelia?"

"Yes, there is another photograph in the hotel. I hope it is not too upsetting for you."

"No, I'm okay, Jay. I know she'd be pleased I'm here. And that I flew part of the way myself."

"Yes, I'm sure she would. And she's right; adventure *is* worthwhile in itself," Jay said, although I was not quite sure I agreed in that moment.

The Vic, as everyone called the hotel, was not so luxurious that we felt out of place, so we dined in the restaurant there, and Jay saw several people he knew. Before Jay could even introduce me, each man presumed

I was "Señora Diente de León." I quickly corrected them on the matter. However, I kept my answers to their questions vague. Something made me hesitant to give strangers too many details of my mission.

As I climbed into the bed in my little room that night, I wondered which room had been Amelia's last year. Could she have spent her night in Darwin in this very spot?

CHAPTER 16

"Have you been to New Guinea before?" I asked Jay as we left Darwin behind.

"Yes, a few times. Flying the mail route. There's not a lot of demand for passenger service."

After some hours of flying over open water, the mountainous landmass of New Guinea loomed before us. I recalled seeing the photos Margaret Mead had shown of her fieldwork there in the 1920s. Of course, I had read her book *Growing Up in New Guinea* when it was published in 1930, but I would have brushed up on it had I any inkling I'd be visiting this vast, largely unknown island.

We flew for about two more hours to reach Port Moresby on the southeastern part of the island. Jay circled the waterfront town twice before landing at the jetty, and I could see houses perched on the steep hills surrounding the bay. Jay fastened Lula to the pier, and I jumped ashore. A sloppily-dressed man with thinning hair and a bushy ginger mustache eventually sauntered down the jetty toward us.

"Allo, mate!" the man said as he recognized Jay. "Have you brought the missus for a holiday?"

"No such luck, Señor Bruce. This is Professor Ivy Linden. From America. She's all business," Jay replied.

"How charming to meet you, miss," the man said, taking my hand. "We don't get many ladies for a visit. I'm Bruce Buckthorn. Come up to the hangar, and we'll get you settled with some tea." He pulled me along to a low shack while Jay conversed with a mechanic.

"Tommy, get the lady some tea," Bruce said to a Papuan man with dark curly hair. The man silently complied. I wished I could spend my one night in New Guinea with Tommy and his family, not in the company of Bruce, but I knew that was not to be.

"How long will you be with us, miss?" Bruce asked.

"Just overnight, I think. Jay has us on a tight schedule. We're leaving for the Solomons tomorrow."

"Good gracious, why would you ever want to go there? That's no place for a woman. Well, neither is New Guinea," he said, slapping my knee with a chuckle.

"I'm a professor of ethnobotany at an American university, Mr. Buckthorn. I'm going there for a plant collecting expedition. And I've been in many other places just as remote, so I'm sure it's no problem."

"Ethno what?"

"Botany. Ethnobotany. It's a combination of botany and anthropology," I said. I felt my patience evaporating in the stagnant heat of the little shack.

"A lady professor? Like that lady anthropologist from America who asked the natives about all sorts of naughty things?"

"You mean Dr. Margaret Mead. Yes. But I ask them about plants and what they do with them, especially to cure diseases."

"Well, that's something, all right, miss," he said, slapping my knee again. Jay walked in just then to my great relief.

"This is some passenger you got here, mate. Pity you're not staying awhile," he said to Jay. "It's nice to have a European woman to talk to."

"No, Señor Bruce, we leave tomorrow for the Solomon Islands. We'll fly to Tulagi and then to Vanikoro in the Santa Cruz group."

"Crikey, that's a funny place to go. Surely they got the plants you need somewhere more civilized than that. Look out for the crocodiles and sharks there, miss."

"Thank you, Bruce. I'll be sure to do that," I said, standing up. "Shouldn't we be going to the hotel, Jay?" I hoped there was, indeed, a hotel to go to, and we would not end up as the guests of Bruce.

"Yes, Profesora, that is a good idea. We have another early day tomorrow. Good night, Señor Bruce."

It was a short walk to the Papua Hotel, an unassuming two-story structure with many windows covered by louvered shutters. A desultory ceiling fan pushed the humid air around the lobby. A pair of lizards scampered under the bed when I opened the door to my shabby room. At least they would eat the mosquitoes.

I didn't mind the early-morning departure the next day, as it meant we missed Bruce, who had not come to the jetty to see us off. But the mechanic was there, and Lula was fueled and ready for the trip. We flew east along the southern coast of New Guinea and over a chain of small islands at its tip. Soon we were over the Solomon Sea.

"I've never flown here before, Ivy. Tell me when you

see land again," Jay said. Perhaps the open water should have worried me, but I felt inexplicably confident in his navigational abilities. After a few hours, I spotted green on the horizon.

"Look, Jay. Is that something?" I said, pointing to the growing dot.

"That must be Guadalcanal," Jay said, looking at a chart. The island loomed larger as we approached it from the southwest side. The coast looked mountainous and inhospitable with a densely covered ridge running along the middle of the island. We crossed over the high jungle terrain and saw grassland below, with small settlements and gardens on the flat land near the northern coast and a large plantation of coconut palms. It was obvious the island held rich plant life. And probably unusual animal life, too. It looked like the perfect repository for a lost world of prehistoric creatures that had escaped extinction.

"I wonder if it's down there," Jay said, looking at the rugged land below us.

"If what is?"

"The gold. King Solomon's mines."

I was about to tell him he was being ridiculous, but then I recalled that a moment before I'd been imagining dinosaurs and massive centipedes crawling beneath giant tree ferns. "Maybe, Jay. Who knows what's down there."

But we would not be exploring Guadalcanal. We continued flying over a span of water poetically named Sealark Channel to a cluster of islands, the Florida Islands, according to Jay's map. Tulagi, our destination, was a little slip of an island protected by a larger one almost surrounding it. Jay made several passes to assess the landing conditions, as he'd never landed there before.

There were neat rows of white bungalows with red corrugated tin roofs, shops, official-looking buildings, and warehouses clustered around a small, but busy port with several piers and jetties. Jay chose one jetty without a ship anchored there as his destination.

When Lula's propellers ceased spinning, Jay tied her to the pier. I jumped out after him and patted her on the nose myself, this time. We retrieved our overnight bags and headed ashore. Not surprisingly, the sound of our engines had attracted some attention. A small group of white-suited men, one even wearing a pith helmet, had gathered to meet us.

"Welcome to Tulagi," the man in the pith helmet said with a clipped British accent. "I'm Resident Commissioner Nigel Bentley. Whom do we have the honor of greeting?" Although he had looked me up and down, he was clearly addressing Jay.

Nevertheless, I stuck out my hand and answered, "I'm Professor Ivy Linden from Cornell University in America, and this is Mr. Jacinto Diente de León of Qantas Airways."

"Ah, you've brought the mail. Brilliant. I'll get some boys to unload it."

Shaking the middle-aged man's hand, Jay said, "Please call me Jay. I have not brought the mail, I'm afraid. This is a chartered flight for the professor. We are en route to Vanikoro and plan to stay here for the night if there are accommodations."

"Yes, well there are some hotels in Chinatown, but they would be thoroughly unsuitable for you. You will stay in the guest rooms at my residency. If we had known in advance of your arrival, we could have prepared properly," he said. "Go tell Mrs. Bentley to have our houseboy prepare the rooms," he added, dispatching one of his assistants.

"Please don't go to any trouble," I protested. I suspected I would have preferred the anonymity of an unsuitable Chinatown hotel to the stuffy evening we'd surely spend with the commissioner and his staff.

"No trouble at all," he said. Of course, it wasn't him who would be going to any trouble. "I'll have some boys come for your luggage. We'll go to the Tulagi Club for refreshments in the meanwhile."

Jay stayed behind to refuel the plane, and I followed Bentley and the other British officials away from the shore.

"Tulagi is the capital of the British Solomon Islands Protectorate," Bentley explained. "The island was unoccupied when we settled it, and you'll see we've made a very nice proper town here." He began throwing out various facts and figures as we walked along neat pathways of crushed white coral. The buildings were landscaped with carefully tended gardens of hibiscus, frangipani, and croton with yellow spotted leaves.

"We have a golf course and a cricket ground, a modern hospital, a court house, jail, a post office, and a wireless station. Burns Philp steamers put in regularly, and we have several nice stores in case you'd like to go shopping."

"I don't think I need to do any shopping, but I am interested in the wireless station. Can I have a message sent to Vanikoro?"

"Certainly. It's right next to the club. We'll stop in there first. Now this here is what we call 'The Cut,'"

Bentley said as we approached a manmade passageway cut into a central ridge of rock to make a shortcut to the other side of the small island. "My residency is up there," he said, pointing to a large red-roofed bungalow on the ridge. "The ladies would all like to have you to tea and play some tennis, I'm sure."

"Perhaps on the way back we can spend more time here, but we've got to go to Vanikoro tomorrow."

"Ah, yes. Now just what is your interest there?"

"I'm to collect plant specimens for the U.S. Department of Agriculture," I said, trying to sound official. And that was what I was going there for, as far as I knew.

"And you're expected?"

"Yes, that's right. But the date was not fixed, so that's why I'd like to send a message on the wireless to say we'll be there tomorrow."

We walked past the cricket field and tennis courts surrounded by well-tended lawns and artfully arrayed palm trees. The entire island appeared to have been landscaped and manicured, with no natural areas left. From this side of the island I could see Guadalcanal in the distance again and a closer small, round island to the west.

"Savo Island," Bentley explained. "It's volcanic. Hasn't been active in decades, though. Not much reason to go there. Then again, there's not much reason to go to Vanikoro unless you want the kauri trees." We entered a tidy, whitewashed building with an antenna on top. A young man idly leafing through a magazine sprung to attention.

"Sparks, we have a guest from America. Miss Linden

here would like to send a message to Vanikoro. Call them up for her, will you?" Bentley said.

"Certainly, Commissioner," the radio operator replied, getting a pad and pencil ready. "What would you like to say, miss?" he asked me.

"Please say, 'Professor Ivy Linden arriving tomorrow by seaplane. To meet Boye as instructed by Johnson and Smith.'" Sparks jotted down the message.

"I'll call them up straight away, miss, but I believe Mr. Boye is in New Zealand on business."

"Oh. Well, please send the message anyway," I said with increasing anxiety. I did not want to wait around on Tulagi for his return.

"Let's go to the club while Sparks sends the message, Miss Linden," Bentley said as he led me out of the wireless station toward a large, white building next door. We climbed the steps to a spacious verandah further shaded by shutters and went inside. There was a small bar, a billiards room, and even a reading room. Trophies, carved masks and shields, deep-sea fish, and a taxidermy boar's head adorned the walls. A few people sitting at small tables rose when we entered and greeted Bentley formally. He installed me at an empty table and went over to the Chinese barman to order drinks.

"We'll sit out on the verandah," Bentley said, leading me back outside. The palm trees surrounding the club swayed in a pleasant breeze. Soon the bartender came out with a pint of beer for Bentley and, regrettably, a steaming cup of tea for me. I accepted it without complaint, though I would have preferred a gin and tonic.

Bentley launched into his lecture on the history of the

Solomon Islands with renewed enthusiasm. He was happy to have a captive audience, and it was clear that, to him, history only started when the British acquired the islands. My mind wandered as I sipped the tea. It was a great relief to see Jay approach, accompanied by two sinewy Solomon Islanders wearing khaki lava-lavas, something like a kilt, with wide leather belts and carrying rifles. He shook hands with the men, and they departed.

"There's your pilot, miss," Bentley said needlessly. "Looks like the boys from the police constabulary showed him the way." I stood up and waved, in case Jay couldn't see us in the shade of the verandah. He waved back and bounded up the stairs. Bentley got up and led him into the club. In a few minutes, they came out with fresh pints of beer and sat down at the table.

Sensing I would not be missed, I excused myself and returned to the wireless station to enquire about a reply to my message.

"Yes, miss. Vanikoro answered on the spot," Sparks said, retrieving his notepad. "The message is 'Eagerly await your arrival. Mind the reef.'"

I thanked him and went back outside. The sun was beginning to set. I would have liked to walk along the beach, but I went back to the club. Bentley and Jay were deep in conversation, so I passed them and went inside to order myself that gin and tonic. Sipping it, I sat back down with the men, who hardly noticed. Jay was asking Bentley about gold prospecting in the islands.

"Miss Linden, your pilot here must be descended from Mendaña himself the way he's interrogating me about gold strikes," Bentley said with a laugh. "We'll have dinner here in a few minutes. Here comes Mrs. Bentley."

A tall, well-dressed middle-aged woman ascended the stairs, and Bentley rose to kiss her on the cheek formally. He introduced us, and she led me inside the club.

"How delightful to have guests. I do wish I had known sooner, though. We would have held a proper dinner at the residency for you, but we'll have to make do with the club tonight. We'll sit in the reading room until the other wives get here."

We sat down in rattan club chairs, and Mrs. Bentley began lamenting the heat, insects, and lack of reliable help. I listened politely, not wanting to offend my hostess for the evening, but I wished more and more for the Chinatown hotel, no matter how dilapidated.

Finally, some other women arrived, and we sat down together at a table in the main dining room. Jay and Bentley had also entered and sat at a different table with several of the other officials. For dinner we were served bland chicken and tinned vegetables, followed by more tea. It seemed the Britishers had not incorporated the local produce into their diets, and I gave up on the idea of asking the women if they used any local plants as medicines.

As the evening wore on, couples trickled out of the club until only Jay and I were left with the Bentleys.

"Let's get you settled in for the night so you'll be well-rested for your trip to Vanikoro," Mrs. Bentley said, and we climbed the ridge to their home, the Resident Commissioner's residency. The house was encircled by a broad verandah and had a lovely view of the palm trees and water from its perch on the hill.

"And this will be your room," Mrs. Bentley said as we came to the doorway of a large and pleasant guest room with simple furniture. Our luggage was already inside. Both my bag and Jay's sat at the foot of the double bed. I felt myself flush and glanced at Jay. He looked amused.

"I'm sorry to be a bother, Mrs. Bentley, but is there a second room, as well?" I asked.

"Oh dear, I thought you and Mr. Leon were husband and wife. Am I mistaken?"

"Yes, I'm sorry I hadn't explained that," I said, though I saw no reason for the assumption.

"It's no trouble at all. You'll have this room, and I'll have my houseboy put Mr. Leon in the next room. That one doesn't have screens on the verandah, but it'll have to do. It's lucky we don't have any other visitors tonight," she said, scurrying away. Jay retrieved his bag and followed her to the next room.

I washed up in the attached bathroom and got ready for bed, although I wasn't tired. I sat out on the verandah watching the stars for some time until I saw shadowy movement on the adjacent section of the porch, separated by the mosquito screen.

"Ivy, you are still awake," Jay's voice came as a whisper.

"Yes, Jay. I'm still awake, too."

"Mrs. Bentley said breakfast will be at seven o'clock tomorrow morning. We'll leave by nine. It should be about a four-hour flight."

"Thank you, Jay. I radioed ahead, and they know we're coming. The reply message said to mind the reef."

"Very good, Profesora. I will be gentle with Lula. *Buenas noches.*"

CHAPTER 17

I spread thick orange marmalade on a scone and sipped some piping hot black tea. The view from the Bentleys' verandah was lovely in the cool morning air. Mrs. Bentley seemed very pleased to have company for breakfast, and she chattered away about the social events she and the other officials' wives hosted for visitors and the staff at the hospital. It seemed a circumscribed existence on the small, almost artificial island, especially with the allure of the larger, untamed Florida Island almost encircling it in the background and the vast expanse of Guadalcanal just across the channel. I noticed Jay was gazing at that brooding island pensively. I hoped he hadn't gotten any more ideas about ancient gold mines there.

"Should we be going soon?" I asked Jay, interrupting his reverie and Mrs. Bentley's monologue.

"Ah, *sí, Profesora*," Jay agreed, glancing at his watch. "We should be on our way."

I tried to help clean up the breakfast dishes, but Mrs. Bentley assured me her houseboy would take care of them. That was what I was hoping to avoid, but it was the custom in this outpost of the Union Jack. I pressed my luck further and asked what I owed for our accommodations and meals.

"Don't be ridiculous, Ivy. It's been our pleasure to have such interesting guests. We hope you'll come back to Tulagi when your business on Vanikoro is done," she replied. Mr. Bentley agreed heartily and accompanied us across the island to the spot where Lula had spent the night. I sensed Jay breathe a sigh of relief when he saw her gently swaying in the water.

Jay inspected the aircraft, and we took our places in the cockpit. We taxied away from the pier, and we were off again, heading southeast over the channel running between the two chains of islands. Finally we cleared the last island, San Cristoval, and flew over open seas. After a few hours of nothing below but water, we approached the Santa Cruz Islands group. Although it was part of the British Solomon Islands Protectorate, it was almost closer to the New Hebrides on Jay's chart.

Vanikoro emerged from the sea, the steep, jungle-covered peak of its interior shrouded in mist. Jay flew around its perimeter several times to assess landing conditions. A much smaller islet was separated from the main island by a narrow passage. The pair was surrounded by a coral reef creating a lagoon close to shore. There were breaks in the reef, but sailing through would be challenging for a ship. There was a sheltered bay on one side that Jay thought was a promising place to land, but as we descended, I pointed out the dense mangrove swamps on the shore. There was no beach or settlement in that area. Circling the island again, I saw a vast swath of bare land on the mountainside, a place where the trees had all been cut down. My heart sank at the sight of the massive pale tree stumps. Whatever grew up in place of the large trees would not be the same. Perhaps some rare plants or animals would even be lost. Close to this point, we spotted the settlement near the mouth of a river, a small cluster of houses, some built on stilts out in the water. That appeared to be where we had to land.

"I'm going to set down inside the lagoon, rather than outside and trying to navigate in through the reef," Jay explained. It seemed like a good plan, and I trusted him to take good care of Lula, and me by default. We flew over the lagoon again for Jay to note smaller outcroppings of coral to avoid. Fortunately, the water was clear, and the reefs were easily visible from the air. I held my breath as Jay eased the aircraft into the water. He deftly maneuvered around some coral until we came to a small jetty.

As was now customary, our arrival had attracted some attention. However, our welcome party was quite different than at our prior stops. A tall, robust figure strode briskly toward us, waving. And wearing a dress.

Jay jumped out with the rope to secure Lula, and I scrambled past him as fast as I could.

"Good day, mates! Welcome to Vanikoro!" the woman shouted at us in a hearty Australian accent. "You must be the professor," she said, wringing my hand. "I've been expecting you! I'm Ruby Olive Boye." It seemed RO Boye was, in fact, a girl. For once, it was my turn to be surprised.

"Hello, Ruby. I'm Ivy Linden. This is Mr. Jacinto Diente de León from Qantas Airways."

"Please call me Jay, Señora," he said, flashing the

woman his charming smile and taking her hand.

"You did a fine job navigating the reef, Jay. Your aircraft will be perfectly safe here. Let's get you up to the house, possums. It's such a rare treat to have visitors. Especially while my husband is in New Zealand on company business and my sons are at school in Australia."

We followed the woman along the jetty to the shore. She was as tall as Jay, but more sturdily built. She wasn't stout, but solid, like the kauri trees whose gigantic stumps I'd seen from the air. Vanikoro was a good deal less developed than our previous destinations, and I guessed her vigorous constitution was an asset in this wild place. She led us to a modest, but well-constructed wooden house near the beach.

"Come inside, and I'll show you to your rooms," she said as we climbed the stairs and crossed the verandah to the front door. The rooms were simply furnished with heavy wooden furniture, no doubt made from the island's kauri trees.

"This will be your room, Jay," Ruby said, motioning him to the first bedroom we came to. As he went inside to put down his bag, she whisked me further down the hall to the next room and pulled me inside.

"Your pilot, can he be trusted?" she asked me in *sotto voce.*

"Trusted?" I parroted back. "Yes, I think so. Well, I trusted him to fly me here from Singapore, so I suppose so." I didn't know what she was driving at.

"Good, just making sure, my chookie," she said, patting my arm and leading me back to the sitting room. "Let's get you both some tea and biscuits." I offered to help, but she declined and sat us down at the table as she prepared the tea. She had short, neatly-coifed dark hair with a few gray strands and was perhaps close to fifty years old. She had a very maternal air about her and exuded competence. I felt instantly comfortable with the woman.

We sat around the table sipping tea and munching on shortbread cookies from a tin. I regretted not bringing provisions from the stores on Tulagi, but I hadn't known what to expect.

"Ruby, have you lived here long?" I asked.

"We moved here just two years ago. Before that we'd lived on Tulagi since 1928. My husband Skov was a plantation manager for Lever Brothers there. I was happy when he took this job with the Vanikoro Kauri Timber Company. Tulagi was too stuffy for my taste. Too much cricket and tennis and bridge games with all the pommies. Things are different here. Real. I have important things to do here," she said with pride. "I take care of the workers and their families. They come from all over the islands to work here cutting the trees. I do a bit of everything. Doctor, teacher, gardener, calm down any disputes. And of course, the radio," she said slyly.

"The radio?" I asked.

"Yes, when I got here I learned how to use the radio. Even send and receive Morse code. The wireless operator wanted an apprentice so he could leave the island occasionally, and I volunteered. It's good fun. Of course, most of the messages are just about ships coming to pick up the timber and sending out some weather reports. But sometimes there are more interesting messages, if you know what I mean," she said, winking.

"No, Ruby, I don't know what you mean. In fact, I don't really know why I'm here," I confessed.

"Oh, that's a good one, Ivy," she said with a hearty laugh. "But we can talk freely here. There's nothing to worry about. And you told me your charming companion can be trusted," she said, looking at Jay who seemed as bemused as I did.

"I'm here to collect some plants, maybe ones with antimalarial properties. At least I think that's why I'm here. Why do you think I'm here, Ruby?"

She looked at me quizzically. "I got the encrypted message from your agents."

"My agents?"

"Johnson and Smith, of course. Fine dull names to use. I must say yours and Jay's are a bit more creative constructions."

"Constructions? But they are our names. At least mine is," I said, suddenly eyeing Jay warily.

"I assure you I come from a long line of Diente de Leóns, and I'm named for *mi abuelo*, my grandfather," Jay said with amusement. "How do I know you are indeed Profesora Ivy Linden?"

I sighed. "Ruby, what's going on here? Please tell us what you know."

"Righto, possums. Let's go to the wireless station. I've got the communiqués secreted there."

We followed her out of the house and toward the river where a rickety suspension bridge reached to the other bank.

"Watch your step, and do mind the crocs. They'll be sleeping now, but they wake up with an appetite in the evening. Best to keep a shotgun or pistol with you, just in case. You do have one with you, I trust?"

"Yes," Jay and I answered in unison; we both stopped midway across the bridge to stare at each other. I shrugged apologetically, and we continued making our way gingerly across the river.

There was a small wooden shack on the opposite bank, and Ruby ushered us inside. A bulky radio receiver and transmitter set-up composed of several boxy cabinets sat on a wooden table. A vase of white flowers was placed incongruously on top of one of the radio components. She pulled up two more chairs and motioned for us to sit beside her. She surveyed the small room, as if someone else could have slipped inside without our notice, and then extricated a flower from the back of the bunch. She plucked out the stem and began to unfold the 'petals.' They were made of paper.

"I learned this from a Japanese trader," Ruby said with delight. "It was supposed to be just for decoration, but I found a rather ingenious use for the skill, don't you think?" she said, beaming. She flattened out the paper, and Jay and I leaned in for a look. The page was covered with a series of dots and dashes. I looked at her blankly.

"You can't read it?" she asked. I shook my head. "But you can read it, Jay?"

"Well, I did learn Morse code some years ago, but never had a reason to remember. Maybe with a pencil and paper and a few hours I could figure it out."

"Oh dear, I'll just read it to you." Ruby looked around the shack again, cleared her throat, and read: "To Agent RO Boye, Vanikoro. Expect Professor Ivy Linden on assignment. She may not be alone. Assess reliability of companions before relaying following message: Find

Totenkopfinsel, obtain items of value there, and bring to USDA for further study. Retrieve from other interested parties using any means necessary. Johnson and Smith."

I looked at Ruby blankly. "*Totenkopfinsel?*"

"It's German," she said ominously.

"Yes, I know. The first part means 'death' and then 'head.' But what's the rest?"

"*Insel* is island," Jay added. "Skull Island."

"Are there islands with German colonies around here, Ruby?" I asked.

"No, there was a German part of New Guinea and some of the islands in the northern part of the Solomons, but they lost them in the Great War. I have heard of an island in the Solomons that people call 'Skull Island.' Maybe that's where they mean."

"Where is it?"

"I'm not quite sure. Somewhere in the western part of the Solomons. Further north and west from Tulagi. Skov might know, but he won't be back for several weeks. We'll have to figure it out ourselves."

"I'm not sure I'm going at all. I've already been on a wild goose chase for Johnson and Smith. I doubt there can be any important plants there. And why would they tell me the name in German, anyway?"

"My guess is that's the name they picked up in their intelligence reports," Ruby suggested. "They obviously trust you to figure it out and be motivated to go there."

"Well, they overestimated my interest. There's nothing I want there."

"Even if a certain blond-haired woman wants it, too?" said Jay.

I scowled at Jay. "There are enough plants in the

world for both of us. I don't have to go chasing after her."

"Plants, oh Profesora," Jay said, laughing. "The items of value can only be one thing, of course. Gold."

"Not the gold again, Jay. If there's one thing I'm not interested in, it's gold."

"But Ivy, we have come all this way. Do you not think we should investigate?"

"Fine, Jay. We'll go to Skull Island. We can fly back to Tulagi tomorrow and find someone to take us there."

"I don't think going back to Tulagi is a good idea. The men talk of gold all the time. Many men will try to follow us. It's too dangerous," Jay said.

"I agree with Jay," said Ruby. "You will find yourself with an entourage of hangers-on ready to cash in on your discovery."

"But we can't go alone. I don't speak any languages here, not even pidgin."

"You'll need a guide you can trust. I'd go with you myself if Skov were here and I could get away. I do have an idea, though. In the meantime, let's figure out where Skull Island is," she said, pulling a sheaf of charts from a drawer. She split the pile in three, and we each took a stack. The futility of the task soon became evident; there were hundreds of small islands in addition to the main ones.

"You said your workers come from all over the islands, Ruby. Can't we just ask them?" I suggested.

"Yes, I suppose so. Many of them are from Malaita and the Santa Cruz group, but there are a few from the western islands. Let's go back to the house, and I'll summon them."

We followed Ruby back across the swaying bridge

and waited while she spoke to one of the supervisors in pidgin. Then we sat on the verandah, and Ruby brought us glasses of limeade to drink. I wanted to ask her for a tour of the logging area, but I despaired at what I would see and doubted they would welcome my forestry input.

After a while, the supervisor came back with three muscular Melanesian men. They appeared nervous at being singled out and brought to the manager's house, but when they saw Ruby, they broke into wide grins. She greeted them warmly and introduced us to Jacob from New Georgia, Peter from Santa Isabel, and David from Kolombangara. We crowded around the table inside while Ruby made a fresh pot of tea.

She chatted with the men in pidgin for a few minutes, and I gathered she was asking them about their families. Just enough of the words were English that I could grasp the gist of the conversation. If I heard it spoken enough, I could pick it up quickly, but for now Ruby would have to translate.

When the tea was ready, Ruby opened another tin of biscuits. "What would you like to ask?" Ruby said, offering us a cookie.

"Please thank them for coming to talk to us, and tell them I study plants and how people use them," I instructed, and Ruby obliged. The men nodded with interest. Seeing no point in beating around the bush, I added, "Please ask if they know of an island that might be called 'Skull Island.'"

At this the men looked at each other, no longer smiling. Finally, Jacob murmured, "Kundu Hite." The other two men nodded and repeated the name softly.

"Are there important plants on Kundu Hite?" I asked.

Ruby translated, and the men chuckled. I took that as a no.

"What's on Kundu Hite? Why is it important?" Ruby repeated my questions in pidgin. The men spoke amongst themselves in another language for some time and then in pidgin to Ruby.

"They say Kundu Hite is a sacred island. It is a tiny island, too small for people to inhabit. But the spirits of the great Roviana chiefs and warriors live there. That's where their skulls are kept. And they guard the seashells. No one goes there without permission. It would be very bad luck to go without permission, and nothing must be taken from the island, or there would be grave consequences."

"So there are no special plants there?" I asked again. The men emphatically shook their heads.

"But what about gold?" Jay added. Ruby translated, and the men laughed. Jacob said something to Ruby.

"He says there's no gold. The island is too small for that. But what is there is much more valuable than gold."

"Can you show it to us on a map?" I asked. Ruby asked the men, and they nodded solemnly. Jacob added that we had to promise not to go there without permission from the local chief and not take anything. Jay and I readily consented, though they would have no reason to trust us.

I regretted leaving the maps in the wireless shack, as the six of us crossed the river once more. But the bridge held, and the crocs went hungry. We crammed inside the small room, and the men pored over the charts, talking amongst themselves. Finally, they agreed on a barely visible speck that was not even labeled on the map.

"Kundu Hite," Jacob announced.

Ruby peered at the map and penciled a star over the tiny islet. "It's in Vonavona Lagoon," she said. "Between the islands of Vonavona and New Georgia. You can fly to Munda and take a boat from there."

"If we go," I cautioned.

"Of course you're going, possums! And I know who can go with you." I expected Ruby to name one of the men who had just been so helpful, but she said nothing more. She folded up the map and gave it to Jay. We followed her out into the humid air once again and across the river. Ruby went inside her house, brought out some cigarettes to thank the men, and sent them on their way. She turned back to us, grinning like the cat who ate the canary.

"Come back inside, and I'll tell you my plan," Ruby said, taking our arms and leading us back into her home. She began preparing a fish dinner for us, insisting we relax. She appeared to be enjoying the mounting suspense. Finally, she set plates of freshly caught fish and roasted yams in front of us. Once we had taken our first bites and complimented her, she could hold back no longer.

"Righto, possums, here's the plan," she said, leaning toward us conspiratorially. "You'll go to Vella Lavella first and pick up Merle Farland."

"Is he a planter?" I asked.

"No, silly goose, Merle is a nurse at the Methodist Mission. A sister."

"*Otra mujer, Dios mío,*" Jay muttered under his breath. I shot him a sharp look.

"I like the plan already," I said. "Tell me more."

"It's the perfect cover. Merle knows the islands and speaks pidgin. Everyone trusts her. You'll say you're taking her to minister to the sick. You can even stop at Tulagi to refuel and pick up supplies and tell everyone they are for the mission hospital. In fact, it won't even be a lie. They always need supplies. And I'm sure patients will, indeed, turn up for her care wherever you go."

"I admit that does sound like a good plan," Jay conceded. "No one will want to follow us or suspect we are after something else."

"But how do you know Merle will agree to come with us, Ruby?" I asked.

"I'm sure she won't turn down the opportunity for some excitement. And she'll have a real chance to treat the ill people of the other islands. But I'll call her up on the wireless just to make sure."

By now it was dark, and Ruby handed us each a lantern to light the way across the bridge. The wisdom of putting the radio shack on the opposite side of the river was opaque to me, but we made our way across without incident. Once inside, Ruby switched on the wireless set and let it warm up for a few minutes. She plucked the flower with the message from Johnson and Smith again and gave it to me to keep. She put on the headphones, took hold of the microphone, and turned some dials.

"Calling Vella Lavella, calling Vella Lavella. This is Mrs. Boye from Vanikoro calling." We couldn't hear it, but she must have received a reply since she continued, "Read you loud and clear, Vella. Message for Nurse Farland, message for Nurse Farland. Take note." And then she began tapping furiously on the telegraph key. It seemed unnecessary to send the message in Morse code, but I could see she was enjoying the intrigue of it all.

When she completed the message, she listened for a few moments, nodding her head to the unseen operator on Vella Lavella. Then she added, "Righto, will expect reply from Nurse Farland at 0800 tomorrow morning. Over and out." She took off the headphones and switched off the radio.

"I used the Playfair cipher," she said with a self-satisfied grin. I looked at her blankly. "For security. I used both Morse code and the Playfair cipher. If anyone intercepts the message, it will seem like gibberish."

This whole expedition seems like gibberish, I thought with a sigh.

"We'll get our reply tomorrow at eight o'clock in the morning. I'm sure Merle will agree. And she'll send a list of items to bring back from Tulagi."

At least bringing the mission some medical supplies would be worth the trip, I supposed. And if she treated people, I could ask them what kind of plants they used as medicines. It wouldn't be a complete loss.

The lanterns illuminated our way back across the bridge. I tried to only pay attention to my footing on the creaking planks, but the red glow of pairs of eyes below us was a distraction. I was still holding the white 'flower' with our first message on it when a board cracked. I grabbed the rope railing, and the white paper fluttered from my hand. Before it could reach the water, a loud snap caused us all to jump. It wasn't a board breaking, but the powerful jaws of a crocodile seizing the paper in midair. The animal slid silently under the water again, no doubt disappointed with its catch. We scurried across the rest of the bridge.

"That's one way to make sure a secret message doesn't fall into the wrong hands!" Ruby said, laughing with delight. In spite of myself, I laughed, too. Vanikoro was definitely more exciting than staid Tulagi.

Ruby settled us into her sons' bedrooms, fussing over us like a mother hen. I regretted having to leave so soon. I think Ruby regretted it, too, but was pleased at being of service to our mission, whatever that really was.

In the morning, Ruby was already preparing a breakfast of fried eggs, bacon, canned baked beans, and fragrant papaya when I emerged from my room. Jay followed soon after.

"The foreman can give you some fuel for your aircraft while Ivy and I receive the message from Merle," Ruby said to Jay. He agreed, and after breakfast, she entrusted him to the foreman while we made our way across the river. In the daylight, the cracked plank was easy to avoid, but I shivered at the thought of how one misstep in the darkness could have resulted in a sated croc.

We sat at the desk in the wireless shack, and I watched with interest as Ruby set the dials. "I can let you make the call if you want," she offered.

"I don't know how to use a wireless. Other than listen to *Your Hit Parade* or Jack Benny, of course."

"They didn't teach you to send and receive messages? You really don't know any codes?"

"I'm an expert on plants. That's it. No one taught me anything about this. Or even told me what *this* is."

"So you really are a botany professor? It's not just your cover?"

"I'm afraid it's no cover, Ruby."

"Oh dear. Well, I am glad Merle's going with you, then," she said, placing the headphones on. At the stroke of eight, she leaned into the microphone and said, "This is Mrs. Boye on Vanikoro. Receiving you loud and clear. Proceed with message when you're ready." She then began to rapidly jot down a series of letters on her pad of paper. After a few minutes of writing, she said, "Message received, Vella. Nurse Farland should expect delivery tomorrow. No further message. Over and out."

"Just give me a few minutes to decipher this," Ruby said to me. I watched her transpose the message onto a fresh sheet of paper, the letters now forming coherent words.

"Oh good, Merle is raring to go! The message says, 'Nurse Farland accepts assignment with enthusiasm. Can leave immediately. Hospital requires following supplies: bandages, gauze, cotton, mosquito nets, quinine, aspirin, milk of magnesia, iodine, Lysol, Antinea lotion. Also, sugar, tea, and anything else that might be of use. Bring trade goods for islanders.'"

Ruby gave me the decoded message and, with a wink, folded up the original sheet into a new flower for the vase.

"I wish I were going with you, Ivy. But you'll be in good hands with Merle."

"I wish you were coming, too, Ruby. You seem to know just what to do."

"It will all work itself out, I'm sure, chookie. Let's get you and Jay on your way."

I followed Ruby across the bridge for the last time; I knew I would not miss that when we left. Jay had secured some suitable fuel and was giving Lula a once-over.

When he was certain she was ready for the flight, we loaded up our bags and said goodbye to Ruby. She crushed each of us to her in a bear hug.

"Good luck, possums!" Ruby shouted to us as we settled in the cockpit. She gave the propellers a spin and backed away as the engines started. Jay peered at the water intently to navigate around the coral patches as we picked up speed. When we finally rose from the water, I realized I'd been holding my breath and let out a long sigh. We circled back around, and Jay waggled our wings at Ruby, who stood below waving vigorously, strong and straight as a kauri tree.

CHAPTER 18

Landing at Tulagi was old hat for Jay now and a piece of cake compared to Vanikoro, but I still felt some trepidation as Lula approached the water. Not because of the landing, but at who would greet us at the dock and the stories we'd have to tell. When the engines stopped, Jay tied up the aircraft, and we jumped out. Sure enough, pith-helmeted Mr. Bentley was walking toward us with a look of dismay.

"I say, back already? We didn't expect you again so soon."

"Hello Mr. Bentley, so sorry to arrive unannounced. We didn't expect to be back so soon, either," I said. "But the plants I was looking for are not producing fruit now, and there was no point in staying." The first lie had come easily enough. "But Mrs. Boye got word from the mission hospital on Vella Lavella that they could use some supplies, so Jay offered to deliver them."

"That's splendid of you, old chap," Bentley said, slapping Jay on the back. It seemed he'd bought the story.

"At Qantas we are always happy to be of service to the Empire," Jay said.

"There's just one problem, I'm afraid," said Bentley.

"We already have other guests at the residency. If I had known you were coming back today, I would have told them to stay elsewhere. I can't very well turn them out now, I'm sorry to say."

"That's no problem at all," I said, hoping my delight was not too evident. "Of course, we'll miss Mrs. Bentley and your gracious hospitality, but we'll stay at a hotel in Chinatown. We have to purchase supplies for the hospital, so we'll be quite busy and won't be very engaging guests."

"Say, I just had a brilliant idea, Miss Linden! Why don't you stay here with the ladies, and I'll accompany Jay to Vella Lavella? I haven't been there in some time, and it would be good if I made an inspection."

"That's a very kind offer, Mr. Bentley, but I really must go. I have to make a requisite number of plant collections on this trip, and I won't be able to do that unless I go," I said with a shrug.

"Well, I'll come with you then. There's room for three in your aircraft. And it can't hurt to have another white man along to protect you," Mr. Bentley stated, looking at Jay for approval. I was dumbstruck for a moment. I was about to list the many places I'd been without needing any man of any color to protect me, but Jay spoke first.

"Mr. Bentley, I regret it won't be possible to take you. The weight of the extra medical supplies we must transport will make carrying a third passenger impossible. Perhaps I can return another time and fly you on a tour of the colony," Jay said diplomatically. Bentley seemed unconvinced and surprised at not having his command obeyed.

"Yes, another time then," he said brusquely. "I do hope you have a pleasant stay in Chinatown." We watched him stalk off toward one of the administrative buildings.

Once Bentley was out of earshot, I asked Jay, "Is that true? About the weight being too much?"

"No, of course not. I don't much like his kind. It's clear to me what he thinks of the natives and the Chinese here. He thinks I am Spanish, but if he knew I am from México, just another land to be exploited for its resources, he might feel differently about having me as a guest."

"Thank you, Jay. I don't much like his kind, either. Let's find that hotel." We walked away from the wharves and toward the cluster of low warehouses, shops, and red-roofed buildings that made up Chinatown. We soon found there were two hotels, Sterling's and Sam's. We opted for Sam's and climbed the stairs to the shaded verandah. Inside, the little lobby had a few rattan chairs and a slowly spinning ceiling fan. I rang the brass bell on the unoccupied desk, and a minute later a Chinese man hurried out from another room.

"Hello, do you have two rooms for tonight?" I asked.

"Ah, yes. You are in luck. We have two empty rooms. Are you sure you do not want just one room?"

I assured him we wanted separate rooms, and he handed us a pair of keys. He explained that the room he'd come from was the restaurant and bar, and it was the best Chinese restaurant on Tulagi. We promised to come back for dinner and went outside to find our rooms. They were adjacent to each other and opened onto the verandah. I entered my room, and the largest cockroach

I'd ever seen darted from under the bed into the small bathroom. It was easily over three inches long, not including its feelers. I peeked in the bathroom, hoping to see the fascinating creature again, but it was nowhere to be found. I put my bag on the end of the shabby single bed. It was definitely not the Resident Commissioner's spotless residency, but it would do.

I met up with Jay outside, and we began our search for supplies. There were half a dozen small stores crammed with an assortment of goods. Once we'd visited each one to assess the merchandise, we returned to make our purchases. After acquiring two armloads of medical supplies, we went back to Lula to put them in the cargo hold. I returned to the shops for another load, while Jay stayed behind and refueled the aircraft.

In the next store, I picked out a dozen mosquito nets, lengths of brightly printed fabric, cheap celluloid combs and mirrors, necklaces of colorful glass beads, and rubber balls. Jay soon joined me and chose some pocketknives, several bush knives, fishhooks, and tobacco. We deposited our treasures in the airplane and came back for more.

We went to a general store with a good supply of groceries and stocked up on tea, coffee, sugar, rice, and tins of meat and fish. I selected Pepsodent toothpaste, toothbrushes, Palmolive soap, laundry soap, Rexona ointment, and Cloverine salve. When Jay wasn't looking, I added jars of cold cream, face powder, packages of Modess and Kotex sanitary napkins, and a few tiny metal tubes of lipstick. Perhaps Jay would think these items frivolous, but Merle or any other women we met might appreciate some feminine luxuries.

Once we had crossed everything off our list, we secured all the bundles in the plane and returned to the hotel. It was a bit too early for dinner, so we freshened up in our rooms, as much as possible given the surroundings, and met in the bar for a drink. A few other patrons, the class of which would not have been welcomed in the residency, already occupied several barstools. We chose a small table, and the bartender brought each of us a gin and tonic. I reflected that Jay seemed to have given up on his principle of not drinking alcohol the night before flying, but it didn't seem to affect his abilities, and the quinine in the tonic water was advisable given our remote destination.

We studied the map that Ruby had given Jay. Although the flight would be short, less than three hundred miles, the number of islands between here and there seemed daunting to me. But Jay was not concerned, so I tried not to be, either. When the restaurant opened for dinner, we relocated to a small corner table there. We didn't want to draw too much attention to ourselves and have more people asking about our plans. The clientele was a mix of Chinese traders, down-and-out white men, and a few unattached women who seemed to be assessing their prospects for the night. We were, perhaps, out of place, but I was glad to avoid the scrutiny of the Bentleys.

The waiter brought us hot tea and the dinner special, a mix of vegetables and meat of indeterminate origin in a spicy sauce over rice. Later, he came back to collect our empty plates and placed the check facedown on the table. Jay picked it up and grimaced.

"Too expensive? I'm paying, remember?" I said, laughing. He wordlessly handed me the bill. Below the total for our meals was written: "Look out for the Japanese shell trader. He is not what he seems." I pocketed the slip of paper and left some money on the table.

"Let's go now, Jay." We walked back to our rooms. A trio of men leaned idly on the verandah railing with their drinks. I wanted to talk to Jay about the note, but not out here. I unlocked my door and pulled him inside my room.

"Profesora, this is not how I imagined it," he said with a sly grin.

"Imagined what? Never mind. What do you make of that note?"

"I suppose someone is just concerned for us," he said with a shrug. "Maybe he saw us looking at the map."

"But why should we care about a Japanese shell trader? And why would the waiter care about us?"

"The Chinese are not very fond of the Japanese, to put it mildly. And the Japanese seem to have a preference for a very unpleasant man in Germany with a ridiculous mustache. Perhaps they know we do not."

"Well, I guess it's nice that we have someone looking out for us. But I wish we were really just going to drop off medical supplies and then leave. Whatever this is isn't our problem."

"I thought the same, Ivy. That I could outrun it. But it's going to become everyone's problem someday," Jay said grimly. "Let's go to bed." For a moment I thought he was suggesting he stay the night, but his hand was on the door, and he opened it to the humid night air. "*Buenas noches*, Ivy. I will see you tomorrow at seven for breakfast."

"Good night, Jay," I said as he walked out the door. I heard one of the drunks on the verandah remark to his friend, "That was fast." I slammed the door.

I went into the bathroom to wash up, expecting to see the massive cockroach scurry away when I turned on the light. Instead, it had met its demise. It lay belly-up on the floor, and dozens of tiny ants were swarming over it. The sight should have disgusted me, but I was fascinated, and watched the busy workers efficiently dismantling the huge carcass. It was at times like this I was especially glad to be a biologist. Nevertheless, I peeled back the sheets carefully, looking for any of the dead roach's friends and family before I got into bed.

CHAPTER 19

Another spectacular sunrise gave way to a brilliant blue sky. We bid adieu to Sam and the invertebrate guests at the hotel and returned to Lula. No one had bothered to come see us off this morning. We settled into our customary positions in the cockpit and started off toward the melodious Vella Lavella.

"Why don't you take the controls, Ivy?" Jay suggested once we'd leveled off. I took the stick and happily piloted Lula while Jay looked at the maps, correcting our course periodically. We flew west over little round Savo Island and then continued northwest over open water. Another cluster of islands came into view, which Jay said were called the Russell Islands.

"What glorious weather we've had for all our flights, Jay," I remarked as we passed over the green jewels below. "No rain at all!"

"*Profesora! Dios mío*, why would you say such a thing? Now you will bring us bad luck. You will jinx us. That is what you say in America, I think." I glanced at him to make sure he was joking, but his face was stern.

"Oh Jay, you're not serious, are you? Don't tell me you believe in bad luck?"

"It doesn't matter if I believe in it or not. It happens. Just like good luck. Do you mean you don't believe in luck? Or fate?"

"No, of course not. I'm a scientist, Jay. I know we make our own luck and choose to call it good or bad. Nothing is fated."

"Profesora, do you mean you have never experienced something you cannot explain?"

"No, there's always an explanation. Maybe we haven't discovered it yet, but I have faith in scientific progress."

"But what about coincidences? Have you never felt a guiding hand was helping you?"

"They're just random chance, Jay. People only notice coincidences and think they mean something because they want to."

Jay shrugged. "Maybe you're right, Profesora. But imagine how many little things had to line up just right to put you here in this airplane with me, flying over the Solomon Islands. Do you think that was merely random chance?"

Now I shrugged. I supposed he had a point. This wasn't where I had expected to be at all, yet somehow here I was. "And maybe you're right, Jay. We'll never know." There was no point in disagreeing too adamantly with the person I was now so dependent upon. We flew on in silence for some time.

"Let me take the controls again, Ivy," Jay said. I let go, and he grabbed the yoke.

"Is everything okay?"

"I'm sure it's nothing," he said, motioning to a darker point on the horizon.

"Is it an island?"

"No, it's a cloud. A storm."

"You're just teasing me."

"I wish I were, Ivy. We should have radioed ahead for a weather report before we left. But I have a feeling this storm had not formed then," Jay said, glancing at me sideways.

Was he actually blaming me for the storm? It was just a coincidence. An unfortunate coincidence.

"Can't we fly around it? Or above it?"

"Maybe. Keep an eye out for the next group of islands. They are volcanic with high peaks that might be obscured."

Obscured? I didn't know if he was serious or just trying to frighten me. But as we continued on, wisps of cloud began to float by the window. They became more abundant until the view in front of us, above us, and below us was limited. We were entombed in a dense cloud. A flash of lightning jumped in the distance. Jay was relying solely on the instruments to fly now.

"Hold on, Ivy. It will be rough."

"A friend once told me it was just like driving on a bumpy road. I'm not frightened," I said. The last part was a lie.

"Don't worry, Lula will see us through. She's never let me down yet." The turbulence increased, and the little plane shook. We dropped down abruptly in an air pocket, and I remembered when Amaryllis and I rode on the Cyclone at Coney Island. She had wanted to ride on the rollercoaster. I tried to discourage her, but she convinced me to come with her. I didn't want her to think I wasn't brave enough. Now she was safely at home in the confines of the library, while I was being jostled through the air over a very different island with no boardwalk or ice cream cones below. I felt the airplane climb and change direction.

"I'm trying to find the edge of the storm," Jay explained. "It will put us off course, but we should have plenty of fuel to find our way back." He seemed at ease, and I wondered if it was just a show of bravery. I decided not to question it and continue with my own show. We bounced along for several more minutes. The clouds began to thin out, revealing glimpses of sunlight above and blue water below. I released my grip on the sides of my seat cushion, unaware that I'd been holding on with white knuckles. We emerged into a clear blue sky again, with no sign of the storm. Or any land below us. My relief at returning to calm air was quickly supplanted by a fear that we were lost. But I kept that concern unspoken, afraid Jay would chastise me for jinxing us again. And perhaps a tiny bit afraid I actually had jinxed us.

"Take the stick again, Ivy," Jay said as he looked at the charts. I took it as a good sign that he trusted me with the plane. "I believe we have gone past New Georgia and Vella Lavella. If I am correct, we are about to come to the Treasury Islands," he said, pointing out a pair of islands on the map. "Once we spot them, I'll turn around and go back toward Vella."

I stared intently at the blue water. We both breathed sighs of relief when the mist-shrouded peak of Mono Island appeared ahead of us. Back at the controls, Jay made a circle around the soaring interior mountain of Mono and flew over the small, flat island named Stirling just off its shore.

"Treasury Islands," Jay repeated. "They must be

named that for a good reason. Treasure." I guessed he was thinking about the gold again and stayed silent. We left whatever treasure was down there behind and flew southeast toward Vella Lavella.

It was impossible to miss the steep, densely forested ridges that ran down the length of Vella Lavella. We flew along the eastern edge of the island, and as each geographic feature on the coast matched our chart, I finally felt at ease. We progressed toward the head mission station and hospital at Bilua on the southern end of the island, passing small settlements along the way.

A stone wharf marked our destination at Bilua. Lula swooped down once for a look, then eased onto the water and taxied up to the carefully built structure. Jay jumped out with the rope to secure the aircraft. By the time he'd tied up Lula and I'd hopped out behind him, our welcome party had arrived. A group of children had first watched us shyly from the shore, but crept closer and closer. Then, shouting *"Halo! Halo!"* as they lost their reserve, the children ran toward us on the stone jetty. Their modest white outfits, no doubt the influence of the Methodist missionaries, stood out in stark contrast to their dark skin. Only the youngest went bare, which seemed an entirely sensible thing to do in the midday heat. Most of the children had masses of dark hair curlier than any permanent wave could achieve. However, a couple girls and boys had striking blond ringlets that would have made Shirley Temple green with envy. I would have to ask what they used to dye it.

The children stared at the plane wide-eyed, and I knew Jay would have some eager passengers if we were around long enough. By now our arrival had attracted more attention, and two orderlies from the hospital, also dressed in white, approached with friendly waves.

"Hello! Welcome to Vella Lavella," a young man said. I was relieved he spoke English, and I would not have to try out my pidgin just yet.

"Hello! Thank you! I am Ivy, and this is Jay," I said, motioning to each of us. "We are here to see Nurse Farland and deliver some supplies to the hospital. Can you take us there?"

"Ah, yes, Sister said to expect you. I am Daniel, and this is Isaac. Come with us," the young man said. With the children parading behind, we followed Daniel and Isaac to the shore and past a series of neat, whitewashed wooden buildings including a simple church. We stopped at a sizable structure, and Daniel gestured for us to accompany him inside. We entered a single large room painted white with two rows of beds, some occupied by patients. A nurse in a white uniform stood at the far end of the ward, her back to us. She turned around at the sound of our entry.

I let out an involuntary gasp and grabbed Jay's arm for support. I felt dizzy and thought I might faint. The nurse crossed the room quickly and was in front of me in an instant.

"My goodness, are you all right? You look as though you've seen a ghost. Sit down right here," the nurse said, leading me to a nearby chair. "Do you need some smelling salts?" I shook my head no. Now that I'd heard her New Zealand accent and seen her up close, I was sure I had not seen a ghost. But until then, I was not quite so certain. The nurse had short, tousled light brown hair and a face that I had last seen in the cockpit of a

Lockheed Vega at the Ithaca Airport. For an instant, I thought I'd made an amazing discovery: Amelia Earhart had merely run away from civilization and become a nurse here on this remote island. It wasn't entirely farfetched. She had volunteered as a nurse in Canada tending to the wounded of the Great War before she became a famous aviatrix.

"Thank you, I'll be fine now. I'm very sorry. It's just that you look like someone I was not expecting to see, and it took me by surprise," I said with embarrassment.

"I'm Merle Farland," the nurse said. "I think I'm expecting you."

"Yes, of course. I'm Ivy Linden, and this is Jacinto Diente de León of Qantas Airways."

"Right, Qantas," she said, winking as Jay took her hand.

"Please call me Jay, Sister."

"And please call me Merle. No need for Sister or Nurse Farland between friends."

I felt better and stood up. "We have some supplies for you. I hope we got everything you needed."

"I'm sure you did. Anything is a help to us here. Daniel, Isaac, please help Jay unload the medical supplies from the airplane." The men led Jay out, leaving me alone with Merle and the patients, who seemed mildly interested in the activity in their ward.

"Ruby tells me your pilot can be trusted?" I nodded in agreement. "Good. Say, if it's not prying, who did you think I was just now?" Merle asked.

"Well, you bear some resemblance to Amelia Earhart," I said sheepishly, adding, "She was a friend. I guess I still keep hoping she's alive somehow."

"Oh dear, I am sorry for the fright. I've never been told that before. It would be a little amusing if it hadn't upset you so much," she said, giving me a hug. "We all hoped she would be found last year."

"I guess I was still shaken up from the storm," I said, trying to explain my melodramatic reaction.

"Storm?"

"Yes, we flew through that terrible storm on the way. We had to fly around it and got off course."

"There was no storm here, Ivy. We've had blue skies all day."

"Oh, that's good," I said with a shrug, wondering how it had not affected the island.

The men returned with the first load of supplies from the plane. I spotted the bundle of items I'd chosen just for Merle.

"Here are a few things I thought you might not get regularly," I said, handing her the package. She undid the covering and smiled at the makeup, cold cream, and sanitary pads.

"Oh, you are a dear, Ivy. You're right; we don't get things like these all the time. I hesitate to ask the men to bring them with the other necessities. Thank you."

The men finished unloading the cargo, and I helped Merle to arrange the new medical supplies. Then she took us to meet the doctor in charge of the hospital, Allen Rutter, and his wife, Elizabeth, who happened to be a bacteriologist. They offered to host Jay in their home, while I was to stay with Merle in her little cottage.

Later we met Reverend Silvester, the head of the mission at Bilua, and his wife Moyna. Everyone seemed quite eager to show off the good work of the mission in educating the children of Vella Lavella and improving the health of the islanders. We were treated to an excellent dinner of pork, yams, and sweet potatoes with refreshing bush limeade to wash it down. The conversation was stimulating, if not exactly pleasant. Dr. Rutter, Elizabeth, and Merle enthusiastically shared their work treating yaws, a bacterial infection that causes festering ulcers on the skin. It seemed half of the islanders suffered from the disease, and they were trying injections of different drugs to combat it. Elizabeth was especially excited to explain that it's caused by a spirochete very closely related to the one that causes syphilis. This would most definitely not have been appropriate conversation for the women at the Tulagi Club.

Jay offered to fly Merle to some of the outlying islands to administer more injections, Dr. Rutter readily consented, and our cover story was set. At least some local people would actually receive medical treatment, even if our quest for whatever treasures Skull Island held came to naught.

As the evening drew to a close, Merle asked Jay to help her bring a cot from the hospital to her cottage. He carried it inside the little white structure, and finally we were all alone to discuss our plans. We sat around a small table, and Jay flattened out the creased map that Ruby had given him.

"Kundu Hite," Merle said, pointing to the tiny dot on the map. "That's not a place too many people want to go. Just what do you expect to find there?"

"I'm really not sure," I replied and filled her in on the trip to Tioman, the missing *Rafflesia*, and my suspicion that Emerald Asche-Böhrer was seeking something on

Kundu Hite.

"Well, she won't be looking for plants there. It's much too small for that. I've never been there, but I've heard about the island. Before the missionaries came, the natives had their own religion, of course. They worshipped their great ancestors and tried to harness their power, or *mana* as they call it, to use in this life. They believed the *mana* was located in the head, so they built little houses for the skulls of their ancestors. These shrines used to be located all over the islands in this part of the Solomons.

"Naturally, the missionaries discouraged them from these primitive beliefs. Most of the islanders saw the light, but some refused. There was a great chief, Ingava, who resisted the missionaries' efforts and never would convert to Christianity. He was afraid the missionaries, or even just white curio collectors, would destroy the skull shrines or steal the skulls and other sacred artifacts there. So he and some of the other chiefs moved the most important shrines to little Kundu Hite, and that's how it became Skull Island."

"Are the shrines still there?" I asked.

"Yes, as far as I know. The last great chief to have his skull housed there was Ingava, himself. He died in 1906. And so he and his *mana* protect the island and the sacred items there. The surrounding villages converted after he died, but everyone still holds the shrines as sacred, and we leave them alone."

"Do some people still adhere to the old religion?" Jay asked.

"No, not officially. But unofficially, who can say? There have been a lot of changes here in just one generation. It's not realistic for them to abandon all the old ways of thinking so fast, especially among those who still live in the bush," said Merle.

I wanted to add that it was just swapping one set of superstitions and myths for another, but I kept quiet. Instead, I said, "I don't understand what interest this could possibly hold for Emerald Asche-Böhrer. It doesn't seem there's anything of botanical value there."

"And that's why we should go there ourselves to find out. And if I can treat some natives for yaws, then so much the better," Merle replied.

"What is the best way to get there?" Jay asked.

"We can't just go to Kundu Hite ourselves. It's *tambu*. Taboo. We need an elder to take us there. I think we should fly to Munda," Merle said, pointing to a spot on the island of New Georgia. "We can discreetly ask around there and figure out where to get a guide to take us to Kundu Hite."

"That sounds like a good plan," I said. "It's a short flight. Maybe we could go tomorrow morning and be back by the evening."

"Maybe, Ivy, but we had better plan on being gone for a few days at least," Jay said. "We'll leave at nine o'clock tomorrow."

With that we bid Jay goodnight, and Merle and I got ready for bed. She insisted I take her bed and she sleep on the cot. The arrangement in her little bungalow felt like a cozy slumber party or my dorm room at Bryn Mawr. Maybe it was this feeling of familiarity that prompted me to ask, "Merle, where are you from in New Zealand?"

"I was born in Christchurch, on the South Island, but we moved to Auckland on the North Island when I was a child. Have you been there?"

"No, not yet. That's where I was supposed to go originally. I have a colleague there. A professor at the University of Otago. I was supposed to meet him before I went to the Three Kings Islands to look for a particular tree. Maybe you know him? His name is Heath Bracken."

"Hmm . . . no, he doesn't sound familiar. It's a small country, but not everyone in New Zealand knows everyone else," she said, laughing.

"No, of course not," I said, laughing too, but feeling a bit disappointed. For some reason, I felt so at ease with Merle that I found myself confessing, "I guess I have a crush on him."

"Well, who could blame you with that dark wavy hair and that roguish smile? He *is* charming."

"Professor Bracken? I don't even know what he looks like."

"Oh, I thought you meant Jay. He's quite attractive."

"Jay? Yes, I had noticed. But there's nothing between us. It's strictly professional."

"Hmmm. Well, best we get some sleep, not stay up all night gossiping like a couple of schoolgirls. Good night, Ivy."

"Good night, Merle."

CHAPTER 20

"There, that ought to do it," Merle said, handing Jay the last of the medical supplies to stow in the airplane. She had dispensed with her nurse's uniform and was now dressed like me in slacks, a long-sleeved blouse, and sturdy hiking boots. We shoved our luggage with enough clothes and tinned food for a few days in next and climbed aboard.

Merle had never flown before, so I urged her to sit in the cockpit with Jay. I took the seat behind her and marveled at her profile. She just needed flying goggles and a leather jacket to be Amelia's twin sister.

Elizabeth and Dr. Rutter waved as we taxied away from the stone pier and picked up speed. Soon we were airborne, and Merle squealed with delight, her calm demeanor melting away at the thrill of seeing her home from the air. We flew south over the Vella Gulf, between Kolombangara and Gizo, and then along Vonavona Island. The turquoise water between Vonavona and nearby Arundel Island was scattered with dozens of tiny islets, spilled out like green beads from a broken necklace. Kundu Hite was one of those emerald gems.

Soon we reached Munda Point on the larger island of

New Georgia. Lula eased back into the water and came to rest at a jetty. As Jay tied her up, Merle and I unloaded some of the supplies.

"There's a mission station here, too," Merle explained. "And a school and a small dispensary. We teach the children proper English and how to read and write in their own language, Roviana. I thought I'd be stationed here, so I learned Roviana on the steamer voyage over. On our part of Vella Lavella the native language is Bilua, so I had to learn that, too, when I got there. But knowing Roviana comes in handy sometimes, like now."

Some islanders had come to greet us wearing spotless white, Western garments like at Bilua. Merle said hello in their own language, and we followed them to the small medical building which was set back from the shore amidst a grove of palm trees.

"Nurse Farland, what a pleasure to see you," a young man dressed in white said in perfect English.

"Hello, George. These are my friends, Ivy and Jay. They're helping me bring medical supplies to some of the more distant villages. I thought we'd stop here first and see if you need any help."

"Thank you, Sister. There have been no patients today, but once word gets around that you are here, we may have some."

"We'll stay for a few hours before we take off for our next stop. I figured we'd visit Sipisai, Mamburana, Kundu Hite, and Vonavona."

"Kundu Hite, Sister? No one lives there."

"Oh, yes. Of course not. But maybe we'll stop there anyway, just to look around."

"No, Sister, you must not. It's *tambu*. Of course, we know that is the old way, but there are still some in the bush who have not received the Word yet, and they would not want you to visit. Especially you and your friend Ivy."

"What do mean?" I asked.

"Women are not allowed to visit Kundu Hite because it is sacred. Only men can go there," George explained. Somehow this only made me more determined to see just what was so special about this island. But Merle and I let the issue drop as patients began to trickle in. Jay excused himself and left the little medical shack when it began to get crowded. I would have left, too, but Merle suggested I stay.

"It's not every day we have a lady doctor here. You can help me with the first aid."

"But I'm a doctor of botany," I said, laughing. "That's not too useful for your patients. But they might be useful for me if they tell me what plants they use to treat their ailments."

People from the nearby villages came in with a variety of ulcers and infections, exacerbated by the humid climate. I helped Merle disinfect and dress the wounds. Occasionally a person presented the characteristic lesions of yaws, and Merle gave them an injection of neoarsphenamine, a synthetic arsenic-containing drug used in the treatment of syphilis. It seemed like a harsh remedy. Maybe a natural cure, derived from some plant or fungus, would one day be found to take its place.

A young mother with a teary-eyed little girl came in next. I was relieved to see she was only suffering from a universal affliction of childhood, a skinned knee. Still, such a scrape could turn serious if it became infected. The girl sat on my lap and put on a brave face as Merle gently swabbed the affected area to clean it. As Merle worked, I admired the child's blond curls, which were such a contrast to her dark skin. The girl managed a smile when Merle was finished and scampered off, no doubt to scrape the other knee.

"Why do they bleach some of the children's hair?" I asked.

"It's not dyed. Not that girl's hair, anyway. Some of the adults with dark hair bleach theirs with coral lime. But that little girl is a natural blonde. I've seen enough babies born here to be sure," Merle explained.

"But her mother had dark hair. Is her father a European?"

"No, I doubt that. I've seen parents with dark hair have children with a mixture of hair colors. Mostly dark, but a blond child pops up now and then."

"Fascinating," I mused. "It's just like in peas. It must be from a recessive gene. It's only evident when a child has two copies of the blond gene, one from each parent. It's hidden in the parents by the version of the gene for dark hair." I'd have to remember to tell Barbara McClintock about this. I always felt a surge of pride because the basics of genetic inheritance had been worked out first in plants, not animals, by Gregor Mendel with his peas.

Merle gave a few more injections, bandaged a machete cut, and treated a toothache. "I think that's it for our patients here. Let's find Jay and go to the next village," Merle suggested.

We found Jay sitting with George and some of the

other local men, shooting the breeze.

"Ladies, finished with your duties already?" he asked.

"Yes, Jay. We'd best be moving on to our next stop. Let's go to Mamburana," said Merle, pointing out a small dot of an island on his map. "Can you land there? It won't have a jetty like this. If not, we can take a boat."

"Of course I can land there. Lula can take us anywhere," Jay replied with confidence. We piled back into the aircraft, waving at our new friends as we taxied away from the little pier.

"Well, what did you find out?" Jay asked.

"Find out? We were just treating people's medical problems," I said, somewhat irritated that he'd been relaxing while we worked.

"Ah, then I'm especially glad I was gathering intelligence," he said.

"What intelligence was that?" I asked.

"The men were a bit more forthcoming with information about Kundu Hite with me. They assured me there were no plants of value there. And no gold. They told me someone could guide me there to see the shrines as long as I didn't take anything."

"Well, that's not acceptable. I need to have a look myself."

"As you wish, Profesora. But that may prove challenging."

"I like a challenge."

"I'd like to see it, too," Merle added.

"That is fine with me, of course. I also asked the men if they have had any visitors lately. Especially any Europeans who don't live here. Any Germans. They all agreed no one has been here recently. Only the usual traders they see. A few Chinese traders collecting bêche-de-mer. And the Japanese shell trader. They said his name is Ito, and he's been visiting the islands for years. Very friendly, they say."

The flight to Vonavona Lagoon lasted just a few minutes as Jay spotted the correct islet, shaped a bit like a sea turtle emerging from the water. We circled a few times for Jay to assess the best place to land, and then Lula set down in the water opposite a cluster of thatch-roofed homes. Jay retrieved an anchor from beneath the back seat, jumped onto the float, tied its rope to a strut, and dropped it into the crystal clear water. In the time it took to do this, islanders in four dugout canoes arrived to greet us, sailing right up to the aircraft. We waved, and Merle shouted a greeting in Roviana. She spoke to them for a few minutes, then instructed us to pass some supplies and whatever we needed for the night to the man in the first canoe. Once that was loaded, he paddled back to shore, and Merle, Jay, and I each boarded one of the remaining canoes for a quick ride to tiny Mamburana.

The whole of the village, about eighty people, turned out to greet us, led by the chief, Liliti. Merle conversed with him in Roviana, then translated to us that we were welcome to spend the night. Liliti directed the villagers to sit down and listen to Merle. It seemed they all spoke Roviana, but not much English. Merle introduced Jay and me and explained she would treat any medical problems among the villagers. Then she asked if they had received any other visitors recently. They all agreed no outsiders had been to the island.

"Has anyone even just seen strangers from afar?" Merle asked them, repeating it in English for our benefit.

One man waved at us and began talking excitedly. When he finished, Merle nodded and thanked him.

"What did he say?" I asked.

"He said he saw the Japanese shell trader, Ito, on his sampan a few nights ago. He usually stops by the village to buy any fancy shells they have to sell, but this time he didn't. They called out to him from the shore, but he ignored their greeting. They were going to sail out to his sampan with some shells, but then they saw the other occupant of his boat and ran away from the water. When they finally came back to look again, his sampan was gone."

"Who was the other occupant?"

"A ghost."

"Oh, brother," I said with a sigh.

"A lady ghost. All white with long white hair flowing in the moonlight."

Liliti pointed out a hut that we could use as a dispensary for the day and told the people to line up for medicine. As the villagers began forming a queue, I asked Merle to enquire if Liliti could take us to Kundu Hite. She obliged, and I could see the answer was no. She didn't force the issue, and I began to consider sending Jay alone.

Once we were set up in the little hut with a variety of supplies, the islanders began to come in one by one again, just as they'd done at Munda. Merle gave a few more injections for yaws, dressed different skin infections, and treated some other minor complaints. The stream of patients dwindled, and then it seemed we were done. As we started to pack up the remaining supplies, an older woman entered the hut. She was perhaps about sixty years old with close-cropped, curly dark hair with a sprinkling of gray strands.

Merle said hello in Roviana and asked what ailed her. The woman looked around and, satisfied she was alone with us, replied in English.

"I can take you to Kundu Hite. I heard you ask the chief. He said no because you are women, and it is *tambu* for women to visit the shrines."

"Thank you," I said. "We would appreciate that very much. But why is it not *tambu* for you?"

"It is *tambu*, but I do not care. My father is there. I am Pula, the daughter of Ingava. He was the last of the great chiefs. He will protect me and not let any harm come to me if I visit his shrine. But we must not take anything from the island."

"Of course," I reassured her. "We will just look and pay our respects to your father."

"We will leave at midnight. It is a short canoe ride across the lagoon."

"Thank you, Pula," I said, pulling a bundle of printed fabric from one of the pouches of supplies and handing it to her. She smiled in gratitude, revealing teeth stained a shocking red. I knew the color came from chewing betel nuts, which came from *Areca catechu* palms, along with the leaf of a vine, *Piper betle*, and lime formed by burning coral. The resulting mixture was an addictive stimulant, like tobacco. While the practice was fascinating from a biochemical and anthropological standpoint, Westerners discouraged it for medical reasons. Or perhaps because it subconsciously reminded colonizers of the cannibalism that had been periodically practiced in these islands.

We found Jay outside with the men, somehow speaking the universal male language of fishing. We motioned him over to us.

"We're going to Skull Island tonight," I said softly. "The daughter of Chief Ingava will take us at midnight. His skull is there, so she does not care it is *tambu* for women."

"Very good, Ivy. I was not making any progress in finding a guide to take you and Merle. I will stay here or come with you, as you wish."

"You should come, too, if Pula will permit you. We must all show respect to her father's skull, for it has great *mana* in their old belief system," said Merle.

The village of palm thatch buildings on the tiny island was idyllic, the perfect setting for a Hollywood South Seas romance. Merle asked the women to give us a tour of their garden patches while Jay went back to fishing. Later, the islanders shared a meal of fish, taro, and bananas with us, and we handed out small items to each person as a token of thanks.

Liliti indicated we could sleep in the hut we'd used for a dispensary, and his wife brought us a pile of woven mats to sleep on. We hung mosquito nets over each mat and settled in to await Pula. I must have drifted off to sleep, as a scratching at the door woke me with a start. Jay opened the door, and the old woman came inside.

She was dressed differently than earlier in the day, wearing the new cloth we had given her wrapped around her body with variegated dracaena leaves tucked here and there into the folds. Around her head was a wide band of braided red fiber adorned with a large white shell disk overlaid with an intricate pattern cut from tortoiseshell.

Stacks of several white shell armbands decorated both arms above her elbows.

"Thank you for coming, Pula," I said. "Will there be room for Jay to join us?"

"Yes, Mr. Jay can come. Four of us will fit in my canoe. Follow me and do not talk."

We silently trailed behind Pula through the village, the moon lighting our way, until we reached the shore. A dugout canoe was at the water's edge. She pushed it forward and held it steady until we'd all climbed in. Pula took her place at the helm with an oar. Jay picked up the second oar, and we began to skim noiselessly through the water. The paddles and the stern of the canoe left a glowing wake behind us, caused by luminescent organisms in the water. The single-celled source of the light was as vast and fascinating as the stardust of the Milky Way that spilled out above us. I found myself wishing I had both a microscope and a telescope to have a closer look at each glimmering realm.

We snaked around the island to the opposite tip and set out away from the land. After some time, I could no longer discern the form of Mamburana behind us. Although I couldn't see where we were heading, I felt confident in Pula's sense of direction. However, I began to imagine what creatures might be unseen below us. I tried to focus on the glittering trail in the water, but images of sharks nipping at the paddles plagued me until Pula stopped rowing for a moment and pointed straight ahead at a barely-visible shape in front of us. "Kundu Hite," she said reverently.

We approached the shore of a tiny islet that made Mamburana look expansive by comparison. It was barely more than a clump of foliage with a few tall palm trees punctuating its leafy outline. Pula navigated us toward a diminutive beach of white sand where two shorter palm trees grew a few feet apart, forming a sort of doorway. Pula jumped out of the canoe with unexpected spryness and held the prow steady as we disembarked in the shallow water and helped her pull it onto the sand. Once it was secure, she reached in for several cloth-wrapped bundles that had been at our feet. She unwrapped them to reveal taro and *ngali* nuts from a tree I knew as *Canarium indicum.*

"These are offerings to my father and the other great warriors and chiefs. We cannot come empty-handed," Pula explained. She gave each of us a bundle of offerings. "Follow me."

In single file, we followed Pula through the threshold formed by the palm trees toward the heart of Skull Island. By now our eyes were adapted well to the dark, but the foliage blocked out a bit more of the moonlight, and it was hard to see the path. Our feet crunched over dried leaves, small sticks, and loose coral pebbles. My foot caught on a root, and I pitched forward, but Jay grabbed me before I fell. We ducked under a low palm frond, and the path widened in front of us. Pula stopped and raised her hand for us to stop, too.

Ahead of us, there was a large pile of rocks heaped up to about the height of a dining table. Structures made of smaller rocks rose from the base in several spots. Pula said some words in Roviana that I couldn't understand. Her intonation was that of a prayer or incantation. Perhaps she was reciting a list of names. We waited silently and didn't step any closer.

Finally, she said in English, "This is the great shrine at Kundu Hite, established by my father Chief Ingava to preserve the *mana* of the wisest and bravest of our ancestors and protect it from the outsiders who come to our islands to take what they want. Here are the skulls of our great ancestors, my father among them. Their spirits, *tomate* in our language, protect the sacred valuables made from the rare old shells of the giant clams. They guard the powerful seashells whose sound can summon the gods. The *mana* of the ancestors guarantees success in all things, in growing crops, in fishing, in war for those who possess its power."

We listened to Pula reverently, as if we were in a cathedral. The arching palm fronds above us might as well have been the flying buttresses of Notre Dame, as it was clear that to her people, this place was as sacred as any Christian church.

Pula spoke in Roviana again as we stood motionless. "Come," she said finally, beckoning us forward. "You may place the offerings at each of the small shrines. I will tell you about the ancestors."

When I stepped closer to the mound of rocks, I realized it was composed of jagged chunks of fossilized coral turned a dark gray with scattered patches of moss and algae softening the surface. Pula led us to the first structure on the bed of rocks. It was kind of a little flat-roofed house made of three slabs of rock. On the ledge in front of it were several large, light-colored rings, like bulky bracelets. They must have been the valuables crafted from the shells of the giant clam.

Pula placed her offering in front of the opening of the little structure and motioned for me to do the same. I placed a *ngali* nut on the rock and peered into the cavity. Blank eye sockets stared back. Four complete skulls and one lower jawbone were crowded together in their little house. I moved aside, and Merle presented her offering. Then Jay did the same, crossing himself the way Catholics do, as he put his taro down.

Once we had placed the offerings in front of the shrine, Pula said, "These are the skulls of some of our greatest warriors. Here are Gumi, Gemu, and Wange. And others whose names have been lost to time. They led many raids to other islands and captured the *mana* of many heads for the canoe houses. Now that *mana* dwells here in their skulls and the valuables they protect."

We stood in silence to show our respect. It seemed an odd custom until one thought of the ossuaries and reliquaries so common in European churches. These shrines weren't really any different than the crypts, catacombs, and purported relics of saints that the faithful visited. Placing a nut here was surely no more primitive than lighting a candle before an icon of the Virgin Mary, yet I knew not many would agree with me.

After a few more moments, Pula motioned us forward again. This time, we came to a different style of skull house, about two feet tall with a peaked roof. This one even had an intricately carved door propped against the opening of the A-frame structure. Pula spoke in Roviana at length. Finally she said to us, "This is one of the shrines for the chiefs. In here is my father Ingava's skull, the center of his *mana*. He was the last of the chiefs to uphold the old ways in the face of the outsiders coming to our islands. I will open the door, and we will put our offerings inside."

Pula moved the triangular carved door aside to reveal the interior of the shrine. Merle, Jay, and I leaned forward for a better view, but were startled backward by the sound of an otherworldly moan.

The chilling wail was coming from Pula. "He is gone," she cried in despair.

Jay grabbed the sagging woman and eased her down to the ground. I reached into my bag and pulled out my flashlight. I switched it on, and a beam of yellow light illuminated the empty interior of the small house.

"You had an electric torch all this time?" said Merle.

"It seemed disrespectful to use it," I said with a shrug.

We peered into the skull house. There was no sign of its expected inhabitant. Now Pula was up again, half marveling at the light coming out of the metal tube and half in shock at the empty shrine. I held the flashlight out to her, and she took it, shining the light all over the house and rocks beneath it. Then she went to the next house on the pile of rocks and let out another wail. "They are gone, too."

"Who is missing from this one, Pula?" I asked as we looked at an empty flat-roofed house.

"Not a who. There were no skulls in this house," she explained. "This is where the trumpet shells were kept. The shells to summon the spirits. Now whoever has the skull of my father can use his *mana* to sound the shells."

I was glad my face was hidden in the dark, as I suspected my incredulity was plain. But Pula's distress was real, no matter how ridiculous I might find her beliefs. And I supposed I would be upset if someone desecrated the grave of one of my relatives, even if I knew they were only organic matter at that point.

"Maybe some kind of animal just dragged them off. I'll stay here with Pula, and you and Jay look around the island," Merle suggested.

Pula handed the flashlight to Jay, and we set out to scour the tiny islet for any trace of the skull and shells. Jay focused the beam of light all around the coral rock table, revealing only some decaying taro and *ngali* nuts left as past offerings. Then we abandoned the path and wandered through the underbrush to the opposite side of the island. It was so tiny that there was no danger of getting lost. We traversed the expanse of Kundu Hite several times, but found nothing beyond loose coral rocks and startled hermit crabs who scurried away from our footsteps. The yellow beam of light began to fade, and we went back to the shrines.

"No sign of them," I said. "If an animal carried them off, I'd say it was of the human variety. What should we do now?"

"We must go back to Mamburana," Pula said. We walked back to her waiting canoe. Jay helped her in and held it steady for Merle and me. He got in and picked up one oar. Merle took the other oar, and they began to paddle us back toward Mamburana. Distraught as she was, Pula still knew the way and corrected them occasionally. My stomach was in knots until I saw the outline of Mamburana appear in the darkness. We sailed along its perimeter to the village, pulled the canoe ashore, and walked Pula back to her hut.

"Thank you for taking us to Kundu Hite, Pula," I said. "I am so sorry that your father's skull and the trumpet shells are missing." I knew it was entirely inadequate, but what else was there to say?

"We will find them for you and bring them back to Kundu Hite," Jay said. I stared at him in disbelief. This was not an offer I had thought to make. There was no way we could promise such a thing. But before I could say anything, Pula was clasping Jay's hands in her own.

"Thank you, Mr. Jay. Thank you, Ivy. Thank you, Nurse Merle. My ancestors will help you."

"Should we tell Liliti in the morning?" I asked.

"No," Pula replied. "We must not tell him my father's skull and the shells are missing. He will blame us for visiting the *tambu* place where women must not go. You will find them and put them back before anyone knows they are missing. And before anyone can use the *mana*."

We left Pula and silently crept back to our hut for some sleep, though it seemed the latest turn of events would banish all possibility of a restful slumber.

CHAPTER 21

After a few hours of fitful sleep, I awoke to find Merle and Jay already gone. I dressed quickly and went in search of them. I didn't have to go far, as they were sitting behind the hut crouched over Jay's maps. They smiled up at me with more cheerfulness than I could muster.

"*Buenos días,* Ivy," Jay said, and I sat down next to them.

"Good morning. You two seem awfully chipper after last night."

"We're making a plan," Merle said, gesturing at the maps.

"Jay, I can't believe you told Pula we'd find the skull and seashells. They could be anywhere. Or nowhere. It's impossible," I said.

"We have to help her. I am sure that's why we were sent here. I have faith that we will find them," Jay said solemnly.

The thought had occurred to me that we could just find another skull and some shells somewhere. How could Pula know the difference? But I didn't dare suggest the idea and banished the deception from my mind.

Besides, I knew I'd feel terrible to leave without at least attempting to help. And salvaging the trip to Three Kings was impossible now, so it was not as if I had somewhere else to be until my classes started again.

"Maybe you're right, Jay," I said, attempting to smile. "I'll try to have faith, too. So what plan have you come up with?"

"We're going on to Sipisai as planned," Merle said, pointing at another speck of an island on the map. "We'll ask around at the village there. Maybe they saw something. Then we'll go on to Vonavona. We can leave the plane here in this bay and then go on foot to the villages on the coast. Those seem like the best places to start looking."

"But couldn't anyone from any of the villages have taken the skull and shells?"

"It couldn't have been an islander. Even though many have converted to Christianity, they all still hold the ancient beliefs at some level. No one would dare take them," Merle said.

"But who else would want them?" I asked. "Souvenir hunters could do better than an old skull and seashells."

"No, they must have been taken by someone who values them for what they are," said Merle.

"Or what they can do," Jay added.

"Surely no outsider would think the powers the islanders ascribe to these things are real," I said in disbelief.

"But it's obviously your Emerald Asche-Böhrer again," said Jay.

"No, Jay, she's a botanist like me. I may not like her, but she's a real scientist. She'd never be interested in something like this. A rare plant, yes, but a silly superstition, no," I said with conviction.

"Maybe she's just working for someone else," Merle suggested.

"Maybe. Still, this whole situation seems ridiculous to me."

I was on the verge of suggesting we find a replacement skull when Jay added, "Perhaps there are more things in heaven and earth, Profesora, than are dreamt of in your philosophy."

"Maybe, Jay," I said, trying to mask my exasperation. There was no point arguing. "Should we be going soon?"

"Yes, let's pack up and be on our way," Merle said, rising.

We gathered our gear and gave some of the remaining medical supplies to Liliti. While Merle instructed him in their use, Jay and I went to Pula's hut and called softly to her.

"We are leaving now, Pula," Jay explained. "But we will be back and restore what has been taken." I nodded in agreement, though I doubted we could ever keep this promise.

Some young men rowed us out to where Lula had spent the night in the lagoon, and we climbed aboard. Jay dipped her wings to bid farewell to the villagers waving to us from the shore, and we flew north to Sipisai. The islet was a little larger than Mamburana, another green sea turtle rising from the lagoon. Jay spotted the little village and landed offshore. Once again, our arrival captured the attention of all the tiny island's inhabitants. Within minutes a few canoes sailed out to meet us, and we were rowed ashore.

Merle greeted the chief, Piko, who came to welcome us. She explained we had brought medical supplies and would treat any complaints among the villagers. Piko led us to a covered pavilion, and we unpacked the gear as a small line formed. As she began dressing wounds and administering shots, Merle chatted with each patient, asking them if they had seen any strangers recently or anything unexpected. A few people had left the island for fishing and trade, but no one had encountered any strangers.

After all the patients had been treated, we were offered a lunch of fish and yams. Almost the whole village of a hundred people was clustered around us eating. Merle repeated her questions to the larger group, but again no one acknowledged anything unusual.

"Ask them about the Japanese shell trader," Jay suggested. Merle complied, and the islanders knew him, but said they hadn't seen him in some time.

"Ask them if anyone has been to Kundu Hite recently," I said. Merle repeated my question. Everyone was silent, and men exchanged glances. Finally a couple men answered in the affirmative and spoke a few words.

"Yes, they say they were there about a month ago to make an offering for successful fishing. They didn't want to tell me," Merle explained. She assured them it was all right that they went, even though they were now Methodists, and asked if everything was in order at the shrine. She listened to their reply and then translated for Jay and me.

"They said yes, everything was fine. They made their offerings and had great success for several weeks afterward. But they have not had much luck for the past few days." Merle spoke to them and then told us she advised prayer like the missionaries had taught them instead. It would keep them away from Kundu Hite until we had a chance to recover the skull and shells. I reflected that we'd need our own prayers answered to do that.

It was now mid-afternoon, and we departed in Lula once more for the brief flight south to our destination on Vonavona. The southern part of the island curved around to form a sheltered bay bordered by a thin strip of white sand. Jay set the aircraft down in the calm water and taxied closer to shore. There were a few small grass huts, but no one came out to greet us. After securing Lula with the anchor, Jay inflated a rubber dinghy he had stashed in the back. He paddled ashore a few times with supplies before coming back for Merle and me.

The huts looked abandoned, and we picked the largest one as our lodgings for the night, deciding it was safest for the three of us to be together, rather than spreading out. The lush green foliage behind the huts called out to me, and I announced I'd take a short walk into the bush to look at plants.

"We'll come with you, Ivy. Best we stick together," Merle said, and she and Jay trailed behind me. The bright sunlight dimmed after walking only a few feet into the jungle, and the sound of the surf hushed. I knew Vonavona was quite narrow here according to Jay's chart, so if we walked too far we'd come to the other side of the island. Still, it was the first time we were unaccompanied by a local guide, and the dense foliage was disorienting.

I was crouching to examine a low-growing plant when the sound of movement behind us broke the silence. I spun around, my hand going instinctively to my bag, and I felt the reassuring smoothness of the pistol's pearl handle.

The three of us looked in the direction of the sound, but saw nothing. We stood motionless for a few moments. Then the rustling noise came again. I drew the pistol, just in case. I glanced at Jay and saw he'd had the same thought. He was now holding his own pistol, which was decidedly less feminine than my petite Colt. He glanced at me, and I think I detected a trace of a smile, before he wordlessly moved forward. I followed a step behind him, scanning the bush for whoever was there.

Another sound in the brush drew our attention ahead of us. And downward. We both lowered our pistols but kept our distance.

"Coconut crabs!" Merle cried out in relief. Four massive crabs with powerful claws had emerged from burrows amidst the detritus of the forest floor. I stepped closer and they quickly retreated into their holes.

"They're gigantic hermit crabs," Merle explained. "They don't use an abandoned shell like the small ones do. They're usually nocturnal."

"They will make a good dinner," Jay said. "Let's gather some dried wood for a fire."

"Oh, no, Jay," I said, putting my hand on his arm. "I'd rather not." I couldn't explain it, but I had looked into one crab's beady eyes before it hid in its home and couldn't bear the thought of eating it. "Let's have some tinned food instead."

"I hope that crab remembers your kindness tonight when it comes out in search of food," Merle said. "We'll have to keep the hut secure, or we'll have some surprise guests. They don't call them 'robber crabs' for nothing."

I made a halfhearted attempt to look at the plants again, but felt too unsettled to concentrate. After a few minutes, I suggested we go back to the beach, and Jay and Merle readily agreed. We arranged our mosquito nets in the hut while there was still light and opened some tinned salmon and peaches. Jay whacked the top off a coconut for each of us to drink. We made a picnic on the sand in front of our hut and watched the sunset.

"Let's walk up along the coast to the villages tomorrow. We'll come to a few small communities within three miles or so. Maybe they'll know something. I'm still exhausted from last night, so I'm going to sleep now," Merle said, leaving Jay and me alone on the beach.

"Ivy?"

"Yes, Jay?"

"Have you had that little pistol with you this whole time?"

"Yes."

"Why did you bring it?"

"I didn't plan to. My father gave it to me and insisted I take it. I don't know why." I handed him the dainty, pearl-handled Colt, and he turned it over in his hands. "And yours? Who gave you that?"

"The Astra? The Spanish Air Force, of course. I had it when I was shot down. We always had to carry it when we flew. In case of emergency."

"Do you always fly with it now?"

"No. I hate it. But something told me to bring it this time. In case of emergency."

"Let's get some sleep, Jay. I'm exhausted, too."

We barricaded the door of the hut with all our bags so the crabs couldn't get in and ensconced ourselves beneath our mosquito nets. Merle was breathing softly, and soon Jay was, too. Despite my fatigue, the rasping sound of the coconut crabs emerging from the bush kept me awake for some time. I listened to what sounded like an army of them dragging their great bodies along the sand and scratching at the outer walls and door of the hut. Only once it seemed our defenses couldn't be breached, did I dare to drift off to sleep.

CHAPTER 22

The coconut shells we'd left scattered about in front of the hut were gone in the morning. I hoped the crabs had appreciated the meal. Merle and I foraged for some fruit for breakfast before we departed on our trek. Meanwhile, Jay paddled out to check on Lula and retrieve more supplies from the cargo hold. Carrying some medical supplies, we began walking along the narrow strip of land between the jungle and the water as it curved around the shelter of the bay and headed north toward the settlements.

After a mile or so, we came upon a small cluster of huts. Merle called out in Roviana, and a few women came out of their homes to greet us with curious children trailing behind. Merle explained we could treat any injuries or illnesses, and several women and children presented the ubiquitous tropical sores no one could avoid.

Merle chatted as we worked to clean and dress the wounds, asking about any strangers who had visited. No one had seen anything unusual. She asked where the men were and was told some were fishing and others were hunting wild boar.

"Ask about Kundu Hite," I prompted. Merle did and replied back to me that no one had been there lately. And, of course, none of them had ever been there since they were forbidden as women.

"Do they know anything about the seashells?" I suggested. Merle translated, and the women spoke for a while.

"Yes, they know about the shells," she told us. "If you have enough *mana* you can use them to summon the powerful spirits from the sky, the *mateana*. They will come down in a flash of light and do the bidding of one who can summon them. The *mateana* sometimes come down at the lake. It's not far from here. Kolomateana, it's called, and it's sacred. Although they also assure me they don't believe that anymore now that the mission has come to give them the Word."

We let each woman pick something from our remaining trade goods and then began our trek again. After another mile, we came upon a similar small grouping of huts and repeated the whole process. And again no one offered us any clues. We continued onward, reaching a larger settlement with many more houses and some small garden plots carved out of the bush. Some children spotted us walking toward the village and called out to their mothers before running to greet us. Soon the women appeared, as well as some men. Merle gave them the usual greeting and explanation for our visit. An older man presented himself as Zuvulu, the chief of Mandou village. He led us to an empty hut, and we set up our treatment station. The procedure was becoming routine, and we began treating the ulcers, cuts, and infections like an assembly line.

Merle casually asked each patient about strangers visiting, and again everyone denied seeing anyone out of the ordinary. The last patient was a mother carrying a wailing baby who clearly had yaws. Merle gave the little boy an injection that only caused the child to scream louder. I rummaged through the bag of trade goods looking for something safe to give an infant. I settled on a celluloid backed mirror and tried to distract the distressed child with his image. He grabbed hold of it, and his sobbing stopped as he stared at the baby gazing back at him.

Zuvulu came in and invited us to stay for lunch. We readily accepted and joined a large group of villagers on the beach. They generously passed yams and fish around to us. Merle asked the larger crowd about any unexpected visitors, and they told us that we were the only outsiders they had seen for some time.

"Ask if anyone has been to Kundu Hite," I suggested. No one had been there in some months.

"Ask if they know the Japanese trader," Jay said. Several men replied in the affirmative, but said he had not been around to buy shells from them in many weeks.

"Ask about the lake. Can someone take us there?" I said.

There was some discussion after Merle's question. She listened to their reply and then told us, "No, they won't take us to the lake. The lake is sacred. And the last time someone visited there from the village they saw a light in the water. They were afraid and haven't been back."

It seemed there were no leads here; it was a wasted trip as far as finding where the skull and shells went. At least we had provided medical care to the villagers, which was more important anyway. We handed out the last of our trade goods, glad to be heading back with lighter loads. Retracing our steps back toward our hut in the bay, we passed through the two smaller villages a second time. In each case, the women insisted on giving us some fruit, yams, and fish. We gratefully accepted the generous gifts as it meant not eating tinned food again or having to ponder a dinner of coconut crabs.

We walked along the beach leisurely, admiring the view of the lagoon dotted with dozens of tiny green islets. The sun was low in the sky as we neared the bay. Coconut palms leaned lazily toward the water. It was a scene meant for a picture postcard. Or a Dorothy Lamour movie, I thought with a chuckle.

But as I marveled at the natural beauty of the bay, I failed to notice the absence of something that did not normally belong there. That is until I heard Jay shout, "*Mierda! Dónde está Lula?*" Indeed, the trusty little airplane was gone.

CHAPTER 23

"*Dios mío!*" Jay cried, running to the edge of the water closest to where the aircraft had been anchored. Merle and I dropped our bundles of food in the sand and ran to join him. There was no sign of Lula.

"Maybe she became unmoored and drifted away?" I suggested.

"No, Ivy. The bay is too sheltered for that. It is three quarters of a circle. She couldn't have drifted out into the lagoon."

"Maybe she sank?" Jay glared at me, and I regretted suggesting it.

"No, the water isn't deep enough to cover her there. Someone must have taken her."

"I don't think the natives would have dared steal the plane, Jay," Merle said. "And even if they'd cut the anchor and towed it with their canoes, they couldn't have gone too far. And we'd have seen them if they'd gone north."

"Could someone have flown her away?" I asked.

"Ivy, no. Surely we would have heard the sound of the engines. We were not so far away the whole day. Besides, who could have known how to fly her?"

I felt my stomach drop.

"Maybe I didn't mention this before, but Emerald Asche-Böhrer can fly," I said glumly.

"No, you neglected to mention that fact, Profesora. But can she fly a seaplane?"

"I don't know," I admitted. "But you're right. How could we not have heard the engines or seen her overhead?"

"The baby," Merle said. "The crying baby. We were inside the hut, and the little fellow made an awful racket. We wouldn't have heard the plane just then."

"That seems hard to believe, Merle. What are the chances of that?" I said.

"Chance, Profesora? You know how I feel about that."

"Oh, Jay, I'm so sorry. This is all my fault for dragging you here. I promise we'll find Lula. And the skull and the seashells," I said with more conviction than I felt.

"It's not your fault, Ivy," Jay said, softening his tone. "Yes, we'll find her."

"Let's have some dinner, and then we'll think more clearly," Merle said. "Be on the lookout for clues."

We gathered the bundles of food again and sat down in the sand. Jay surveyed the bay while Merle and I spread out the feast the villagers had graciously shared with us.

"Everything looks just as we left it," Jay said as we ate. "How could someone have left no trace?"

"They must have left some signs. Unless they came by boat," Merle said.

"Maybe they came from the bush," I suggested, and

we all turned uneasily to face the darkening patch of jungle behind us. "We can look for clues in the morning."

The sound of a rustling from the bush interrupted our discussion, and we looked warily over our shoulders again.

"It's just the crabs," I said. "Let's go inside before they become active. Last night they made a lot of noise." We gathered up the remains of dinner and threw the scraps toward the jungle's edge for the crabs to scavenge. Merle went inside the hut, while Jay walked back to the water lapping at the white sand and scanned the horizon again. I followed him and gently placed my hand on his arm.

"I am sorry, Jay. We can get a boat back to Vella Lavella and radio over to Tulagi. Maybe the Resident Commissioner will know something. He can send out his constables to look for Lula. We'll find her."

"Thank you, Ivy. Let's see what tomorrow brings."

After a few more moments of gazing at the empty bay, we walked back to the hut. Jay opened the door for me, and I stepped into the dim interior. I heard a muffled sound and looked around the hut as my eyes adjusted to the darkness.

"Merle, are you all right?" I asked as I withdrew the flashlight from my bag. I hadn't changed the batteries, but the faint yellow light was just enough to illuminate the scene in front of me. I gasped aloud.

"Good evening, Fräulein Linden. Please don't move. That goes for your friend, too," a man said in a calm voice with a German accent. A light came from behind us, a lantern held by another man. Both men had pistols pointed at us.

"You may turn off your electric torch and drop it on

the ground, please," the German man instructed. As I did so, the beam shone on Merle, and she tried to speak, but a gag prevented her from being understood. She was sitting on the ground with her hands tied behind her.

"Put your bag on the ground, please," the man said politely, taking the lantern from the second man. "Ito, search them for weapons, and look in her bag." The other man roughly ran his hands over me first, finding nothing. Then he searched Jay, withdrawing his concealed Astra. The man grabbed my bag, pulled out the little Colt, chuckled softly, and dropped both guns inside.

"Tie them up, please, Ito." The Japanese man produced two lengths of rope and tied Jay's hands behind his back, while the German man kept his pistol trained on us. Next it was my turn, and the man deftly secured my wrists together behind me with the rope. My mind raced. What to do? We were putting up no resistance at all. There were three of us, and only two of them. Surely we could overpower them. But how?

The German raised the lantern higher, illuminating his face better, and I had a flash of recognition.

"You! The man from the Clipper! Have you been following me this whole time? Who are you? Why are you here?" I demanded.

"Ah, forgive me for being so rude, Fräulein Linden. I did not make proper introductions. I am Käfir Ohrwürmer, and this is my colleague Herr Ito. And no, I have not been following you the whole time. I had important business to tend to. I presume your friends are Fräulein Farland and Herr Diente de León?"

"How do you know that? I insist you let us go immediately. The British Resident Commissioner will be looking for us with the full force of the colony behind him. I advise you to untie us right now unless you wish to cause an international incident."

"Fräulein Linden, I doubt that very much. And it is my job to know things. And to find out whatever I need to know by whatever means necessary. Now we are going to take a pleasant evening stroll. I would rather not hear you talk. Unless you wish me to prevent you from speaking, I suggest you say no more. Ito, get her up," Ohrwürmer said, motioning to Merle. Ito roughly pulled Merle to her feet. She didn't seem hurt, but her rage was apparent. He removed the gag but cautioned her to keep silent.

Ohrwürmer motioned us to the door, and we filed past him as Ito kept his pistol trained on us. Both men withdrew large machetes hanging from their belts, and Ohrwürmer led the way with the lantern in one hand and the machete in the other. Merle walked behind him, then me, then Jay, followed by Ito, who had my bag slung over his shoulder and kept his pistol in one hand and machete in the other.

Ohrwürmer led us not toward the easy terrain of the shore, but into the bush. The darkness closed around us just a few feet in, the only light coming from his lantern. He whacked at the foliage ahead of us to clear a path, while Ito randomly slashed the brush with his machete as he walked behind us, pistol in hand. The swishing of the knife was less to clear brush and more to remind us of the ease with which he wielded the lethal blade.

The lantern cast a dim glow on the debris-strewn floor of the jungle. Roots and low-growing vines stretched out like tripwires in our path, impossible to avoid as we stumbled along without the benefit of using our hands for balance. Coconut crabs scurried from our path, as well as other creatures I preferred not to think about. I reasoned that any snakes were more afraid of us than we were of them and would do their best to get out of our way. That was not so from above, however, as flying foxes and smaller bats dipped down to investigate.

The attention required to keep from tripping proved too great to allow me to concoct any sort of plan. Or even to fully comprehend this turn of events. I vaguely wondered if Merle or Jay had come up with any ideas. If only Amaryllis were here, she'd know what to do. She'd seen every film serial that played at the movie theater and knew all the plots. She'd know how the hero gets out of scrapes at the last minute, somehow turning the tables on his evil captors. But this was no movie.

We walked on in silence for at least an hour before Ohrwürmer allowed us to rest for a few minutes. We had barely caught our breath before he and Ito were pushing us onward through the jungle again. I couldn't even contemplate the vast expanse of plants surrounding me, perhaps even many unknown species, as the men slashed their way through the bush. Occasionally the lantern reflected sets of eyes glowing red or green back at us. As unnerving as that was, I knew the tiny mosquitoes that assaulted us were a bigger threat than any other beast we were likely to encounter. Besides the two-legged ones, of course.

After another short respite, we trudged on again. We were not walking fast, but by then we must have walked a few miles. Since we hadn't come to the shore of the opposite side of the island, we must have been walking toward the center part of the island's southern half. We couldn't have been too far from the coastal villages we'd visited, but we were deep in the uninhabited interior where few islanders would go, unless perhaps to hunt wild boar. The chances of happening upon anyone who could help us seemed slim.

Eventually the canopy of trees above us began to thin out. Once in a while, a glimpse of dark sky was visible. Then all at once we emerged from the dense bush. The starlight revealed the shore of a lake ahead of us. Lake Kolomateana, I surmised. It seemed to curve around in the shape of a boomerang. A large, dark form was visible in the water at the end of the lake farthest away from us. My mind went back to lost dinosaurs for an instant before I recognized the shape. Lula!

I looked back at Jay and saw the relief on his face. I allowed myself a flicker of optimism. At least we had a means of escape now. But Ito shoved Jay forward, and we kept walking toward a small cluster of huts along the lakeshore. Ohrwürmer ordered us to stop before we reached the first hut. He walked ahead, still keeping his pistol pointed in our direction, and spoke some words in German at the doorway of the thatched structure. He motioned to Ito, who prodded us forward again. We stood silently opposite the hut for a few moments before a luminous form emerged from inside.

"Fräulein Professor Doktor Linden, how delightful to see you again," the blond woman said with a slight bow. "Ohrwürmer, where are your manners? Untie my guests right now. Ito, get them something to eat and drink." The two men followed her orders, and we rubbed our chafed wrists. I looked at Jay, wondering if now was the time to try to escape. But Ito was back, and both pistols were again pointed in our direction. We reluctantly accepted the water and fruit he shoved at us.

"And Professor, where are your manners? Please introduce me to your friends." I scowled at her, but saw little use in antagonizing her.

"This is Sister Merle Farland of the Methodist Mission at Vella Lavella, and this is Mr. Jacinto Diente de León of Qantas Airways," I said, motioning at Merle and Jay. "And this is Fräulein Professor Doktor Emerald Asche-Böhrer from the University of Göttingen." She barely looked at Merle, but stepped closer to Jay. Her long, platinum blond hair was flowing loose around her shoulders and shone almost white in the moonlight.

"What charming friends you have," she said, running her hand down Jay's arm. "I so enjoyed flying your little airplane. Perhaps we will take a flight together." Jay stared at her with steely indifference and said nothing.

"The strong, silent type. I like that very much," Emerald said, brushing her hand along Jay's cheek. "You all must be very tired from your walk. Why don't you get some rest? Ito, tie them up again, please. I don't want them to get any ideas about leaving us too soon. Sweet dreams, *meine Lieben.*"

Ito bound our wrists again and pushed us toward the next hut. Ohrwürmer followed us inside and shoved us down onto some sleeping mats on the dirt floor. The two men perched atop stools on either side of the door, pistols drawn. There was no way to talk to Merle and Jay without being overheard.

In spite of the discomfort and my instinct to remain alert, I must have slept, because the next thing I knew, sunlight was streaming through the window, and Ohrwürmer was jostling me.

"It is time to wake up, Fräulein Linden," he said, moving on to Merle and Jay. We looked around warily at each other and the bare interior of the small hut. Ito was still at his post by the door. If the two men had slept themselves, giving us a chance to escape, we had missed it.

CHAPTER 24

"I trust you slept well, Professor. I'm sorry I cannot offer you all better accommodations," Emerald said. Though she was addressing me, I could see her piercing green eyes were fixed on Jay. The morning sun reflected on her blond hair, now artfully bound into a chignon. Somehow, she managed to be stylishly dressed in a crisp safari jacket and even wearing scarlet lipstick. That Merle and I were so dirty and disheveled only made the situation more ignominious.

"Untie us now, Emerald. Whatever game you're playing isn't funny. Let us go now, and we'll see that no harm will come to you," I said.

"Game? This is quite serious, Professor. You and your friends are in no position to make promises to me."

"What do you want with us? Why have you and your colleague been following me?" I said, looking at Ohrwürmer, whose visage was as ugly as Emerald's was beautiful.

"Following you?" Emerald said with a laugh. "My dear, it's you who has been following me."

I felt sick as her words sank in. She was right. I'd been following her all along, even if I hadn't known it.

"Now please tell me who sent you. And how did they know where to find us?" she asked.

"I don't know. No one ever mentioned you. I certainly wouldn't have agreed to come if I had known there was any chance of meeting you again."

"Ah, yes, I suppose you don't have fond memories of our encounter last year in Africa. But I expect that's why you wanted to find me again and settle the score."

"There's no score to settle, and I didn't come to find you. I came to find medicinal plants. That's all. The U.S. Department of Agriculture sent me to Malaya to look for malaria treatments."

"We are a long way from Malaya, Professor. I think we both know what you really came to find. And of course you are too late, once again. Now tell me the names of your agents."

"There are no agents. All I know is Mr. Johnson and Mr. Smith from the USDA wanted some antimalarial plants, and I agreed to look."

"That's fine, Professor. I will leave it to Herr Ohrwürmer to extract that information later. That's really more his specialty. But I had hoped we could do things the easy way. Ito, fetch our guests some breakfast."

As the Japanese man backed away, Emerald withdrew a Luger from inside her jacket.

"I don't want you to think about leaving us until we have discussed all the options," she said, casually pointing the pistol in our direction. "You will have breakfast first, and then we can decide on the best course of action."

Ito brought back some small bananas and papayas. He opened three coconuts with his machete and then untied our hands again. We ate the fruit in uncomfortable silence as they watched us.

"There. Isn't it wonderful how the jungle provides everything one needs? Now why don't we start again? Tell me what you've come to find," Emerald commanded.

"Nothing," I said. "Just antimalarial plants in Malaya. And now we're on a medical mission, delivering supplies and treatments to the islanders."

Emerald sighed in exasperation.

"That's not true," Jay said. I stared at him in surprise.

"Do go on, darling," Emerald purred at him.

"We know you took the *Rafflesia* from Pulau Tioman. And we know you took the skull of Ingava and the sacred shells from Kundu Hite," Jay answered. "And we are here to get them back." I was impressed he'd remembered the name of the plant, but I wasn't sure revealing this now was wise.

Emerald sat down next to Jay. "Get them back? I'm afraid that is not turning out very well for you. But I'm sure we can find a way to work together. Just what is it that you plan to use them for?" Emerald asked.

"We are here to return them to their rightful owners. To the people of Tioman and the family of Ingava."

"Herr Diente de León, why are you being as difficult as the professor? You don't really expect me to believe you are just a do-gooder, here to help the natives, do you?" Emerald asked, leaning closer to Jay. "I don't want to give Herr Ohrwürmer a reason to talk with you privately. However, I think my methods of gathering information might be more persuasive in this case," she said with a smile, casually placing her hand on Jay's knee. He looked at her with repulsion, and I felt a wave of relief. Then she turned to face Merle.

"Perhaps I've been asking the wrong people. You don't look much like a 'sister.' A medical missionary makes a very good cover, indeed. In fact, you look rather familiar. Where do I know you from?" Emerald asked her.

"I'm certain I've never seen you before. And I *am* a nurse with the Methodist Mission on Vella Lavella. Reverend Silvester will expect me back by now, and I'm sure he is organizing a search party to find us," Merle said with a confidence that filled me with optimism.

"A reverend?" Emerald said, laughing. "That's even more humorous than thinking that ridiculous Resident Commissioner will save you. No one is coming for you."

"Don't underestimate the Reverend," Merle said. I tried to take her words to heart, although I was more inclined to agree with Emerald.

"Let's start from the beginning, Professor," Emerald said, turning back to me. "Who are you working for?"

"I told you. The United States Department of Agriculture. They sent me to look for antimalarial plants. And Merle and Jay have nothing to do with it. I only just met them. Let them go," I replied.

"Jay? Oh, is what your friends call you, Herr Diente de León? How charming. I'm sure we can be friends," she said in a saccharine-sweet tone. Jay stared at her in stony silence. "Are you really just a pilot for hire, Jay? Then perhaps I can hire you. Of course, I like to do my own flying, but it would be nice to have a co-pilot." Jay didn't respond. "In fact, it might be useful to have a nurse around, especially one of a religious persuasion. And even another ethnobotanist. There is so much work to do. We would make a good team."

"A team? For the University of Göttingen?" I asked.

"Oh no, Professor. This has nothing to do with the university. You are thinking too small. This is a much more important endeavor."

"Then who are *you* working for, if not the university?"

"Why, I am working for our leader. The Führer, of course. I am just his humble servant on this noble mission for the Third Reich," Emerald said with a faraway look in her eyes. "Why not join us now?"

"Never!" I said in disgust.

"Suit yourself, Professor. You will see the light sooner or later. Until then, everyone needs a nemesis, and fate has made you mine. Anyway, it spurs competition," Emerald said with a smile and a shrug.

"I don't need a nemesis. And there is no need for competition. We are both scientists. It's better for everyone if we cooperate for the good of humanity."

"Ah, then you do see it my way. That's exactly what we are doing. Our mission is for the good of humanity."

"The good of humanity?" Jay scoffed. "I've seen your vision for humanity firsthand. At Guernica."

"Don't tell me you played on the wrong side of that game, Jay? Maybe you really are just a pilot for hire. It's not too late to join the winning team. I'm sure I can make you an attractive offer." Jay glared at her with contempt.

"I'm interested in what you might have to offer," Merle said. "But I would need more information to decide." I stared at her in disbelief, wondering if she could really sympathize with the Nazi ideals. I supposed I barely knew her, after all.

"Ah, a change of heart. Here's a reasonable woman. And now I remember who you remind me of. You resemble that aviatrix with the terrible sense of direction. The one who looked like a female version of your great American hero, Lindbergh. Yes, he is proof that some of you can see the promise of the future if we all work together for the goals of our Führer." I bristled at the comparison. Any similarity between Amelia and Lindbergh ended at the physical. Like everyone else, I'd been enamored of the dashing aviator when he made his solo flight across the Atlantic and shed tears when his baby son was kidnapped. But more recently, he was becoming better known for his admiration of Germany. I was certain Amelia didn't share his enthusiasm for the Third Reich, but now I wasn't too sure of Merle.

"I'm sure I have many skills beyond nursing that would prove valuable, Professor Asche-Böhrer. I know the islands well and speak the native languages. Plus, as you say, a medical missionary makes a good cover. What is your interest here, so far from Germany?" Merle asked.

Emerald looked at her appraisingly. "My interest, like Professor Linden's, is chiefly botanical. But I have broadened my views, thanks to Herr Ohrwürmer and my colleagues in the *Ahnenerbe*. It is a particular source of pride that Herr Himmler himself recruited me to join their research institute. It is my great honor to gather the ancestral knowledge of the Fatherland so it can be used to shape the glorious future of the Third Reich."

We stared at Emerald blankly, not understanding what she was driving at.

"The Fatherland? What do the Solomon Islands have to do with Germany?" I asked.

"I see your confusion, Professor. But surely you must know a bit about genetic inheritance. And evolution. I can see how you may dismiss these natives as one of the inferior races, but in truth there is a kernel of greatness in them. It is in the genes. You see the blond hair that some of them have? Our geneticists have determined these people have descended from an Aryan ancestor, like the proper Germans. Of course they are not pure, but that does not mean they are entirely without value."

I still did not comprehend her meaning, but waited for her to continue.

"There are certain beliefs and even powers possessed by the people here that are of use to us. Since they derive from the Aryan stock, it is our birthright to use them in service to the Reich. And we are merely here to collect our birthright."

As her words sank in, I stared incredulously. "You don't mean to say you've come here to steal artifacts like a chief's skull and sacred seashells because you actually think they have some sort of magical powers, do you? I thought you were a scientist."

"Professor, I am a scientist. And when I encounter something that cannot be explained by our current hypotheses, I know I must change the hypothesis, not throw away the data. Perhaps you would do better to keep an open mind."

I didn't know whether to laugh or cry. We were in real mortal danger on this obscure island all because some lunatics actually believed things like skulls and seashells could hold supernatural powers. All I could do was shake my head in bewilderment.

"But what about the *Rafflesia* from Tioman? Surely

you don't think that's magic, too, do you?" I asked.

"No, although there are some legends surrounding it that I would not immediately discount. But in this case, it is the medicinal properties we must harness for our cause. An extract from the flowers makes childbirth easier, and women are able to bear another child much faster after its use. The highest good a German woman can achieve is to bear more children for the Fatherland. This discovery will hasten the assumption of the Aryan race to our proper place in the world. I have heard the Führer himself has taken a special interest in the project," she said with pride.

There was too much nonsense to counter in her assertion, so I stuck to the botanical. "But you may have collected the entire wild population of the species. What makes you think you can get such a difficult plant to grow in cultivation?"

"I have an impressive laboratory and greenhouses at the Ahnenerbe's facilities. My team of plant scientists will discover the ideal growing conditions. And Germany has the best chemists. Simultaneously, they will extract the relevant compounds and find ways to synthesize them in the laboratory. Then we will not need to grow the plants at all. But we could use more experts in our endeavors, and surely you now see the importance of this work. I would allow you to be my assistant on future expeditions."

"No, I would never join you," I said, shaking my head in disbelief at the audacity of her proposal.

"Don't be so hasty, Professor. Why don't you think it over for a while? Ito, tie them up again, and put them back in the hut. I'm growing weary of this conversation."

The Japanese trader began binding our wrists again. Before he started to march us into the hut, Jay asked Emerald, "Why have you told us all of this? You don't really think we will join you, do you?"

"I remain hopeful, Herr Jay, that you will all see the wisdom of contributing to the noble cause of the Fatherland. But if you remain unconvinced, it is of no importance. I don't anticipate you will have an opportunity to tell anyone else about what we have just discussed. Come, Käfir, we have work to do," Emerald said, and Ito shoved us inside the hut.

I hit the ground hard from Ito's rough push. The woven sleeping mat was not much of a cushion to break the fall. He took up his position seated at the door with his machete in his lap and his pistol pointed at us. He stared at us sullenly.

Although we outnumbered him, overpowering Ito was out of the question. The rope binding our wrists together was too secure to work free. He must have learned how to tie knots as a sailor. So I decided to take another tack.

"Don't do this, Ito. They're not really on your side. We see how they order you around. You don't think they consider you an equal, do you? You're not one of their precious Aryans. Untie us, and we'll escape together," I said.

He grabbed hold of the machete and slashed the air inches from my throat. "Silence!" he commanded, flashing a cruel smile that revealed the shine of a gold front tooth. I did not need to be told twice.

There was no way to get Jay or Merle's attention or talk to them under Ito's gaze. And I wasn't sure I wanted to talk to Merle. Was she really thinking of joining them? I glanced at her and found she was staring at me. She started blinking her eyes excessively. Maybe she got some dust in them from the earthen floor. Then she stared intently at me for a few moments before she started blinking again. I watched her and realized a pattern was starting to emerge. She was trying to communicate with me! It must have been Morse code! I observed her effort with incomprehension and frustration. I regretted being so unknowledgeable, but learning Morse code had never been required at Bryn Mawr or Harvard. I gave Merle an apologetic look, and she gave up. Maybe Jay could have understood her message, but he was facing the other way, and I didn't dare speak to him.

With nothing to do, my mind drifted from one thought to the next. Why couldn't I have stayed home? I could be watching a concert at Chautauqua right now. Why didn't I stand up to Johnson and Smith? I could have said no. It was all their fault. Johnson and Smith. Johnson. Smith. The Johnson Smith Company. The time Amaryllis and I saved all our allowance for a year and filled an envelope with nickels and dimes to order novelties and magic tricks from the Johnson Smith catalog. Dad intercepted the overburdened envelope before the postman came, joking we'd give the poor man a hernia. He replaced the coins with dollar bills. And secretly gave us back the coins, warning us not to tell Mother. A box arrived a month later, filled with our squirt rings, invisible ink, sneezing powder, the magic tricks, and a ventriloquist's dummy. We put on shows with the illusions held in "The Conjurer's Casket" for anyone who would watch and gave comedy performances with the dummy, which we'd named Elwood Stumpf. Woody for short. We felt sure we were destined for fame in vaudeville. I hadn't thought about that in years. In truth, we weren't very good, but the adults in the audience humored us. Some of them, I realized now, had been Dad's colleagues in the Botany department. Now they were my colleagues. How embarrassing. Well, it's not like I'll ever see them again, I mused. Thanks to Johnson and Smith. Johnson Smith. Woody Stumpf. The *Art of Ventriloquism* booklet we'd scrutinized so intently that the cheap paper began to disintegrate. It promised that it was "Fun and Easy to THROW YOUR VOICE!" Throw your voice. Throw *my* voice . . . an idea . . .

I glanced at Ito. He was still watching us. It was worth a try, if only to talk to Jay and Merle for a moment.

"Ito, come here right now!" I shouted in my best German accent. Ito looked up in surprise. He didn't look at me but at the window to his right. The sound had come from there! Perhaps the money we'd spent on Woody had been worth it, after all! Ito looked back at us with indecision. I tried it again, being even more careful not to move my lips. "Ito, I need you now. Leave them. Come here!" Ito glared at us, then left the hut.

"That was me, not Emerald," I whispered. "We've only got a minute until he's back." Jay had turned to face Merle and me. "Can you work your hands free? Does anyone have a plan?" I asked. They both shook their heads. "Merle, what were you trying to tell me?"

"That I would never work with these Nazis. I just wanted to get more information and buy us more time," she replied.

"I knew you'd never help them," I said with relief.

Ito burst in again, and we fell silent. It was clear he was angry, but it was worth it. At least I knew I could trust Merle. I saw her fluttering her eyes at Jay, but I couldn't tell if he comprehended the message or even noticed she was trying to communicate with him.

The hours wore on, and although my mind was a jumble of thoughts, no more ideas came. The light had started to fade when we heard Emerald call, "Ito, come here." The man didn't move, and a moment later Emerald burst in.

"Ito, I called you. Didn't you hear me? I'll guard them now. Go get your dinner, and bring back some food for our guests," she commanded. Ito sullenly slunk away.

"Well, *meine Lieben*, you've had the whole day to think over your situation. We are leaving tomorrow. Will you be joining us?" None of us spoke.

"Professor? Answer me."

"No, I'm not joining you. I'd never stoop so low."

"I think you will come to regret that decision, Professor Linden. But it is no loss for me. In fact, I wouldn't be surprised if your name were really Lindenfeld. Or stein or berg," she said. "And what about you, Herr Jay? Surely you are not so foolish?"

"I fought against Nazis like you before, and I will again," said Jay.

"Your time to do so is quickly running out. What a pity, as I really do think I could put you to good use," Emerald said with a wink. Jay scowled at her. "And Nurse Farland. It is only natural that you will help the Fatherland. You are more reasonable than your friends."

"I'm afraid I'm not going to be joining you after all, Professor Asche-Böhrer. I'll take my chances with Ivy and Jay," Merle replied.

"Chances? You are all out of chances," Emerald said, as Ito came back with some food. "I've changed my mind, Ito. Take that away. They won't be dining tonight. Tell Herr Ohrwürmer to come watch the prisoners." Ito left, taking the food with him. In a few minutes, Ohrwürmer entered the hut.

"You'll guard them first tonight, Käfir. They have decided not to come with us tomorrow. A pity, really." Emerald shifted her gaze to me and asked, "Fräulein Professor Doktor Linden, what is the fastest growing plant in the world?"

"Bamboo," I answered, puzzled by the pop quiz.

"That is correct. You will help us with a little gardening tomorrow before we depart, so you need your rest. Ito!" she called, and the man entered the hut. "Please blindfold and gag our guests. I don't want them to have any ill-advised ideas overnight. Like trying to mimic my voice or communicate by blinking." She turned and left us to Ohrwürmer's vigilant glare while Ito carried out her command.

CHAPTER 25

At least the discomfort of the tightly tied blindfold and gag was a distraction from the insistent hunger pangs that gnawed at regular intervals. I knew if I could just fall asleep, the hunger would subside, but that seemed a remote possibility. And yet I was jolted awake some time later by Emerald's voice singing out, "Rise and shine, *meine Lieben,*" followed closely by a sharp kick from her boot.

"Ito, our guests will need breakfast before they get to work in the garden. Go get their food. Herr Ohrwürmer, you can remove the blindfolds and gags."

I felt the blindfold being ripped off and opened my eyes to the morning sunlight streaming in the hut. And to the sight of Ohrwürmer's steel-gray eyes regarding me with contempt while Emerald stood over me with her Luger at the ready. As Ohrwürmer turned to Merle, Emerald bent down and untied Jay's blindfold herself and removed the gag, caressing the rough stubble of his cheek with a crimson-tipped finger.

"Good morning, sleepyhead," she said, tousling his hair. "I do hope you have changed your mind about being my co-pilot."

Jay answered by spitting in her face.

In reply to the affront, Emerald calmly slapped him hard across the mouth. "*Hurensohn,*" she said, stalking out of the hut. I caught Jay's eye, and he flashed me a quick smile, despite a ruby droplet forming at the corner of his lips.

Ito came back and pulled us to our feet. He pushed us out the door to some waiting fruit, yams, and fish. He opened three coconuts while Ohrwürmer kept his pistol fixed on us. He pushed us down to the ground in front of the food and untied our hands. Ohrwürmer and Ito watched us greedily devour the food and drain the coconuts dry. Ito bound our wrists again and pulled us up once more. We stood for a few moments before Emerald emerged from her hut, machete and Luger in hand.

"Now we will walk to the garden," she said, leading the way. Ito and Ohrwürmer prodded us along behind her, around the shore of the lake toward the end where Lula floated in the placid water. I glanced at Jay and saw him looking at her with anguish. But before we reached the airplane, Emerald turned toward the jungle. She began slashing a path through the foliage, and we followed her into the dim brush. Behind us, the two men waved their machetes to remind us they, too, wielded lethal blades.

As we walked on, I noticed the plants: climbing rattan palms with arrays of sharp spikes, pandanus with rosettes of great saw-edged leaves, and vigorous vines with huge variegated green, yellow, and white leaves more commonly known as a small, tame houseplant called devil's ivy. Columns of red ants marched along tree trunks, colorful spiders as broad as my hand bounced on intricate webs, and centipedes scurried away from our approaching steps. Even in the daylight, my beloved jungle did not seem to welcome us.

At least observing the plants kept me occupied. I spied a bamboo plant and then another. We had come to a thicket of bamboo with very few other plants able to compete in its shade. Emerald and the men stopped slashing with their machetes. There was no need to clear a path as one could easily walk through the stand of bamboo. We trailed behind Emerald as she weaved past the tall, jointed green stalks trimmed with a fringe of leaves above. Once we reached what must have been the middle of the thicket, she commanded us to stop.

"And here we are, *meine Lieben.* The garden. But you see it is overgrown. I want to give the young shoots a chance to reach the light. Fräulein Professor Doktor Linden, how fast can a bamboo shoot grow?"

"I don't know. It depends on the species."

"Why don't you make an educated guess?"

"Some can grow two or three feet in a day."

"And what about this species?" she asked, gripping one of the sturdy canes.

"I don't know." I was in no mood for her game.

"I suppose that is what you will be finding out in your final experiment. Now there is work to do. Ito, untie them," she said, leveling her Luger at us. "Kneel down on the ground. You right here, Professor. You over there, Nurse Farland. And you here, Herr Jay."

I could barely comprehend what was happening. They each had their pistol aimed at one of us. They were going to shoot us now. That was it. But instead, Emerald commanded, "Get to work clearing the ground. Brush aside all the fallen leaves and debris to uncover the new shoots."

We stared at her in disbelief for a moment before beginning to follow her order. I pushed the top layer of dry leaves away, revealing a rich decaying layer underneath. Ordinarily I would have been captivated by the diverse array of insects and fungi living below the leaves, but I could only mechanically dig away the decomposing vegetation, bracing myself for the crack of the pistol. But it did not come, even as I exposed the newest shoots of bamboo to the light.

"Very good," Emerald said. "You may all stop now." Emerald walked around the three newly exposed patches of dirt and examined the green tips just barely visible at the surface of the soil. She carefully considered the tall stalks around each clearing. She then tied a length of palm leaf fiber into a bow around four stalks surrounding each of the areas of bare earth. "Ito, cut down all the bamboo except the ones I've marked," she barked. Ito made quick work of the thicket, slashing the stalks close to the ground with a single swipe of his machete. In just a few minutes, the area was clear, leaving the canopy open and sunlight streaming in.

"Herr Jay, I want you to clear out those canes. Pile them all right there," she said, motioning to an empty spot with the muzzle of her pistol. Jay glared at her and made no motion. She walked over to him, pressing the Luger to his ribs. "Come now, we haven't got all day. We're leaving after this. Just one more destination before we can go home."

Slowly Jay began to pile up the rigid stalks of bamboo. Emerald watched his every move with rapt attention. "Faster, please, Herr Jay," she said with amusement. When the fallen canes were cleared away, the three areas of bare dirt were visible again, each with four remaining sturdy stalks marking the corners of a rectangle.

"I do hope my estimates were correct. Perhaps I should have measured. But no matter, we will make it work. Herr Jay, since you've been working so hard, you deserve a break," Emerald said, taking him by the hand to the largest of the three clearings. She ran her fingertips down the front of his dirty, sweat-soaked shirt. "This is your last opportunity to come with me, darling. I wouldn't have given just anyone so many chances. But I must say you are surely the finest specimen Professor Linden has ever collected." Jay scowled at her. "No? Ito, tie him up."

Ohrwürmer pushed Jay down to the ground while Ito tied his wrists and ankles to the remaining upright stalks of bamboo. A wave of comprehension swept over me, and my head began to swim. The bright sun grew dark, as if a fast-moving eclipse were blotting it from view.

"Professor! Wake up, Professor," Emerald said, waving a pungent leaf under my nose. My head cleared enough to see the horror of our plight again.

"Secure the nurse next, Ito." Merle submitted stoically. "Your turn, Professor," Emerald said as she pushed me down onto the bare patch of earth. Was it my imagination, or were the tender new shoots I'd just uncovered peeking out of the soil a bit more already?

Ito made quick work with his knots. I didn't have to move to feel how secure they were. My leather boots protected my ankles, but the rope was already cutting into my wrists. I closed my eyes to the overhead sun. A blindfold would have been welcome now.

"There. The garden is complete. Now we just have to wait for it to grow," Emerald said with a laugh.

"You can't just shoot us and leave us here. They'll find us. You won't get away with this," Merle said.

"Shoot you? Dear Nurse Farland, I fear you misunderstand the situation. We have no intention of shooting you. What a waste of bullets. We just need to let nature take its course. A decaying human body will have all the nutrients a young shoot needs to thrive. It will rise up strong and tall like the youth of the Fatherland. Of course, it will take a day or two for the growing tip to see the light again, but the darkness will be worth it in the end," she said with a smile. "My only regret is not being able to stay and watch our garden grow. But the three of you will get to watch it grow. And more importantly, feel it grow!"

Emerald walked around to each remaining upright stalk and made certain the knots were secure. "Goodbye, Fräulein Professor Doktor Linden. It seems I will need a new nemesis already. You hardly lasted long enough to make this a challenge. Herr Ohrwürmer, Ito, it is time to go." Emerald melted into the forest with the two men trailing behind her.

"You won't get away with this!" Merle shouted again. A faint muffled laugh floated back in response. Or maybe it was just the sound of some jungle bird.

CHAPTER 26

"I'm sorry, Jay. I'm sorry, Merle. I'm so sorry I dragged you into this," I said, self-reproach piercing me as sharply as the bamboo shoots would soon do from below.

"I came along willingly, Ivy," Jay said.

"Me too, Ivy," Merle added. "My family told me becoming a medical missionary in the Solomons was too dangerous. But they sure never imagined I'd be killed by a tree."

"Actually, bamboo is a grass," I said. I couldn't help myself.

"Oh. Somehow that seems even worse. But surely the shoots beneath us really can't still grow?"

"I'm afraid they can, Merle. They know which way is up and want to see the sunlight more than anything. Plants are more active than people give them credit for. Did you never see a persistent weed push its way through asphalt paving? The apical meristem, that's the growing tip of the shoot, will find little to stop its progress in our soft bodies." As much as the thought filled me with horror, I had to admit a perverse feeling of admiration for Emerald at utilizing such an ironic method of dispatching us. Or at least me. A botany professor impaled by her own object of study was rather clever.

"Well, what are we going to do about this? I have no intention of letting an overgrown blade of grass finish me off," Merle said with defiance.

"Maybe we'll die of thirst first. Or some hungry wild boars will come along," I suggested, rather unhelpfully.

"That wasn't what I'd had in mind," Merle said. "Isn't there some way to stop the shoots from growing?"

"Maybe if we could move enough to damage the tips. But that would just activate other shoots below ground to start growing."

"Still, it's worth a try," Merle said. "Try moving your shoulders and back against the ground." The three of us began wriggling around in place like some of the creepy-crawlies we'd unearthed in our digging. "Maybe if we keep doing that every few hours–"

"Shhh," Jay interrupted. "Do you hear that?"

I listened intently and then picked up a faint sound that quickly grew louder. The sound of engines.

"Is it . . . Lula?" I asked, barely able to get his affectionate name for the airplane out.

"Yes, I'd know her anywhere." The pitch changed as the aircraft took off from the lake. Then we heard it overhead. In a moment it was circling the clearing and dipped down as low as possible. The wings waggled a mocking wave at us before the plane turned away and sped off. I saw Jay pulling at the tight bindings in rage, but to no avail.

"I'm sorry, Jay," I said again, aware I could never make an adequate apology.

"It is not your fault, Ivy. If anything, it is mine. For

leaving Spain. For not going back to the Air Force. It was my destiny to be killed by those evil Nazis, and I thought I could outrun them. But that is not how destiny works."

I was about to disagree, but Merle said, "At least they're gone. We should save our strength. One of us should shout for help every ten minutes. Maybe a native will be passing by and hear us. I'll start first." She yelled at the top of her lungs. It was plenty loud, but I was sure the sound was swallowed up by the dense vegetation surrounding us. "There. Now I'll count out ten minutes, and then it'll be your turn, Ivy."

It seemed pointless, but at least it was something to try. On cue from Merle, I shouted to no one. "Good," she said. "I'll tell you when ten minutes are up, Jay." At the appropriate command, Jay raised his voice. I was not enthusiastic for a second round of shouting, but humored Merle. At least it passed the time.

The sun had mercifully moved past its zenith, and the glare was no longer unbearable, although my thirst was becoming acute. "Merle, can we take a break from yelling? Would the villagers even be walking in the bush at night?" I asked.

"No, I suppose you're right," she conceded.

"Did you mean it about Reverend Silvester coming to look for us?"

"Oh, he'll notice we haven't come back and come looking, all right. I'm sure of it," Merle said with confidence. "There's no way he'd find us here, but I'm sure he'll look."

"Ivy, Merle, for whatever reason it is our fate that we are all here together. And die together," Jay said softly. "It is not ours to understand. We should not deny it."

"I deny it very much, Jay," I said as emphatically as I could muster with my waning strength. But maybe he was right. Then a humorous thought came to me, and I couldn't suppress my amusement.

"What's so funny, Ivy?" Merle snapped, irritated at my sudden laughter.

"I was just thinking how pleased some of my students would be. I'm sure the ones who failed my plant physiology course would be delighted by my botanical demise. Maybe they even have a voodoo doll in my likeness which they regularly spear with bamboo cocktail skewers," I said, giggling.

"I could go for a cocktail right now," Merle said wistfully. "A gin and tonic would be nice. Or a whiskey sour. Or even a pint of Guinness."

"Or a Gin Sling. Or a Pimm's," I added. "A beautiful man once bought me a Pimm's. At the Long Bar of the Raffles Hotel, no less." Had I just said that aloud? I wasn't thinking clearly. It must have been dehydration. It seemed like a thought would start on one side of my head, but couldn't quite make it to the other side.

"And a gimlet," Jay said.

"Yes, waiter, one gimlet, please," Merle said.

"Just a Coca-Cola for you, Jacinto. Don't forget you're flying in the morning," I added helpfully.

"Make that two Cokes, please," Merle said.

"I'm afraid I got off on the wrong foot with Hyacinth," I stated.

"Who's she?" Merle asked.

"No, Profesora. You are mistaken," said Jay.

"I wasn't afraid of snakes and insects and bats, was I?"

"You were no trouble at all," Jay murmured.

We fell silent as the sun dipped below the fringe of bamboo leaves encircling us in our green cage.

The next time I opened my eyes, the sun had set completely, revealing a smattering of stars above, the Southern Cross just visible above the horizon of leaves. I felt a bit more clearheaded than before in the cool evening air. I thought I heard a rustling in the bush. The sound came again.

"Jay! Merle! Someone's coming!" The noise stopped at my voice, then started again. "Hello? Help!" The movement ceased again. After a few moments, the footsteps resumed. No, not footsteps. A shuffling sound. Something dragging along the ground. Many somethings. The coconut crabs.

I stared in horror as a group of them entered the clearing.

"Merle, Jay, it's the crabs," I wailed.

"I see them, Ivy," Merle said.

"Maybe it's better this way. Quicker," Jay added.

The pack of crustaceans dragged themselves toward us with their powerful claws and spiky legs. Soon we were each encircled by several massive crabs, their antennae waving with curiosity.

"Shoo! Shoo! Get away!" Merle cried.

The crabs were undaunted and shuffled closer. A huge one shambled toward my face. I closed my eyes. I felt a gentle touch on my cheek. The tip of one feeler. I opened my eyes to see the great crab's face just inches from my own, separated only by its powerful claws. I stared into the black beads on the end of its eyestalks and wondered what he could see. Or she? Dinner, probably. She regarded me for some moments longer, then softly brushed my cheek again. I braced for the inevitable crushing claw. But the crab started backing away. She scooted in reverse and turned around toward the bush. One by one, the other crabs began to recede, too. The whole pack disappeared into the vegetation again.

I exhaled deeply, unaware I'd been holding my breath for so long. I realized Jay was whispering something barely audible. I listened closely and heard snatches of Spanish. "*No nos dejes caer en la tentación sino que líbranos del malo. Amén.*" And then, "*Dios te salve, María. Llena eres de gracia . . .*" He was praying.

Then I realized Merle was reciting something almost noiselessly, too. "Yea, though I walk through the valley of the shadow of death, I will fear no evil: for thou art with me; thy rod and thy staff they comfort me. . . ."

A wave of panic, regret, and a curious envy washed over me. They were giving up. I should, too. But they had these prayers to comfort them now. Did I even know a prayer to say? Let's see, there was the one that terrified me as a child. Now I lay me down to sleep. Until I'd heard that prayer, it had never occurred to me that I might go to sleep and not wake up again. Somehow I hadn't absorbed the comforting bit about the Lord taking my soul. In fact, that part sounded scary, too. Take it where? I wanted it to stay right where it belonged and wake up at home with Mother tending to her garden and Dad writing at his desk and Amaryllis sleeping in the next bed. In fact, that was just what I wanted most right now.

But now I wouldn't see Mother, or Dad, or Amaryllis again. Or Rama and Osiris. I'd never drive Tut around Ithaca. I'd never see my students again. I'd never see

Elspeth Huxley, or Osa Johnson, or Ethel Bailey, or any of my other friends again. I'd never meet Heath Bracken or find that rare tree. But worst of all, Jay and Merle would never see their families and friends again, either. All because of me. All because I didn't stand my ground and say no to Johnson and Smith. My remorse and self-pity stabbed as sharply as the insistent shoots that were now making contact with my lower back. I felt the trickle of moisture coursing down my cheeks.

My meandering thoughts drifted away from all the things I would never do again to everything I had done. Walks in the forest with Mother and Dad and Amaryllis. Growing up and going to school. To Bryn Mawr and Harvard. Studying plants. Becoming a professor. I'd had adventures in South America and Africa. And this one. This final one. It was more than most people got to do. It was enough, I decided. It had to be enough.

At least Merle and Jay seemed to have some faith to comfort them now. A faith in something after this life. I envied them, but I knew better. I knew the molecules released by the decomposition of our bodies would return to the soil to be absorbed by plants, fungi, and bacteria. Maybe pass through the digestive tracts of birds and crabs and lizards. We would be distributed all over the island. Become part of the island. Maybe that was a sort of afterlife, really. That didn't sound so bad. To live on within a towering tree, or flying fox, or cockatoo.

Maybe I should try that prayer again. How did it go? Now I lay me down to sleep. To sleep, perchance to dream. Ay, there's the rub. The undiscovered country. I wouldn't be returning from this one. No, that wasn't how the prayer goes. If only I'd gone to Sunday school to learn some prayers. But instead Mother and Dad had taken us for walks in the woods on a Sunday morning when all the other families were in church, dressed in their finery. What was it that Dad used to say as we tramped along the trail together? "Keep your eyes on the ground, and treasures will abound." That was it. Amaryllis had come up with a second verse upon receiving a telescope for her twelfth birthday. "Keep your eyes on the skies, and treasures will arise." I mumbled the phrases to myself. It kept the other thoughts at bay. The pale cast of thought. Maybe I'll look at the stars just one last time before . . .

With effort, I opened my eyelids a crack, the pool of tears distorting the constellations above me to an indistinct glow. But the light wasn't coming just from overhead. It was coming from much closer to the ground. At my feet even, but I couldn't lift my head to see. There was no point in trying, anyway. I felt something at my right ankle. And a moment later at my left. The crabs? A snake? A wild boar? I didn't want to know and repeated my rhymes in a whisper.

Then the glow was closer. A sensation at my wrist. I blinked away the tears to clear my vision. A shape crouched at the bamboo stalk, a faint aura illuminating it. I felt the tension at my left wrist ease as the form darted behind my head to my other wrist. The kneeling figure repeated the motion, and my right wrist fell free of the tight rope.

The form turned toward me. Merle!

CHAPTER 27

"Merle! How did you get free?" I cried. She took my hand, and an untapped reserve of adrenaline surged through my veins. I gingerly tried to move my stiff limbs. As I attempted to rise from the ground, Merle darted in the direction of the path, a faint glow trailing behind her. She must have picked up some phosphorescent microbes from the soil. "I'll untie Jay," I said.

Unsteadily, I got to my feet and stumbled to his form sprawled out on the ground. "Jay, Jay, we're free," I cried, as I started to pick apart the intricate knots that held him fast. First one ankle and then the other. Then the right wrist. Then the left. But he said nothing. "Jay! Wake up, Jay!" I said, shaking him. I pressed my hand to his neck and put my ear to his lips. I felt a slow beat and soft breath.

"Jay, wake up! Open your eyes!"

"*Un ángel del cielo,*" Jay murmured, his eyes fluttering open for a moment.

"No, no, it's me. Ivy. *Profesora. Trata de recordar, Jacinto,*" I pleaded. I was about to slap him – that's always how they bring someone around in the movies – until I remembered Emerald's cruel slap. That wouldn't do. Oh! Amaryllis had dragged me with her to see *Snow White and the Seven Dwarfs* at the State Theatre earlier this year. Since my lips were already in the right vicinity, I decided to try that approach first. I bent down closer and kissed him softly.

"*Profesora ángel,*" Jay said, his eyes opening fully. "*Estamos en el cielo ahora,*" he said with a smile.

"No, Jay, we're not in heaven. We're still here. On Vonavona. But we're free. We've got to go," I said, pulling him up to a sitting position. He looked around as he regained his senses.

"How did you get free, Ivy?"

"Merle untied me. She got loose somehow. She's waiting for us. Let's go now," I said, helping him up. Leaning on each other for support, we staggered toward the cut in the vegetation that led back to the lake. There was still a faint glow ahead. As we were about to slip out of the bamboo grove and onto the jungle path, we heard a voice from behind us.

"Wait! Don't leave me here!" It was Merle. I whirled around, and there was Merle on the ground, still bound to the bamboo stalks. My mind reeled in confusion.

"But Merle, you untied me!" I cried as I stumbled over to her and started to unfasten the knots.

"What?"

"You got free somehow and untied me. I saw you," I said feebly. "It was you. It looked like you." I shook my head as if that could clear out what felt like a tangle of cobwebs impeding my thoughts.

Merle tried moving her limbs and sat up slowly. Beneath where she had lain, a cluster of shoots had poked through the soil. I looked at the patches of earth where

Jay and I had been bound and saw the emerging bamboo stalks. I felt a surge of admiration for the tenacity of the plants. But I was glad not to become fertilizer just yet.

"Come on, let's get back to the lake," I said, helping Merle to her feet. The three of us entered the dark jungle passageway, the canopy of leaves blotting out the starlight. Yet a soft glow illuminated the path ahead, just out of sight. We tramped along, vegetation pulling at our arms and legs, until we approached the end of the trail. We burst out of the jungle and into the clearing near the shore of the lake.

A figure stood at the edge of the water, with a hazy light illuminating its outline. Her outline. It was Merle! But Merle was still standing between Jay and me. We gaped at the glowing woman for a few seconds. She was wearing slacks and a leather flying jacket. I ran toward her. She winked at me and faded into the water, but not before I got a good look at her short, tousled hair and mischievous grin.

After a few moments, I realized Merle and Jay had joined me at the water's edge.

"Was that . . .?" Merle said, her voice trailing away.

"*Un ángel del cielo*," Jay said matter-of-factly. "A guardian angel. From the sky. From Heaven."

"Yes, Jay," I agreed, gazing from the moonlight reflected on the lake up to the ethereal stream of the Milky Way. He put his arm around me for support, and I leaned against him as we walked slowly back to the now-empty huts. Emerald and her henchmen had taken everything with them. There was nothing left to eat or drink. We considered the lake water, but decided not to risk parasites.

"We can't be too far from the coast and the villages we visited," Merle said. "It must be that way. Let's try to get there."

We found a gap in the vegetation that seemed to be a disused trail. As we walked along, I rubbed my wrists, realizing for the first time how painful they were. The rope had cut into the flesh, making the kind of abrasion that could become infected very quickly in this environment. Jay must have noticed my concern.

"Let's rest for a moment," he said. "Stay right here." He walked back on the trail a few yards and bent down. He returned clutching a length of vine with heart-shaped leaves. He stripped off a bunch of leaves and gave some to Merle and me. He took a few leaves in his hands. "Roll them around in your hands like this," he said, demonstrating. "It will release the medicine. Now we will put them on the cuts." He pulled a handkerchief from his pocket and ripped it into strips. "Put out your wrist, Ivy." He gently tied the leaves around the raw skin. He did the same for Merle, and she neatly tied the leaves in place for him. "They will help to heal the cuts and prevent infection," Jay explained.

Indeed, the lacerations immediately felt better. My bewilderment at the glowing figure by the lake was supplanted by surprise at Jay's sudden burst of ethnobotanical knowledge.

"Jay, what plant is this?" I asked, examining the unfamiliar leaves and stuffing a few more in my pockets. "How did you know it would help?"

"I don't know what it is called, Profesora. I'm sure it has a scientific name. But I recognized it as similar to one I have seen before. A long time ago, when I was a boy.

Mi abuela, my grandmother, showed it to me. My mother's mother was a *curandera.* A healer. She knew all the traditional medicines of her people. The knowledge was passed down to her over many generations from long before the Spanish arrived. She chose me to be her student when I was just a boy and began to show me the plants and what they could do. But my father opposed the lessons. It was his wish that I go to Spain and receive a proper education, not learn the old superstitions of my mother's family. And so the lessons stopped," he said with a shrug. "But maybe I still remember a few things."

"You never mentioned that before."

"I have not thought about it in years."

"But how did you even notice that plant?"

"I didn't. It noticed me. It called out to me when we walked past and said it could help. I haven't heard the plants since I was a boy," he said simply. "I suppose I stopped listening, so they stopped talking."

I stared at him in astonishment. I'd heard things like this before from the traditional healers I'd met in the Amazon. But as willing as I was to accept their knowledge of medicinal plants, I'd never put any stock in how they claimed to have acquired that knowledge. That part was surely just a quaint explanation for how centuries of trial and error had led to an understanding of the healing properties of certain plants. But what if they *had* simply listened to the plants?

"Let's keep moving," Merle said. "We've got to get to the coast." We trudged on awhile longer. Then the vegetation started to thin, and we could hear the roll of the surf. We emerged from the bush onto a soft white sand beach, but saw no village. We must have been a little farther north of the settlements. We started walking wearily along the shore. The coastline curved a bit, and as we rounded the bend, we were greeted by a welcome sight: a canoe! Filled with men!

The canoe was enormous, about fifty feet long. There must have been twenty men in the canoe, but it could have held even more. The body of the canoe was narrow and black, and the prow and stern curved high up out of the water. The prow was intricately carved and decorated with seashells. Cowrie shells and mother-of-pearl inlay studded the ebony wood. A powerfully built man stood at the helm, dressed in traditional clothing. In fact, all of the men wore traditional garb.

The man at the bow waved at us. He was motioning us toward him! Jay and I ran forward. I was already splashing in the surf when I realized Merle had remained rooted to the spot on the beach. "Come on," I called to her. She reluctantly approached the canoe.

We scrambled aboard. There was plenty of room for us. Now I got a closer look at the man at the prow. He wore only a brief garment knotted around his middle. A stack of shell armbands covered most of both upper arms above the elbow. Around his neck on a cord of red braided fiber hung a breast ornament fashioned from a ring of giant clamshell and embellished with a fringe of shell beads and teeth from some small animal. Hollow loops of the man's earlobes hung down like rubber bands, having been distended from wearing a large ornament in them. He had not adopted the missionaries' preferred style of dress.

The man at the helm motioned to bundles wrapped in banana leaves at the bottom of the canoe and said something. I looked at Merle to translate. "He says to eat and then sleep," she said.

We each undid a bundle as the men began to paddle away from shore. Inside we found taro and *ngali* nuts. The man commanded us to eat again and pointed to coconuts to drink. I didn't need to be told twice and was devouring the food in an unladylike manner until I realized Merle was just looking around between the food and the men.

"What's the matter?" I whispered. "We shouldn't offend their hospitality."

"This is a *tomoko*," she answered. I gave her a puzzled look. "A war canoe. For raids. Head-hunting raids."

I stopped eating, as did Jay. I involuntarily rubbed my neck. "You don't really think they'd . . ."

"No. No, of course not. It's not that. It's that I've never seen them sailing one before. The British government and the missionaries put a stop to the raids a generation ago. They don't make these canoes anymore. I didn't think there were any seaworthy ones left. The government sent some away to museums and destroyed the rest. The native men used to keep the *tomoko* in canoe houses filled with the skulls of their enemies. The *mana* from the skulls assured future success. We took all that down, of course."

"Well, they must have kept one hidden," I concluded.

"I guess so," Merle agreed.

"I would rather have my head chopped off with a full belly than starve while being impaled by bamboo. We might as well follow his suggestion," Jay said, pushing the food toward Merle. She began to eat, and when we were all sated, we curled up in the bottom of the canoe and let the gentle rocking of the sea lull us to sleep while the well-muscled men propelled us along.

CHAPTER 28

I awoke with a start when the bottom of the canoe scraped the shore. We were no longer skimming along the water, but beached on a thin strip of white sand. I felt remarkably refreshed, although the sun was not quite above the horizon. I looked at the man who still stood at the prow. He was a commanding presence. Had he stood there all through the voyage like some sort of living figurehead?

Jay and Merle were also roused by the bump.

The man at the helm of the canoe spoke a few words to us in Roviana.

"He says this is our destination. And to take the food with us," Merle translated.

The man pointed at the beach, and it was clear he meant for us to depart. We each grabbed a banana leaf-wrapped bundle and climbed out of the canoe. We stepped a few feet onto the shore before turning around in time to see the *tomoko* dissolve into the spray of the surf.

"Where are we?" I asked Merle.

"I don't know. It doesn't look familiar to me, but there are so many small islands. I guess we must still be in

Vonavona Lagoon or maybe Roviana Lagoon. We couldn't have gone too far."

"Let's wait until the sun rises and get our bearings," Jay suggested, and we sat down in the sand. I gingerly pulled the poultice of leaves away from one wrist. The laceration was just a faint discoloration now. I looked at my other wrist. All of the cuts had healed.

"Merle, Jay, how are your cuts?" They both examined the skin under the heart-shaped leaves and found the abrasions were all but gone.

Merle gaped. "I've seen wounds go bad in a matter of hours in this environment, but never the other way around. This plant could really be of use." We gathered up all of the leaves, and I tucked them in my pockets, hoping I could find more growing or at least identify the plant. Maybe there was a therapeutic compound that could be extracted from its leaves.

We watched the surf, but there was no sign of other canoes. I would have been content to observe the tiny hermit crabs that traversed the sand, as adorable as their coconut crab cousins were formidable, but we had to keep moving. Brushing ourselves off, we started to walk along the shore with the hopes of coming to a village. The sand was littered with seashells, driftwood, and clumps of seaweed. It seemed to be a small, flat island, rather than a volcanic one, with palm trees nodding over the beach.

We could see other small islands in the distance, but no signs of settlements. We followed the curved shoreline for about a mile before coming to a sheltered cove. And there, at the point furthest away in the little bay, was a most welcome sight: a twin-engine biplane on floats bobbing in the aquamarine water. It was also a sight most distressing. It was Jay's beloved Lula, although a freshly painted swastika now sullied her tail.

"*Gracias a Dios*," Jay said as he started toward his airplane. Merle and I both held him back.

"No, Jay. If your plane is here, that means Emerald and her lackeys are, too," Merle said.

"Let's get a closer look, but it's not safe to walk out here in the open," I said. We slipped in among the vegetation bordering the beach. It wasn't dense jungle, but there was enough foliage to give us some cover as we approached Lula with caution.

"There's no one around," Merle said as we crouched down behind a shrub and assessed the situation.

The sight of the swastika was infuriating. The Nazis had appropriated the auspicious symbol used in numerous ancient cultures and even religious traditions like Buddhism and Hinduism and made it synonymous with their brutal aspirations. I could only imagine how the insult to Lula must have enraged Jay.

"Let's make a run for it. We can take off before they spot us," I suggested.

"No, we can't," Jay said. "We have to find them first. The skull and the seashells. We made a promise to Pula."

"Oh Jay, you can't be serious! It's a miracle we're still alive and found your plane. We've got to get out of here," I said.

"I am serious, Ivy. It is a miracle. Which is why we have to keep going."

"Okay. I see your point," I said, although it seemed insane to throw away our chance to escape. "What do you think, Merle?"

"I agree. Let's keep going," she said.

We started to walk parallel to the shore again, hidden in the brush.

"We don't even know how large the island is. They could be anywhere," I said.

"Yes, we have to look for clues. Keep your eyes on the ground," said Merle.

"*Y los tesoros serán revelados,*" Jay said.

I stopped and caught Jay's arm. "What did you say?"

"It was something *mi abuela* used to say when she took me walking in the forest."

"Keep your eyes on the ground, and treasures will abound."

"Yes, you could translate it that way. I like that it rhymes in English."

"Look at that," Merle interrupted, pointing to a low shrub.

"*Tesoro dorado,*" Jay said, plucking a golden hair from a branch. "They must have come this way."

We continued on cautiously looking for more signs. After a while, we approached a clearing bordering the beach: a garden! We crept around the perimeter of a patch of taro and sweet potatoes. Beyond it was an isolated hut and then a cluster of thatch-roofed structures. We crawled up as close as we could, concealing ourselves behind some low-growing vegetation. From our vantage point we could observe the little village. We heard muffled talking, but saw no one.

Then a figure stepped into the center of the village. It was Ito. He was speaking pidgin, but I couldn't understand what he was saying. I heard a reply from an unseen villager. Then Emerald and Ohrwürmer strode into view. They both had their guns drawn. A native man came forward holding something in each hand. Ito motioned to him to place the objects on the ground. The man hesitated, and Emerald and Ohrwürmer moved closer to him. He set the items on the ground. They appeared to be stones the size of a small coconut with a crystalline streak that sparkled in the sunlight. The islander said something to Ito, clearly in protest.

At this point, Jay began to rise from our concealed position. Merle and I both pulled him down.

"What are you doing?" I whispered.

"We can surprise them. Let's go," he said.

"This is no time for individual heroics," Merle cautioned. "Let's get back to the plane and go get help. They'll be trapped here until we come back."

"But what about the villagers? They could shoot them in retaliation when they see the plane is gone," I worried.

"It's a chance we'll have to take," said Merle.

As we whispered to each other, Ito had gathered up the two stones, wrapped them in cloth, and placed them each in a canvas sack.

"They have what they want now. They'll be going back to Lula. We need to get there first," Jay said.

We slunk back through the underbrush, making as little noise as possible. When we got back to the cove, Lula was still alone, anchored offshore. We looked around for a few moments. There was no sign of a canoe or the rubber raft.

"We'll have to swim to her," Jay said.

The surf had just washed over the tips of our boots as we approached the water when a shout came from behind. "*Nein!* Stop!" Emerald cried. "Put your hands in the air." A bullet whizzed past. We did as she said and turned around.

"How did you get free?" she demanded. "How did you get here? Never mind." Ohrwürmer herded us back onto the sand in front of Emerald and Ito. She looked at us with curiosity.

"Well, Fräulein Professor Doktor Linden, maybe I underestimated you. But we don't have time for games now. Shoot them, Herr Ohrwürmer." He raised his Luger.

"No! We have something you want. Something your Führer needs!" Merle cried.

Emerald put up a hand to Ohrwürmer. "And what might that be, Nurse Farland?"

"A plant. A plant that can heal wounds. In a matter of hours. Just think how that might be of use to the Fatherland. Your soldiers would be invincible. Unstoppable on the battlefield."

"Go on, Nurse Farland," Emerald said with interest.

"I've never seen anything like this. Show them your wrists," Merle said to Jay and me. We slowly lowered our arms and stretched them out for Emerald to inspect. "We had deep lacerations and abrasions from the rope," said Merle. I glanced at Ito, and he flashed his gold-toothed grin again. "We put the leaves of a plant on them, and the cuts were healed within hours."

"What plant?" Emerald asked.

"I don't know what it is. But you might recognize it," I said. "I saved some leaves. They're in my pockets."

"Hands in the air again, Professor. Ito, search her pockets," Emerald ordered.

Ito dropped the canvas sacks onto the sand. He roughly dug into my pockets and pulled out handfuls of the now-wilted, heart-shaped leaves. As he handed them to Emerald and Ohrwürmer, Merle darted down and grabbed one of the sacks. She swung it with all her might against Ito's head. He pitched forward, falling onto Emerald. As she lost her balance and the two tumbled to the sand, Jay's right fist made contact with Ohrwürmer's jaw. He staggered backward. I dove for Emerald's Luger. Merle dealt Ito another heavy blow with the sack. He was out cold now. Merle grabbed the Nambu pistol tucked in his waistband.

I raised the Luger at Ohrwürmer. "Drop your gun," I said to him, as Merle kept Ito's pistol trained on Emerald. Ohrwürmer let the pistol drop to his feet, and Jay retrieved it.

"Professor Linden, it seems the tables are turned. For now, anyway," Emerald said. She almost seemed to be enjoying the moment.

"What's in these sacks?" I demanded.

"Just some magic stones," Emerald said. "Nothing a scientist like you would be interested in, I'm sure. The people of Nataghera village here on Santa Ana used them for healing diseases. Before the foolish missionaries came around and stamped out their culture."

"Hmm, seems like they're better for causing afflictions than healing them," Merle said as the canvas sack she wielded smashed against Emerald's platinum blond head. Ohrwürmer's cold gray eyes briefly showed surprise before Merle knocked him out with a perfunctory swing of the sack. The three bodies lay sprawled out on the sand. Merle checked their pulses. "They're still alive," she said.

"What do we do now?" I asked as I opened up one

canvas sack and took out the stone. It was the color of caramel with lighter streaks and a vein of clear crystal running through it. Merle unwrapped the other one that had served her so well.

"Let's put these over there, away from the water," she said, spreading them out on the empty sacks.

"Where is Santa Ana?" Jay asked.

"It's off the tip of San Cristoval. Far to the southeast," Merle replied.

"But we can't be there. We never could have gotten here by canoe in such a short time," I said.

"Even in a *tomoko* that vanished after we disembarked?" Jay said.

"I see your point," I replied. "So what do we do with them?" I asked, looking at the motionless trio on the sand.

"We could leave them to the justice of the islanders," Merle suggested.

"That might prove to be harsh justice," said Jay.

"Exactly," said Merle.

I crouched down and gathered up the healing leaves that fluttered around the unconscious bodies and stuffed them in my pockets again.

"Let's go," Merle said. "We aren't far from Vanikoro. If we can make it there, Ruby will help us. We can radio for the constabulary to come and pick them up. If there's anything left of them by then."

We started to wade out to Lula. "Do you think there's enough fuel?" I asked Jay.

"We'll find out," Jay said. He went ahead, needing to swim only the last few yards. He reached Lula and pulled himself up onto her float. Merle and I hung back while he dipped under her wing and inspected the engine. He gently caressed her nose, and I could see he was talking to her. Then he crossed onto the other pontoon to examine that engine. He came back around to the side with the door, shaking his head in disgust at the symbol that defiled her proud tail.

Jay opened the door to the cabin and motioned for Merle and me to come aboard. We waded as far as we could and swam the last distance. He reached down and helped Merle onto the float first. She went inside the cabin to the cockpit while Jay gave me a hand. Merle let out a scream, and we froze on the pontoon for an instant before scrambling to the door.

"What's wrong? Merle, are you all right?" I cried. She answered with a nervous laugh and leaned into the rear cabin.

"I was just startled by the pilot, that's all," she said, holding open a canvas bag. Two blank eye sockets stared back at us.

"It must be Ingava!" I said. I climbed into the cabin. Another large sack lay on the rear bench. I opened it and took out three cloth-wrapped parcels. I unwound the wrapping on one to reveal a huge triton shell, about the size of a football. It was aged to a dull gray with green stains of algae. "These must be the sacred shells from Kundu Hite."

"We will keep our promise to Pula," Jay said. "See if you can find the chart that shows Santa Ana and Vanikoro while I go turn the propellers. Then I'll raise the anchor, and we'll get out of here."

Merle handed me a sheaf of paper, and we started to riffle through the charts.

"I think this is it!" I said, holding out a map to Merle.

"Yes, this is it, Fräulein Professor Doktor Linden."

I whirled around to see a bedraggled Emerald Asche-Böhrer perched in the doorway of the plane, the barrel of a small pistol pointed straight at my heart, its mother-of-pearl grip shining in her hand.

CHAPTER 29

I froze as my gaze shifted between the little Colt vest pocket pistol and the wild look in Emerald's eyes. Before I could say a word, Jay came up behind her, balanced on the lower wing.

"Start the engines!" Jay shouted. Emerald spun around as Jay grabbed her. "Start the engines, Merle!" he yelled again. "Raise the anchor!"

I grabbed at the rope and started pulling at it frantically, as Emerald and Jay struggled on the wing. Then I heard one engine sputter to life. I drew in more rope, and the heavy anchor emerged from the water. As I heaved it inside the cabin, the other engine began to roar. We were moving. I heard a sharp crack as one engine backfired. But it wasn't an engine. I saw a stream of red flowing down the white surface of Lula's wing. Emerald was motionless on top of Jay.

And then she slowly raised herself up over Jay, my pistol still in her hand. Seeing the spreading red stain on Jay's grimy shirt, I instinctively swung the anchor with all my strength. It struck Emerald, and she lost her balance. She splashed into the water with a scream.

"Jay, Jay, can you hear me?" I shouted as I started

retrieving the anchor once more. I leaned out onto the wing as far as I could and grabbed Jay's hand. His eyes opened.

"No kiss this time, Profesora?" he said weakly.

"You have to come inside!" We were slowly moving away from shore again. With effort, Jay sat up and took my outstretched hands. I pulled him into the cabin, and he tumbled on top of me. Merle looked back from the cockpit.

"There's no time for that now!" she called to us. "How do I take off?"

I rolled Jay onto the cramped floor of the cabin. He was pale, and his blood stained my shirt now, too. I leaned over to close the door, and there was Emerald, paddling toward us again with an impressive breaststroke.

"The seashell, Ivy," Jay said, his eyes closed now. The seashell? The tritons!

I grabbed a shell that had rolled under the seat. I raised it to my lips and blew. A low, eerie sound emerged from the shell. I blew it again and a third time. I slammed the cabin door shut as we picked up speed. Just as I saw Lula's float clear the water, a dark triangle rose up from the depths. A dorsal fin. With a scream, Emerald vanished beneath the waves. A moment later, her outstretched right hand shot out of the water as if giving one final Nazi salute before disappearing again. I watched the spreading red stain on the surface of the water with horror for a moment before I remembered the red stain on Jay's shirt.

We were now airborne. Somehow Merle was flying the plane. And I was now in the position of nurse. I was about to suggest we switch roles when I remembered the leaves in my pockets. I hastily unbuttoned Jay's shirt and pressed down on the seeping wound. I took the cloth wrapping from the triton and wiped away some blood. The gunshot had made a small hole. Better the petite Colt than the nasty Luger. I wadded up some of the heart-shaped leaves and placed them on the wound. The bullet must have just missed his heart.

I pressed down on the cloth, and the red blot ceased to grow. I felt for Jay's pulse and bent over to listen to his ragged breathing. I let my lips brush his rough cheek. He opened his eyes.

"You're going to be okay, Jay. We're going to be fine," I said. *If* we could figure out how to get to Vanikoro. *If* we didn't run out of fuel. *If* we could land Lula.

"*Sí, Profesora. Estaremos bien,*" Jay murmured.

"Merle, do you want to trade places? I put the leaves on Jay's gunshot wound, and it seems to be helping. But it would be better if you take a look." I squeezed into the cockpit and took the controls. Merle slipped into the cabin and began rummaging around. She found some gauze and antiseptic we had not left at one of the villages. She cleaned the wound thoroughly and dressed it, packing some leaves in first.

"I think he'll be fine," she said, joining me in the cockpit again. "Now we just have to figure out where we are and how to land."

"I've seen Jay do it so many times now. He makes it seem easy. How did you take off, anyway?" I asked.

"My co-pilot helped, I guess," she said, nodding toward the sack at her feet. She picked it up and carefully placed it on the seat behind her. "Don't want anything to happen to him now after all this."

I focused my attention on keeping the plane on course for where I thought Vanikoro should be, while Merle looked at the map and scanned the empty blue expanse below. I monitored the array of gauges and dials on the control panel reporting our speed and altitude as best I could. But I studiously avoided looking at the left-most gauge, the one that said: FUEL. There was nothing I could do about that one, so I vowed to ignore it.

After a while, Merle pointed to the horizon. "I think there's land ahead!" she said. A green form took shape below us. I circled around for a better view. "It looks like Santa Cruz Island," Merle said. "Vanikoro isn't far." I adjusted our course south, and soon we passed over another small island. "I see that one on the map. Vanikoro should be next." That news should have relieved me, but the impending need to land Lula rose to the forefront of my mind.

"I've never landed on water," I confessed, feeling perspiration rising from every pore.

"You can do it, Ivy. It can't be that different from landing on the ground," Merle said.

"I've never landed on the ground, either."

"Oh."

A moment later, the peak of Vanikoro rose up out of the sea ahead of us.

"That's it," I said. Now what?

"Mind the reef," came a voice from behind in reply to my unspoken question.

"Jay, you're awake!" I cried with relief. I glanced back into the cabin. He'd pulled himself up to a sitting position on the floor. He was no longer so pale. "You're just in time to land the plane."

"No, Profesora, you land Lula. I'll tell you what to do if you need help," he said, closing his eyes and reclining against the edge of the back seat cushion.

I circled around the island as I gently began our descent. I spotted the jetty near Ruby's house. "That's where we need to land," I said, pointing it out to Merle. "Jay set down inside the lagoon before, so we'll try that." I circled back around and aimed us on a course parallel to the coral reef as I continued to decrease our altitude.

"Slow down a bit more, Profesora." I pulled back on the throttles. "Good. Raise the flaps. Keep her nose up." I pulled up on the yoke. Suddenly the water rose up to meet us in a rush, and we bounced along the surface. "Brakes, Profesora. Watch out for that bit of coral on the right." I applied the brakes with the rudder pedals and maneuvered away from the jagged white coral visible just below the surface. I felt sufficiently in control of the aircraft again to take my eyes off the windshield and look back at Jay, expecting to see him leaning up between the seats, but he was still reclining with his eyes closed. "*Muy bien, Profesora*," he murmured.

We approached the jetty, and Merle and I both heaved sighs of relief. I think we had held our breath for the entire landing. "You did it, Ivy," Merle said, giving my hand a squeeze. I cut the engines, and the propellers slowed to a halt.

"I'll tie us up," I said as I climbed into the cabin and over Jay. It was a tight fit. I grabbed the coil of thick rope and swung open the door. And I found myself staring into the barrel of a shotgun.

CHAPTER 30

"Ivy, it *is* you!" Ruby said, lowering the shotgun. "I saw the swastika on the tail and thought you'd been compromised." Then her eyes moved to my bloodstained shirt. "Good gracious, have you run into trouble? Throw me the rope," she said, putting down the rifle. She began to secure Lula to the jetty, and I jumped out. "Oh, chookie, what's happened to you?" she said, engulfing me in her ample embrace. I melted into her motherly refuge for a moment before remembering Jay and Merle.

"I'm fine, Ruby. It's so good to see you. We did run into a bit of trouble. Merle is here," I said as she leaned out of the cabin. "She's fine, too, but Jay is hurt. He's been shot, in fact." Merle jumped out, and Ruby gave her a hearty embrace.

I climbed back into the cabin to tend to Jay. He was sitting up on the seat now, looking around.

"How do you feel, Jay? Are you strong enough to leave the plane on your own?"

"I think I can make it, Ivy. I feel much better now," he said, gingerly rubbing the bandaged area of his chest. He eased himself out of the cabin and onto the wing, which still had a faint red stain. Ruby reached out to help him onto the float, then the jetty.

"We'll get you all fixed up, love," the imposing woman said tenderly as she supported Jay with her muscular arms. She led him up the jetty to her home, Merle trailing behind.

I slid onto the wing again and carefully made my way to the front edge of the pontoon. I caressed Lula's nose and thanked her for getting us here safely.

The fuel gauge had been on zero for the entire time I was flying.

I raced up to Ruby's house and found her already putting on water for tea.

"I want to hear every detail, possums. Oh, how I wish I'd been able to go with you," Ruby said. "But first, let's get you some tea and biscuits. And then a bath. You all look frightful. We'll have a good look at Jay's injury, and you'll be fit as a fiddle in no time. Is there anything I can get you, dear?"

"Yes, Ruby. Some white paint, please. I need to remove that monstrosity from Lula's tail," Jay said.

"Of course, love. You're in no shape for that. I'll have the boys do it."

"Can they put some fuel in her, too?" I asked.

"Yes, chookie. Let me go see to that. Merle, when the water boils, please make the tea. Help yourselves to the biscuits in the meantime," she said as she strode onto the verandah. I watched her sturdy form march down the stairs and wished that she'd been with us, too. Emerald and her flunkies wouldn't have stood a chance.

We were munching on shortbread cookies and downing our second cups of tea by the time Ruby returned.

"We've got your airplane all sorted out, Jay. Now let's have a look at that injury of yours," she said, bringing over a small first aid kit. Merle and I looked on as she gently removed Jay's blood-soaked shirt and the dressing Merle had applied on the plane. Ruby looked bemused by the green leaves clinging to his skin. She wiped them away and peered at the wound. "Oh, that's not so bad at all. I thought Ivy said you'd been shot. But where did all this blood come from, then?"

Merle and I came closer to inspect the wound. There was no dark hole seeping blood now. It was healed over, though a bit reddened. I reached in my pocket and found one remaining leaf.

"It *was* a gunshot wound, Ruby. Not from a very large pistol, fortunately, but it was serious. This plant caused rapid healing," I said, smoothing the crumpled leaf and holding it out to Ruby. "Do you know what it is?"

"Can't say that I do. Maybe some of the boys know it. Or the chaps from the timber company. But if anyone knew about its healing properties, I'm sure it would be in wide use by now."

"Can I have some paper, Ruby? I want to press it so I can take it back with me. Maybe someone will recognize it. And I can have some of the chemists at the university analyze it." Ruby gave me an old *Pacific Islands Monthly* magazine, and I placed the heart-shaped leaf among its pages.

"Why don't you all get cleaned up, possums? I'll give you some fresh clothes to wear. While you're washing, I'll see that dinner is prepared."

"Can you send a message to Reverend Silvester and Dr. Rutter for me?" Merle asked. "Please tell them I've been delayed, but not to worry."

"Righto, Merle. Any other messages?"

"Can you wire Tulagi, too? Please tell them you heard rumors of suspicious activity on Santa Ana, and they should send some men from the constabulary to check things out," I said. Ruby's eyes widened.

"My dear, this sounds like quite a story. Whatever were you doing on Santa Ana? Do you want me to try to get a message to your Johnson and Smith?" she asked.

"No."

"Very well. Off to your bath now. I'll be in with towels and something to wear in a moment."

Later, we sat around Ruby's table again, clean for the first time in days. Ruby had given Jay a pair of her son's pajamas to wear, while Merle and I each floated in one of her ample nightgowns.

Once our plates were full of roasted chicken, sweet potatoes, and tinned peas, Ruby looked around warily, as if a spy could be lurking in the kitchen. "Now tell me everything, chookies."

Jay and I relayed the events that happened since we'd left her home, with Merle joining in once we came to her entry into the story. As we went on with our narrative, it dawned on me how ridiculous it all sounded. Surely she'd think we were making it up. Anyone in his or her right mind would think we were making it up. Or at least not in our right minds. I finished the story with opening Lula's door only to see Ruby, rifle in hand.

She was silent for some time before nodding slowly. "I believe you, possums. I believe you. So you mean to say you have the skull of old Chief Ingava and the sacred tritons in the airplane right now?"

"Yes, that's right. They're in canvas sacks," I replied.

"That won't do. I'll have one of the boys make kauri wood boxes for them. But I won't mention what they're for. No one would be too pleased to find out all the women who've handled them, much less dared to blow the triton. Now let's get you all tucked in bed."

Merle and I cleared the table and began to wash the dishes as Ruby settled Jay into her son's bedroom. She came back and insisted we go to bed, too. She led us to her other son's room, where she'd made up an extra cot next to the single bed. Merle and I obediently slipped between the sheets. I could barely remember the last time I slept in an actual bed. Ruby arranged the bedclothes around us, saying, "I'm so proud of you girls. You really saved the day. I do wish I could have come along, though. I suspect that's the most adventure these sleepy islands will ever see." She turned off the light, and we slept like proverbial logs, mighty kauri ones.

CHAPTER 31

Coffee, bacon, and eggs greeted Merle and me in the morning. Jay was already dressed and puttering about Lula. Ruby called him to breakfast, and he came back carrying our bags. It seemed Emerald had not dumped anything from the plane. He handed me the satchel Ito had taken. To my delight, my journals were still inside. After breakfast, I began to write up a narrative of our last few days. And in my field notebook, I set down the following scientific description of the healing plant: low-growing vine, leaves cordate, blade 10 cm long, 6 cm wide, on a slender petiole 4 cm long, base broadly cordate, tip acuminate, margins dentate, surfaces nearly glabrous, seven-veined from base. And yet the botanical terms were clearly missing something vital, I realized as I tucked the remaining flattened leaf inside the book.

"Here you go, possums," Ruby said, presenting us with two small crates constructed of kauri wood. "A much more fitting receptacle for Chief Ingava's head than a canvas sack." Merle and I took the boxes to the plane, and she stood watch while I jumped into the cabin. I used the last remaining cloth we'd purchased at Tulagi to wrap up the three tritons and secure them in one box. I found a silk scarf in my own bag and wound it around Ingava's skull to cushion it in the second box.

I pondered what Ingava had looked like in life as I secured both boxes under the rear seat. As I did so, I noticed another sack in the cargo hold that did not belong to us. With some trepidation, I untied the rope securing it closed. A terrible odor of rotting flesh emanated from the bag. I braced myself for the sight of some decomposing animal or human body part and opened the sack. A blackened, dried up monstrosity lay there. I grimaced and closed the bag up fast. It was not some decaying creature, but a *Rafflesia* flower that had been in full bloom. I rummaged around in the cargo hold and came across another unknown carton. I was not surprised at the smell when I lifted the lid. A dozen egg-sized *Rafflesia* buds bursting from sections of *Tetrastigma* vine were nestled in a bed of dried grass. I very much doubted the ability of Emerald's experts to get these flowers to bloom outside of their natural habitat. Perhaps some medicinal compounds could be extracted. But these buds and the flower would not be seeing the inside of a laboratory. We would return them to their rightful place on Pulau Tioman.

As comforting as Ruby's hospitality was, we needed to be on our way. She insisted on one last round of tea and biscuits before walking us to the jetty.

"Well done, my chookies!" Ruby said as she gave us each a bear hug. "Have a safe flight. Merle, I'll see you on Tulagi, I'm sure. Ivy, Jay, I do hope our paths will cross again someday. You are always welcome on Vanikoro!" She waved emphatically as we taxied away from the jetty. In a few moments we were airborne, and Jay swooped down and waggled Lula's wings at Ruby. We headed northward, and I was happy to be sitting in the back seat with nothing to do but enjoy the flight.

We passed over a large expanse of open water before a small island appeared on the horizon. "According to the chart, that must be Santa Ana. And San Cristoval is just beyond it," Merle said.

"Let's take a peek," Jay said as we flew over the center of the little green island. He dove down over the placid cove. There was no sign of anyone. The spot where we had left Ohrwürmer and Ito was empty. But not far away, two huge saltwater crocodiles sunned themselves at the water's edge. They looked as content as Rama and Osiris after a can of Puss 'n Boots and saucer of milk.

We continued along the north coast of San Cristoval and then Guadalcanal. We began to descend for a brief stop at Tulagi. Jay landed Lula with ease and set about refueling her, while Merle and I made a beeline for the shops in Chinatown. We stocked up on medical supplies and other sundries for the mission hospital and came back to the plane as fast as we could. None of us wanted to be interrogated by the Resident Commissioner or forced to partake in a game of golf or drinks at the club. We loaded up Lula and were airborne again within an hour.

The little green islets that dotted the waters of Roviana and Vonavona lagoons looked like clumps of moss from above. We spotted the turtle's back of Mamburana emerging from the blue. Jay set Lula down in the water, and canoes came to greet us moments later. I handed the wooden boxes to the men in the first canoe, hoping they did not arouse too much curiosity, and then added a bundle of trade goods and medical supplies to their load. Other men gave us a ride to shore, where Chief Liliti greeted us warmly. Once again, the village had gathered to welcome us. I scanned the small crowd and saw Pula peering out from her doorway.

Merle spoke to the villagers in Roviana and began distributing the supplies, while Jay and I retrieved the wooden boxes and snuck into Pula's hut. Merle joined us a moment later.

"We're back, Pula," I said, handing her the smaller box. She took it from me and cradled it in her arms. Jay set the crate containing the tritons down at her feet.

"Yes, I knew you would be back today. And I knew you would bring my father's skull and the sacred trumpet shells with you. Thank you," the old woman said, revealing her shocking red smile.

"We can accompany you to Kundu Hite tonight," Jay said.

"Thank you, Mr. Jay, but that is not necessary," Pula replied.

"Is it safe for you to go alone?" I asked.

"I will not be going alone. I will take my daughter and my granddaughter with me. And of course my father will be with us," she said, patting the kauri box. "He will not let any harm come to us. Just as he protected you. I made offerings of taro and *ngali* nuts to ask for assistance from my ancestors for your safe return. I also asked your ancestors and the *mateana* to assist you."

We murmured our thanks to the old woman. She rummaged in a bag made of plaited palm fronds and withdrew three white shell arm rings.

"These belonged to my father. I would like you to

have a remembrance of him and your time here," she said, handing each of us a heavy bangle. "He wore these at his funeral," she explained. We solemnly accepted the gifts, and she slid each one onto our upper arms. "Some of his *mana* will always protect you."

"Pula, do you recognize this plant?" I asked after fishing the pressed leaf out of the notebook in my bag. She took it and smiled her crimson grin again.

"Yes, I know this plant. I am glad she found you," she answered.

"What do you call it? Is there some growing on this island? What can you tell me about it?"

"I can tell you that you need to ask her the questions, not me," she said cryptically, handing the leaf back to me. I returned it to the pages of the book for safekeeping, nodding as if I understood her meaning.

We bade farewell to Pula and then to the rest of the village. Since there was no need to stay overnight, we headed for Vella Lavella. It was a relief to see the stone wharf and neat buildings at Bilua. Daniel and Isaac from the hospital greeted us when we landed, and a group of children ran to Merle, calling out, "*Halo*, Nurse Farland!" in their mellifluous voices. She told them we had brought some small presents, but they must let us rest first. They obediently went back to playing, and we brought ashore the new supplies. Reverend Silvester and Dr. Rutter were both in the large room of the hospital.

"Nurse Farland, glad to have you back," said Reverend Silvester. "We were getting a mite worried. We didn't think you'd be gone this long. I hope you didn't run into any trouble."

"A few more afflictions to deal with than I'd

expected, but nothing we couldn't handle," Merle replied. "Allen, I have more yaws data for your study. I'll tell you all about it over dinner."

In the evening, we dined with Reverend Silvester, Moyna, Dr. Rutter, and Elizabeth. Merle regaled them with stories of yaws and ulcers and other medical problems she'd treated. However, she left out Jay's gunshot wound and our lacerations from being bound to bamboo stalks.

After dinner, Jay, Merle, and I sat around the little table in her bungalow. "It's good to be home," Merle said. "There was a point when I thought I'd never see this place again."

"Are you going to tell anyone what really happened?" I asked.

"I'm not sure, Ivy. Certainly not Allen and Elizabeth. They would never believe it. I'm not sure if *I* even believe it. But I just might tell Reverend Silvester and Moyna. They've been here longer, and they might be a bit more open-minded."

"I'm not sure who to tell, either. Do you think we need to report what happened to the Resident Commissioner?"

"I don't think so. Ruby will relay any relevant information to the proper authorities. Say, do you want to ask the natives about the healing plant tomorrow?"

"I don't think so, Merle. I think I'm supposed to follow Pula's advice." Besides, I thought, the islanders at the mission in their proper white, European attire have probably forgotten how to listen to the plants, now that manmade remedies like neoarsphenamine do the talking.

"Do you want to go back to Vonavona to try to find

the plant again?" Jay asked.

"No, Jay. I just want to go home."

"Then we will leave tomorrow for Port Moresby. We can make it from here without going back to Tulagi first."

"Good. I can't say I wanted to be relegated to the Tulagi Club reading room again."

We bid goodnight to Jay, and Merle and I settled in to our beds. It seemed impossible to believe we were safe and cozy again after all that had happened.

"I'm sorry I dragged you on this crazy expedition, Merle."

"Sorry? Don't be, Ivy. I wouldn't have missed it for anything. I don't doubt I'll look back on it years from now as my one great adventure. It's not likely anything so exciting will happen in these remote islands again. Not to me, anyway."

"I think I've had my fill of adventure for a while, though," I said. "It'll be good to go home."

"Maybe you'll have a chance to see that young man who caught your fancy before you go back to America."

"Young man?"

"The professor. At the University of Otago?"

"Oh, right. He'd slipped my mind, actually. No, there's no time to go to New Zealand. It'll take awhile to get back to Ithaca, and I have to be there in time for the start of the semester."

"That's too bad, Ivy."

"Well, I guess it wasn't meant to be," I said with a sigh. "Good night, Merle."

CHAPTER 32

A small crowd gathered on the stone wharf at Bilua to see us off. A chorus of children, angelic in their white outfits, sang hymns for us, their voices blending in a heavenly harmony. The orderlies from the hospital, Reverend Silvester and Moyna, and Dr. Rutter and Elizabeth all turned out to bid us farewell.

Merle threw her arms around Jay and then me. "Do keep in touch, Ivy. We can get letters here, so I hope you'll write. And Jay, maybe you can arrange to fly the mail route sometime. You'd always be a welcome guest."

Jay and I climbed into the cockpit while Reverend Silvester gave Lula's propellers a few spins. Jay started the engines, and we taxied away from the pier, waving goodbye to the crowd on shore. Once we were airborne, Jay swooped back down, rocking Lula's wings for his customary farewell. In a few moments, we'd passed over Vella Lavella and were over open water, the Solomon Sea.

"Why don't you take the controls, Ivy?"

"Thank you, Jay," I said as I grabbed the stick. "It's nicer to fly with you beside me in the cockpit, not unconscious in the cabin."

"It is nicer to be beside you. But Lula would have taken care of you no matter what."

"I believe you, Jay. I'm sorry I put you through all this. And you didn't even get to find King Solomon's mines or any other treasures down there."

"You are quite mistaken, Ivy. I did, indeed, find treasures. Did you not?"

"Yes, Jay. I did. In abundance."

We flew on, taking turns at the controls. We passed over some small islands, and finally the large island of New Guinea came into view. Jay took the yoke and guided us to Port Moresby. Once the town was in sight, he told me to take the stick again.

"You land Lula this time."

"Oh, no, Jay. Once was enough."

"Come now, Ivy, you should practice. I'm right here and will help if you need it. And Lula will do all the work."

I reluctantly took the controls again and followed Jay's instructions. The Dragonfly skimmed along the water, and this time there was no bouncing, just the smooth landing of an aquatic bird.

"*Muy bien, Profesora*," Jay said as he maneuvered us along the jetty. "A few more landings and Qantas will offer you a job."

I was very pleased with myself, but my high spirits didn't last. As Jay went to tie us up, I spied that insufferable Bruce Buckthorn shuffling toward us.

"Allo, mate!" he cried to Jay. "You still got that lady professor with you?" As much as I wanted to, I couldn't hide in the plane, and so I jumped out behind Jay.

"There she is! Miss Linden, right? It's nice to have a

proper lady grace our fair shore again, miss," he said, looking me up and down. "I'm pleased to see you look none the worse for wear. I guess those savages in the Solomons didn't give you any trouble."

"I assure you, Mr. Buckthorn, the people of the Solomons were most welcoming. It was the real savages who were the problem," I replied. He gave me a quizzical look.

"It is nice to see you, Señor Bruce," Jay interrupted. "Can you have the mechanic look over the airplane and refuel her? We'll leave first thing tomorrow."

"Certainly, certainly, Mr. Jay. Let me just escort the lady up to the hangar and get her settled with some tea. So nice to have a European woman to converse with," he said, grabbing my hand. I looked plaintively at Jay as the unkempt man pulled me along. "Tommy!" he bellowed, well in advance of the shack that served as his office. "Put some tea on!"

To my great relief, Jay caught up with us, and I was able to extricate my hand from Buckthorn's sweaty grip.

"You two sit right here, and I'll be back in a jiffy," Buckthorn said, calling out to the mechanic as he left the shack. Tommy presented us with cups of weak tea and hard navy biscuits. Soon Buckthorn was back, smiling officiously.

"And did you find what you were looking for, miss? Some type of plant, was it?"

"Uh, yes, I found what I needed." I had no desire to share any further details with him.

"Pity about the Clipper, though," Buckthorn said.

"What do mean? We've heard no news for some time," I said.

"The Hawaii Clipper. It disappeared on a flight from Guam to Manila. No trace of it. Fifteen aboard plus the crew. They've been out looking, of course. Found an oil slick, last I heard. A real shame. Second one lost this year. That's a run of bad luck, all right. Although some say it was more than that."

"What do you mean?" Jay asked.

"Sabotage," Buckthorn said knowingly. Jay and I exchanged glances.

"Who was flying?" Jay asked.

"Terletzky."

"He was their best," Jay said, shaking his head. We fell into silence as the tragic news sank in. It was hard to imagine the sister ship of the China Clipper had vanished. Nothing had seemed unsafe about flying in that luxury aircraft. Its loss seemed about as likely as a posh supper club or opulent hotel disappearing.

"I'm sorry, Jay. Did you know him?" I asked.

"Only a little. A fine pilot."

Buckthorn got up and pulled a bottle from his desk drawer. He poured some whiskey into our empty teacups.

"To the Hawaii Clipper and Leo Terletzky," he said, raising his cup. We clinked our chipped cups together and downed the amber liquid.

"And where are you headed now, miss?" Buckthorn asked.

"Back to Singapore. And then I have to return to the U.S."

"Ah. By way of ocean liner?"

"No. I anticipated taking the China Clipper again."

"Oh dear, surely you won't want to do that now."

"I'm sure it's no problem. Jay, shouldn't we be going

to the hotel?"

"I insist you be my guests tonight," Bruce said, leering at me.

"Oh no, Señor Bruce. That is a kind offer, but we could not put you out. The hotel will be quite sufficient," Jay said firmly.

"Well, if you find you'd like some company, miss, you know where to find me," Buckthorn said, taking my hand again and raising it to his lips. I managed to pull it away before making contact with the bushy mustache.

"Good night, Señor Bruce," Jay said, and we left the stifling shack. The sun was beginning to set, and the air outside was slightly more pleasant as we made the brief walk up the hill to the Papua Hotel.

The Chinese man at the front desk remembered us from our previous visit.

"We have just one vacancy tonight," the man said apologetically.

"One room will be quite sufficient," I said, feeling Jay's eyes on me but not daring to look. The clerk handed Jay the key. He gave it to me, and I started walking to the stairs. Jay was motionless.

"Jay?"

"Profesora?" he said, walking over to me now, out of earshot of the clerk and the few people loitering in the shabby lobby. "Should I go back to Bruce's? Or find another hotel? Or to Lula?"

"I was hoping you'd stay here with me," I confessed. "Only if you want to, that is."

"*Sí, por supuesto,* Ivy. How could I not?"

Jay took my outstretched hand, and we walked up the rickety stairs together.

CHAPTER 33

In the morning, I awoke to find a pair of dark eyes staring intently into mine; a tiny green lizard clung to the wall next to our bed, surveying the scene: limbs entwined like vines, entangled like an epiphyte and its host. Most definitely mutually symbiotic, not parasitic, I thought with a small smile. The lizard blinked, flicked his tongue, and scampered away as I reluctantly stirred.

"Good morning, Ivy."

"*Buenos días*, Jacinto," I said, caressing the rough stubble of his cheek. My hand moved to the spot just above his heart where I had desperately pressed leaves and dirty cloth to staunch the flow of blood just a few days ago. There was only a faint scar there amidst the dark curls now. Anyone would have thought it was an old injury, sustained many years ago. "I wish we didn't have to go," I said with a sigh.

"But we must go back to Singapore. Qantas may wonder what has become of us. And they must worry about you at the museum."

"True. But we'll have to stop overnight in Darwin and Surabaya again, won't we?"

"Yes."

"Good."

In an hour, we were in the air again. Lula had benefited from a thorough going over by a proper mechanic, and her engines hummed along happily. The sky was a glorious shade of blue with an occasional wisp of cloud. I marveled at the splendid weather, but made certain not to remark upon it to Jay, just in case.

We took turns at the controls, and after some hours of flying, we spotted Darwin below.

"You land again, Ivy," Jay suggested. I agreed, happy that I needed even less instruction than the day before. "Beautiful, Profesora. You are an excellent student. Although it's best you not mention the lessons here. The people from Qantas may not appreciate it." I agreed and gave back the controls for Jay to taxi into the harbor.

We walked up to the Qantas hangar at the airfield. While Jay conversed with the mechanics, I wandered over to the autographed photo of Amelia. She smiled out at me, and I almost expected her to give me a conspiratorial wink. Yes, adventure is worthwhile in itself, Amelia. As long as you're looking out for me, that is.

Jay came up behind me and put his arm around my shoulder. We left the hangar and strolled over to the Vic. I stopped Jay before we entered.

"Perhaps we'd better get separate rooms. For appearances' sake. I don't mind wasting Johnson and Smith's money on a room we won't use. It's the least they can do after all we've been through." Jay agreed, and we procured two adjacent rooms, set down our luggage, and walked around the little town for a while before heading back to the Vic for dinner. Afterward, we went back to our respective rooms, and I wrote in my journal until I heard Jay's soft knock on my door at the agreed upon hour.

Although it would have been nice to linger, Jay kept us on schedule in the morning. We departed Darwin promptly for our westward flight to Timor for refueling. I could have easily been persuaded to stay there overnight, but we pressed on ahead to Surabaya as planned. Johnson and Smith spared no expense at the Hotel Oranje. We had two adjoining suites with a convenient door connecting them. Instead of finding a spot in town for dinner, we ordered the most sumptuous items on the room service menu.

In the morning, we found Lula nestled beneath the protective wing of the Imperial Airways Short Empire flying boat. We taxied away from the dock and were airborne again. Just a stop in Batavia for fuel and we'd be back in Singapore by the evening. And then I'd have to find my way back to Ithaca.

"How will you get to Manila to catch the China Clipper?" Jay asked. Perhaps my departure was weighing on his mind, as well.

"I'm not sure. There's no time for a ship. I caught a cargo flight to Singapore by chance, but that's not likely again."

"Well, you could charter a flight. And I just happen to know a pilot who would be available."

"Oh?"

"Yes, there is only one issue. The flight would have to stop overnight. To refuel."

"And the pilot would have to stay overnight in Manila, too?"

"*Por supuesto.*"

"Yes, I think I'd very much like to charter that flight," I said happily. "But there's one more stop. Can we visit Pulau Tioman?"

"Yes, it is not so far out of the way."

"Good. I have to return something. The *Rafflesia*. There's a bag in the back with one flower and a carton with twelve buds."

"Their particular perfume had alerted me to their presence. I assumed they were going back to America with you for study."

"No, I don't want to take them back with me. They don't belong to me. And I don't think I could get them to grow anyway. I'd rather give them back to the people of Tekek. At least they could use them as they always have, even if no more grow in their place."

"Very well, the itinerary is settled then. Would you like to fly until we reach Batavia?" Jay said, taking his hands off the yoke. I took the controls, and we flew on in comfortable silence.

Before I knew it, we were secured at the Qantas dock. I went for a short walk while Jay tended to Lula, and then we were in the air again. The flight to Singapore seemed like just a short hop as Kallang Aerodrome appeared ahead. It was funny how the journey *to* someplace always seemed to take much longer than the identical return trip, whether it was the familiar childhood car ride to visit our grandparents or this unplanned island-hopping expedition.

"You go on ahead to Raffles, Ivy. I will secure your charter flight and arrange for the equipment and samples you have stored in the hangar to be loaded. We'll leave the day after tomorrow. That will give you time to pack up and visit the Raffles Museum again if you want. Will I see you tonight?"

"Yes, of course. Let's have dinner. I think Johnson and Smith are feeling very generous, indeed. I'm in room 315. How about eight?"

"Perfect," Jay said, motioning for a taxi.

Once again, I entered the posh lobby of the Raffles Hotel in a bedraggled state, but I cared not at all this time. I stopped by the reception desk for my key.

"Ah, Professor Linden, you have returned. Here's your key and some correspondence that arrived in your absence," the clerk said, handing me a few envelopes. "Do you require assistance to your room?"

"No, thank you. But I'll be checking out the day after tomorrow." I walked up the grand stairway to the third floor. My room was, indeed, just as I'd left it. I marveled at the clean clothes in the closet and pondered what to wear for dinner. I chose a coral pink silk crepe evening dress, bias cut with a plunging V neckline and flutter sleeves. I'd had no real occasion for such a fancy dress before, and chances to wear it were fleeting.

I undressed and bundled all my dirty clothes together for the laundry, although an incinerator would have been a better destination. I sank down into the deep tub of hot water and let it melt away my remaining cares and any leftover grime.

Afterward, wrapped in a plush white bathrobe, I curled up on a rattan lounge chair in the sitting room with the envelopes. Two telegrams and an envelope that had not come though the mail, but just bore my name in vaguely familiar handwriting. I opened one telegram first.

IVY= HOPE YOU ARE HAVING A GOOD TRIP STOP WE MISS YOU STOP LET US KNOW WHEN YOU WILL BE HOME STOP LOVE MOTHER AND DAD

That was nice. I'd send them a reply tomorrow after I booked my return ticket on the Clipper. Then I tore open the next envelope.

PROFESSOR LINDEN= PLEASE PROVIDE UPDATE STOP WE TRUST YOU HAVE EXTERMINATED ANY PESTS STOP JOHNSON AND SMITH USDA

I rolled my eyes and supposed I'd have to reply to them, as well. Now what was this other envelope? I looked at the handwriting again. It couldn't be, could it? I carefully opened the envelope and withdrew a sheet of heavyweight cream stationery. "My Dear Ivy," I read aloud. Oh no. The letter continued, "I happened to be passing near Singapore and thought I would stop by just in case you were still there. Alas, the clerk informed me I had just missed you and had no knowledge of your return date. I do hope your collecting trip has been fruitful, and I much regret missing the chance to see you in person. I look forward to learning of your discoveries and await your future correspondence with great anticipation. Sincerely yours, Heath."

Oh dear. I had completely forgotten about Heath Bracken over the past few days. And to think, he was right here in the Raffles Hotel. Just to see me. And I had missed him. I felt the smallest twinge of disappointment.

But perhaps fate had other ideas, I thought with a shrug. I shoved the letter and telegrams into my bag and busied myself with getting into the coral evening dress.

At eight o'clock on the dot, I heard a rapping on my door.

"Señor Diente de León," I said, opening the door wide and my eyes even wider. "Please come in." Jay was immaculately dressed in a crisp white suit. We made a very elegant pair.

"Ivy, you look stunning."

"Thank you, Jay. You've cleaned up quite well yourself, I see. Where shall we go for dinner? Johnson and Smith said the sky's the limit. The ballroom is set up for dinner, and there's a formal after-dinner dance later."

"Your suite is practically palatial," he said, looking around. "It seems a shame not to take full advantage of it."

"Room service it is then," I said, picking up the telephone. "We can dine on the balcony. The view of the Palm Court is lovely."

"The view is lovely from right here, as well. It has been from the first moment in the Long Bar."

I felt myself flushing and hastily placed an order for dinner. Later, when the remnants of beef Wellington, *haricots verts*, and *pots de crème* were taken away, we sipped champagne and looked out at the traveler's palms as the first notes of the orchestra floated up to us.

"You know what they say about the traveler's palms, Ivy?"

"Oh yes, they aren't really palms at all. Or even trees. They're related to bird-of-paradise flowers and bananas. And they're native to Madagascar. They are said to orient their leaves in an east-west direction, and water can be found in pockets at the base of the leaves, both useful for travelers, hence the name."

"Very good, Profesora. I don't doubt that is all correct. But do you know what they say about *these* traveler's palms?" I confessed ignorance. "If you stand in front of one and make a wish in good faith, it will come true."

"Well then, I think an experiment is in order," I said, standing up. "Shall we go for a stroll?" Soon we were standing among the stately trunks in the Palm Court. We both stood silently in front of a traveler's palm for a few moments. Just as when I had a flaming birthday cake in front of me as a child, I could not settle on a wish. But then finally, it was to see Jay again someday after we parted in Manila.

"There. Now we'll see if our wishes come true," I said, taking Jay's arm. "Let's go back upstairs."

"Ah, mine was granted instantly, Ivy."

CHAPTER 34

By the time I got out of bed, Jay had already slipped away to his room to get dressed. We met for coffee and pastries in the hotel café and parted for the day. I made arrangements with the concierge for a booking on the China Clipper from Manila to San Francisco. The timing worked out so that I'd spend just one night in Manila. I was worried about securing a place, but it seemed they had some cancellations lately, thanks no doubt to the grim fate of the Hawaii Clipper.

Then I set about sending those telegrams. I told Mother and Dad when I expected to land in San Francisco and that I'd wire them from there with more details. I suspected my mother was beside herself with the news of the Clipper disappearance.

To Johnson and Smith I wrote:

DEPARTING SINGAPORE TOMORROW STOP EXPECT TO ARRIVE IN ITHACA IN A WEEK STOP DID NOT APPRECIATE THE NEED TO USE PESTICIDE WITHOUT PRIOR WARNING

I strolled over to the museum and arrived in the mid-morning. I inquired at the front desk, and soon Fred Chasen and Tweedie came down to greet me.

"Ivy, so glad you're back," Fred said. "How was Vanikoro?"

"It was . . . interesting. Yes, I observed many intriguing things that no doubt require further study. Tweedie, I was able to view some crustaceans up close. Coconut crabs."

"Very good! They are impressive creatures. The largest terrestrial arthropod, you know," Tweedie said with evident pride. "They can kill and eat large birds. But their meat is quite tasty itself."

"I missed out on that delicacy. Fortunately, we agreed not to dine on each other." Tweedie gave me a peculiar look. "Did you happen to get my film developed?" I asked.

"Oh yes, here are the photos," Tweedie said, handing me a stack of small prints. I flipped through the photos of the *Rafflesia*. A few were out of focus, but most showed the flower quite clearly, maybe well enough to establish it as a new species. The last shot was not the smelly flower, but Jay smiling his charming grin. Funny, but I didn't remember snapping that one. I hastily put it at the bottom of the stack again.

"Thanks, Tweedie. I didn't make any new plant collections on Vanikoro. But I did recover a *Rafflesia* bloom and a dozen buds from Tioman. There's no way I can get them to grow again, so I'm going to return them to Tekek."

"That's a shame. Did you run into that German botanist?" Fred asked.

"I did. It's a long story, but eventually she gave up on her expedition. And she handed over the *Rafflesia*. She had a German man with her. From some research institute. She called it the Ahnenerbe, I think. I'd never heard of it, but she seemed to think they were a pretty impressive lot."

"Well, that's the Germans, isn't it? They do seem to think they're impressive," Fred said.

"They weren't just Germans, though. They were Nazis. Honest-to-goodness, swastika-loving, Führer-heiling Nazis. And they were awfully chummy with a Japanese man."

"Yes, that friendship's getting to be a tad worrisome," Tweedie said.

"Indeed, my family back in England is most concerned about the situation with Germany," Fred said. "We're lucky to be here in Singapore. Gibraltar of the East. Impenetrable. Well, good for you, getting that plant back. Can't imagine it could be of much use, though. How long are you staying?"

"I'm leaving tomorrow. It'll take a whole week to get home, and time is running out before the students return."

"Well, it's been a pleasure to have you. Come back and bring your father the next time. Let's have lunch before you go," Fred said. We went to their favorite noodle spot, and to my delight their wives were free to join us for lunch. The conversation was light, and I was able to steer it away from the details of the Solomons trip. Elvira did inquire after Jay, and I assured her he was in excellent health and spirits.

After lunch, I did a bit of shopping and picked up

souvenirs for Mother, Dad, and Amaryllis. I also arranged for bags of rice, sugar, tea, and medical supplies to be sent over to the Qantas hangar and loaded aboard Lula to drop off on Tioman.

I met Jay in the Long Bar for a drink before dinner. A pink Gin Sling for me to say farewell to Singapore and a Coca-Cola for Jay. After dinner in the Tiffin Room, we walked around the town for a bit and retired for the night.

"I wish I didn't have to leave, Jay," I said, parting the mosquito netting that surrounded the big four-poster bed for him.

"I wish you could stay, too, Ivy. But I know you have to go back home," Jay said as he secured us within the protective canopy. "But we still have tonight. And tomorrow night and Manila. Let's make the most of it."

"That makes good sense, Jay. But what about you? Will you go back home?"

"Someday. Not just yet. But maybe soon."

"Ciudad de México isn't that far from Ithaca, really. Maybe we'll see each other again."

"I don't doubt it for an instant, Ivy."

Chapter 35

Jay greeted me in the Raffles lobby with a slight bow as if we had not just parted an hour before. "Profesora Linden, I hope your last night in Singapore was agreeable. I'll escort you to your flight."

"Oh yes, most agreeable, Señor Diente de León. Qantas really does provide excellent service," I said, handing my key to the clerk. "As does the Raffles."

"We do hope you'll join us again in Singapore," the clerk said as a porter conveyed my luggage to a taxi. We left the regal white building and stately rows of palms behind.

At Kallang Aerodrome we stopped in the Qantas hangar while Jay finalized his flight plan and then walked over to the seaplane dock. Lula bobbed in greeting. She was clean, and her paint was touched up. I wondered how Jay explained the extra coat of white paint on her tail. And the faint red streak on her wing.

We managed to wedge our luggage in the cabin and squeeze past to the cockpit. It was a tight fit between my equipment, samples, and the extra supplies, but at least those would stay at Tioman. In short order, we were aloft and circling the city. Singapore disappeared from view, and we flew north along the lush green of the Malaya coast. Before we knew it, we spotted Pulau Tioman and the little jetty at Tekek.

"Go ahead and land her, Ivy." I took the controls and eased Lula down into the calm water.

"*Muy bien*," Jay said. "And you will learn to take off next."

Our arrival attracted the attention of the whole village. Johari, Wira, and Jasmi came to welcome us, with Kasih, Kiambang, Mawar, and Melati following behind. We unloaded the supplies for the village and then located the bag and carton of *Rafflesia*. Jay made a show of carrying the box at arm's length, but I really didn't think it smelled much at all.

Once everything was ashore, Johari had us sit down in the center of the village.

"We have some good news, Johari. We have the stolen *Rafflesia* for you. And the people who took it won't be coming back," I said, pushing the box and bag to him. "I know you can't replant them, but at least you can use them."

"Thank you, Professor Ivy and Jay. And we have good news for you, too. Every morning since you left, I have sent Wira and Jasmi to the top of the tree to look for the flowers, and every day they came back and said there was nothing growing. But today was different. They saw several buds on the vine. We will have more flowers."

"That is wonderful news, Johari. I know the people of Tekek and Juara will continue to tend to the flowers and all the plants and animals that make Tioman their home," I said.

We chatted for a few more minutes before Jay

interrupted and said we had to depart to stay on schedule. We bid the villagers farewell, and Jay promised to return. I did, as well, although that seemed much less likely.

In the cockpit again, Jay started the engines and began to taxi away from the jetty. Once he had Lula in position, he took his hands from the yoke and gestured to the control stick in front of me.

"Your turn, Ivy. I'll tell you exactly what to do." I followed Jay's instructions, and Lula skimmed along the water until we were airborne. "Don't forget to wave," Jay said, and I waggled her wings to the small crowd below at Tekek. Jay looked at a map and told me to adjust our course eastward. It occurred to me I hadn't even asked what route we were taking.

"Jay, how are we getting to Manila?"

"There are two possible routes. One is the mail route along the north of Borneo. We'd stop to refuel twice in Sarawak and stay overnight in Sabah at the northernmost tip of Borneo. The other route is direct to Saigon."

"Oh, I'd like to see Saigon someday. But I'd rather take the Borneo route. My friends Osa and Martin went to North Borneo in their flying boat. That was their last expedition together, although they didn't know it at the time. They gave me this hat when they came back from Borneo, in fact. I can't believe I managed to keep it after all we've been through on this trip."

"Maybe it brought you good luck."

"Maybe. So we'll take the Borneo route?"

"Yes, I figured that was the one you would prefer. More chances for snakes and insects and bats than in cosmopolitan Saigon. We are already headed in that direction."

"I like your reasoning, Jay."

Small islands occasionally punctuated the water below until the northern coast of Borneo appeared. Jay set us down at Kuching at the mouth of the Sarawak River. As much as I would have liked to explore, he had Lula refueled quickly, and I was back in the cockpit for my second takeoff. We snaked eastward around the coast of Borneo until we came to the small settlement at Miri on the easternmost edge of Sarawak. After refueling again, we headed for Kudat at the northern tip of Sabah.

A British North Borneo official met us at the dock, and Jay arranged for refueling. It was nearly dark when we walked to the Kudat Hotel, a two-story, whitewashed structure with latticework decorating the façade, and checked in to a room. We came back downstairs for dinner at a little table for two on the charming verandah before retiring for the evening. If the room had any snakes, insects, or bats, I did not notice.

In the morning we were off again, and I had another chance to practice a takeoff. I asked Jay to take the controls once we were airborne so I could look at the view below. Lula flitted along the thin island of Palawan, a green serpent emerging from the water. We stopped at Puerto Princesa for more fuel, and I made my final takeoff. Jay took over again, and we passed above other small islands and then Mindoro, according to the map. I knew Luzon lay just beyond. Soon enough Manila Bay was visible below. Jay set us down at the Pan American base at Cavite, next to the China Clipper. He hopped out and tied us up.

"Wait here, and I'll arrange to have the cargo transferred to the Clipper," he said.

I climbed out of the cabin, carefully walked to the tip of Lula's float closest to the dock, and gently caressed her nose. "Thank you, Lula. Well done," I whispered.

Jay was back and took my hand as I stepped onto the dock. "They will take care of the cargo. I'll stay here while you check in at the Pan American desk." I left Jay and went into the hangar.

"Welcome to Manila, Professor Linden," the clerk said. "We have you booked on the China Clipper for tomorrow's departure. Tonight you'll be staying at the Manila Hotel. A taxi will bring you back here tomorrow morning at eight o'clock sharp. And Mr. Diente de León has arranged for all your cargo to be transferred to the Clipper. Is there anything else we can do for you?"

"No, I think that should be everything. Oh, wait. There is something. Do you know a Harry Hartman here in Manila? His fiancée Helen was a passenger on the Clipper with me on my way out here. They must have gotten married by now. Mr. Hartman's company has a DC-3 over at Nielson Field. I'd like to get in touch with them, but I don't know their address."

"Oh yes, Mr. Hartman. Let me make a call," the clerk said. In a few minutes, he came back with a note containing their address and telephone number. I thanked the clerk and left the hangar to find a waiting taxi. Jay and I got in back. Wordlessly, he took my hand as we sped away from Cavite. Soon we were in the center of Manila. We disembarked at the Manila Hotel, and porters whisked our bags inside. I checked in and arranged for a separate room for Jay, courtesy of Johnson and Smith.

"Do you know anyone in Manila?" I asked as we

walked up to our rooms.

"A few people. Do you?"

"I met a girl named Helen on the way here. She was coming to get married to a Mr. Harry Hartman. It was his company's cargo plane that took me to Singapore. They were awfully nice. I promised them I'd visit on my way back," I said wistfully.

"Do you want to see them tonight?"

"No, there's not enough time. I think Helen would understand. I'll write her a letter," I said as we reached my door.

"Room service at eight?"

"I'm counting on it," I replied, and Jay continued down the hall to his room. I sat right down at the desk to write Helen a letter, congratulating her on her presumed nuptials, apologizing for missing her on my return trip, and reiterating her appointment as a special correspondent to the "Garden Spot." I told her I'd write more when I got home and hinted at Jay, which I knew would pique her interest. I sealed up the letter and walked back to the lobby to post it. Jay knocked on my door at eight o'clock. Twelve hours passed too quickly, and soon we were in the cab heading back to the Pan American base again.

CHAPTER 36

"You're all set for the flight, Professor Linden," the Pan American agent said, handing me the ticket. "And your cargo is going all the way to San Francisco. From there we have you staying overnight and then departing on the United Air Lines Mainliner to Chicago and then on to Ithaca, New York as your final destination."

"Thank you, that sounds about right."

"We'll announce when it's time to board."

I walked outside and found Jay pacing around the dock. Lula seemed to be sitting higher in the water, no doubt without all my equipment weighing her down. I paced alongside Jay.

"I wish I could stay. I wish you were coming with me."

"I wish the same, Ivy. I wish I were your pilot for this journey."

"Me too, Jay. Thank you for everything. The flying lessons. Everything," I said, smiling to forestall a threatening deluge of tears.

"*De nada, mi tesoro.* Thank you, Ivy. I know we'll meet again."

"I hope so. Please be careful flying back to

Singapore."

"Of course, Ivy. Lula won't let anything happen."

"Yes, I believe you're right."

"The China Clipper is ready for boarding," blared a voice from the hangar. A small group of well-dressed people began forming near the plane. Jay took my hand and brushed it with his lips. "Goodbye, Profesora Ivy. I will miss you."

"Goodbye, Jay. I'll miss you, too. I'll write," I said with a forced smile and joined the small crowd waiting for the steward to escort us aboard the Clipper. I looked back at Jay. He was standing forlornly next to Lula. I ran back over to him and threw my arms around him. After one last long, desperate kiss, we parted. I walked up the ramp, and the steward guided me inside the aircraft. He showed me to a plush seat, and I turned to the window. I waved out at Jay and Lula. Jay waved back, and I thought Lula bobbed just a bit in the water.

Her engines humming, the China Clipper was finally ready to depart. Jay had not budged from the dock. I felt us begin to move away from shore and furiously began waving again until we were airborne. I peered down at the diminishing form of Lula and the spot next to her. I fancied Jay was still waving up at me, but the tears I had held back were now unleashed. I pulled my hat from Osa down low over my face and closed my eyes. On this trip back across the Pacific, I was content to be the mysterious traveler who said little and roused the curiosity of the other passengers.

But my morose spirits only lasted until lunch and an invitation to play cards with the family sitting around me. The mother, father, and young son soon cheered me with stories of their life in Hong Kong. It was not until I climbed into the upper berth of my sleeping compartment that I was alone with my thoughts again. I wondered what Jay was doing. And Merle. And Ruby. But I reminded myself I'd soon be home, and that would be good, too.

The journey eastward across the Pacific was pleasant and uneventful. My fellow passengers studiously avoided the topic of the Hawaii Clipper's disappearance, though it must have been on everyone's minds. I had several occasions to wear my palm tree-print bathing suit, and I was sure Helen would have been pleased I chose that over more academic pursuits.

The bright orange of the Golden Gate Bridge was a welcome sight. My melancholy was receding, replaced by excitement to be so close to home. When we landed at the Pan American terminal at Alameda, I arranged for one crate of pressed samples to be diverted from the Mainliner for transport to the California Academy of Sciences. At the Mark Hopkins, I sent telegrams to my parents and to Jay in Singapore, letting them know I'd arrived safely. I figured Johnson and Smith could wait for news from me. Then I strolled over to Golden Gate Park and popped in to see Alice Eastwood. She greeted me warmly, and I told her about the botanical aspects of the trip and warned her to look out for a crate of samples to mount for the herbarium.

The next day, I departed on the Mainliner, stopping in Wyoming to refuel, before reaching Chicago. As pleasant as the luxurious airliner was, I couldn't help missing Lula's cramped cockpit. And her pilot. Nevertheless, I made the most of it, helping myself to the tiny porcelain salt and pepper shakers with the United Air Lines logo as a souvenir when no one was looking.

Soon I was homeward bound, hopeful all my equipment and collections had made it into the small hold of the Ithaca Airways Electra. In a few hours, we were over the rolling hills, farms, lakes, and forests of central New York. The Ithaca Airport emerged from the landscape, and we touched down with a bump. I'd have to learn to land on the ground, I mused, although it didn't seem like as much fun as on water.

I disembarked from the plane, but saw no sign of Mother, Dad, or Amaryllis. Had I wired them the wrong day or time? I went inside the hangar to find somewhere to stow my trunks and cargo. When a steward accompanied me back to the cargo hold, I was relieved to see Tut crawling along the road toward us. The Scarab stopped, and Amaryllis raced out to the tarmac, with Mother and Dad bringing up the rear at a more dignified pace.

"Ivy! You're home!" Amaryllis cried, throwing her arms around me. "Did you have a good trip? We missed you so much! The summer was swell! It's a pity you weren't here!"

"Oh Ivy, thank goodness you've made it home in one piece. I was sure you'd gone down on that Clipper," my mother said, grabbing me tightly next.

"Welcome home, Ivy," Dad said, giving me a peck on the check. "Glad you made it back quicker than Odysseus."

Once my trunks and crates were loaded into the back of Tut, I was ushered into the rear with Amaryllis. "We want to hear all about your trip, Ivy," Mother said. "But we know you're tired from such a long journey, so we'll wait for you to come over for Sunday dinner to tell us everything."

"I can't wait that long," said Amaryllis. "Let's go to the movies on Saturday, and you can tell me all about it."

"And I can't wait that long, either," Dad said. "You'll come to work tomorrow and tell me all about it."

I knew I wouldn't be telling any of them *everything* about it. They would each get a different version of what happened. Once I figured out exactly what *had* happened.

"Do you want to go straight home now?" Mother asked.

"Yes, I think that would be best. It's been a long trip."

We climbed up the hill to Cornell and through the campus to Forest Home Drive. Soon my little white bungalow came into view. The shrubs were neatly pruned, surrounded by yellow black-eyed Susan and red bee balm blooming in profusion. The cottage had not suffered in my absence. We pulled in to the driveway. Rama and Osiris cautiously emerged from the bushes, then trotted over and rubbed against my legs. Osiris appeared to have grown more, and Rama looked a bit rounder than I recalled. Amaryllis had taken good care of them.

We all went inside for a few minutes, and Mother pointed out some food she had left for me in the refrigerator. Then they climbed into their sedan and waved goodbye. I closed the front door and sank down on the couch. It was the first time I'd been truly alone in a very long time. The cats jumped up to vie for my attention. I hadn't been sure I'd ever see them again. Or my little home. Or my family. But somehow everything had managed to work out. Or had it? I wasn't sure what I was going to tell Johnson and Smith. But I had at least secured some specimens for the herbaria.

I flipped through a pile of letters. One from Elspeth. Two from Osa. I could tell them the whole story, for sure. And they might even believe me.

CHAPTER 37

The next day, I sat in my office at my desk, just looking around, astonished to be back. I had another pile of mail to sift through there. Two letters from Heath. Those could wait. I wandered downstairs to my father's office. He was already there, writing at his desk. I knocked softly to get his attention.

"Ivy! Come in, come in. Sit down," he said, getting up and closing the door behind me. I settled into the burgundy leather chair opposite his desk.

"I want to hear about everything. Did you find any new plants? How was Singapore? How was Tioman? What was the Clipper like? Your mother was beside herself with worry the whole time, especially when word came about that Hawaii Clipper disappearing. Oh, how I wish I could have gone with you."

"Fred Chasen at the Raffles Museum sends his regards. Singapore was lovely. And Tioman was very interesting. So were the Solomon Islands. And the Dutch East Indies. New Guinea, too. Even a bit of Borneo."

"The Solomon Islands? East Indies? New Guinea? Borneo? Whatever were you doing there? You didn't run into any trouble, did you?"

"Trouble? Like the kind requiring a plant physiology textbook to resolve?"

"Uh, yes. You didn't need that textbook, did you?"

"No, it turns out I was right about it being an old edition. I needed something more up-to-date," I said, opening my bag. I placed Emerald's Luger on my father's desk. He gasped audibly.

"Oh, Ivy. How on earth did you get that? We didn't think you would really be in any danger. Larry and I thought–," he said, still staring at the ugly pistol wide-eyed, before I cut him off.

"Larry?"

"Yes, Larry. Dr. MacDaniels. We discussed it, and we both thought you could handle it. . . ."

"Well, I *did* handle it. With some help. But I nearly didn't come back. And my friends nearly didn't, either."

"If we'd have known it would be so dangerous, we never would have let you go," he said, cradling his head in his hands.

"So you *and* Dr. MacDaniels were both in on this with that Johnson and Smith pair? And didn't tell me? No, didn't *ask* me if I wanted to be a part of this?"

"Well, we figured you were the best person for the, uh, expedition, for a variety of reasons, but thought you would say no."

"Of course I would have said no. Well, maybe. Or yes. I might have said yes."

"Are you sorry you went?" he asked in a small voice.

"No," I admitted. "I'm glad I went. But that's not the point. It should have been my choice to decide for myself. And if I had known what I was getting into, I could have been more prepared."

"I'm sorry, Ivy. We should have asked you. But it all worked out in the end, right?"

"Yes, Dad, it all worked out in the end." In spite of myself, I couldn't stay angry with him. "In fact, you might even say that some treasures did abound."

"Treasures? What did you find?" he asked eagerly.

"A new *Rafflesia*, I think. On Tioman," I said, taking out the stack of photos. I was careful to leave the last picture of Jay in my bag. Dad flipped through the photographs.

"I think you may be right. It looks different than the ones I know. Did you get any specimens?"

"No, I didn't bring any material back. The population was nearly wiped out by pests," I said, motioning to the Luger. "I didn't feel right about taking anything away from the people of Tioman."

"Oh, that's a shame. Did you find anything else unique?"

"I did find a plant with wound-healing properties in the Solomons. I don't know what it is. I just have one leaf pressed."

"That sounds promising. We'll take it over to the fellows in the chemistry department and have them grind it up and see what they can extract."

"Here's your Malay phrasebook back. *Terima kasih*," I said, handing the small volume to him. He rose to place it back on the bookshelf.

"If I'd known you were going to the Solomon Islands, I could have given you some other books. Like this one," he said, pulling a dusty one from the shelf and handing it to me.

"*A Natural History of the Solomon Islands* by

Reginald Woodbridge," I read aloud, flipping through the pages. The center featured a section of photo plates. "Can I borrow this one?"

"Yes, of course. Why don't you keep it?"

"Thanks, Dad."

"Go get that leaf, and we'll see what we can make of it," he suggested.

Back in my office, I closed the door and sat down at my desk. I pulled out my father's Solomon Islands book and checked the publication date: 1907. I leafed through the pages again and found the section of photographs. There were huts, canoes, and other artifacts. I stared at one photo closely: a man in native dress wearing a breast ornament made of a giant clamshell on a braided cord and stacks of shell armbands on both of his muscular upper arms. He looked off into the distance regally, the large holes in his stretched earlobes clearly visible. It was him. I was sure of it. The man from the *tomoko*. I read the brief caption over and over: "Chief Ingava of Roviana." I gently closed the book and then peeked inside at the photograph again. It was still there, not just my imagination. Who would believe that?

I withdrew the dried heart-shaped leaf from my notebook. It was well preserved. The thought of it being ground up and dissolved into chemical fractions was unbearable. And not just because it – no, she – had saved Jay's life and maybe mine and Merle's. I felt like I'd be betraying her, somehow. The plant who had offered her help at just the right time. I tucked the leaf in the book with the photo of Ingava. Then I added my photograph of Jay to its pages for safekeeping, too, and placed the book on my own bookshelf. If Dad and Dr. MacDaniels and Johnson and Smith could have secrets, then I could, too. I went back down to my father's office.

"Dad, I don't know what happened to that leaf," I said. "I can't find it anywhere. It must have slipped out of my notebook at some point. It wasn't with the rest of my specimens. It was collected under . . . difficult . . . circumstances. All I have is my description."

"That's too bad, Ivy," he replied, looking at the page of my notebook where I'd noted its physical characteristics. "Cordate. Sounds like nothing special; it could be anything. Oh well, I'm sure the trip wasn't a total loss."

"Not at all. I have a lot of specimens for Ethel to add to the Bailey Hortorium. Plus I deposited duplicates in the Raffles Museum herbarium and the California Academy of Sciences herbarium. Alice Eastwood sends her regards, incidentally. Oh yes, and I learned how to fly. A Dragonfly. A de Havilland DH.90. On floats. I'm sure I'm forgetting something else. . . ."

"My goodness, Ivy. I do want the full account. But I think you had better not mention some of this . . . maybe most of this . . . to your mother."

"My thoughts exactly."

"You might want to pay a visit to Larry, uh Dr. MacDaniels, this afternoon and tell him how the portable drying apparatus worked out. In the Solomons. He'll be very interested and pass it on to the USDA. To Johnson and Smith. And I'm sure he'll want you to use the plant drier in the field again. That is if you want to, of course. He'll be sure to ask you if you want to do fieldwork like that again. We won't make assumptions the next time."

"Yes, Dad, I'll fill him in on the details of the plant

drier," I said, playing along. "I'd likely be willing to use it in the field again, as long as I'm not kept in the dark the next time."

"Very good. I do wish I could go you on any future expeditions that require a portable drying apparatus. Or a plant physiology textbook."

"We'll see, Dad. Let's go have lunch with Amaryllis. She said Mother sent tuna salad sandwiches for all of us."

The next afternoon, I stood in line at the Strand Theatre with Amaryllis.

"Oooh, let's see this one," she said, pointing to a garishly colored poster of a titian-haired young woman looking heavenward as she clutched a handsome man in a flying jacket. "It's new. *Sky Giant.* It's something about dashing aviators with some romance thrown in. You might like that."

"You just might be right about that."

We got our tickets and butter-drenched popcorn and selected seats at the front of the balcony.

"It's too bad you missed the summer in Ithaca, Ivy. I went to the movies every week. And I had dates with some nice young men. An accountant, a civil engineer, and an economics professor."

"I'm glad you had a good summer, Amaryllis. They do sound like very nice young men. Sensible and down-to-earth."

"Did you ever get to see that professor from New Zealand? Heath, was it?"

"No, there was no time. In fact, I missed him. He was in Singapore, but I was away."

"That's too bad."

"It's okay," I said with a shrug. "I did meet someone else, though. I'll tell you about him after the show. We'll go for milkshakes at Woolworth's."

"That sounds intriguing," Amaryllis said. "Oh, the newsreel is starting." The lights dimmed, and conversation faded away.

"Amaryllis? Can I ask you something?" I whispered.

"Yes, Ivy?"

"Have you ever heard . . . uh . . . do you hear . . . plants?"

She looked at me over her sack of popcorn with a bemused expression. "Of course, Ivy. Don't you hear the plants?"

Author's Note

Ivy Linden's adventure is, of course, fiction. However, some of the characters she meets are real people whom Ivy could have known in 1938. Each one had a fascinating life full of excitement and achievement. A small biography follows for those readers who want to know more about Ivy's friends.

Botanist and author **Ethel Zoe Bailey** (1889-1983) was the daughter of famed botanist and horticulturist Liberty Hyde Bailey, who had begun teaching at Cornell University the year before Ethel was born. She grew up in Ithaca, New York and attended Smith College, where she earned a degree in zoology in 1911. Shortly after graduating, she returned to Ithaca and began to work with her father as a collaborator and editor. They co-authored the important plant reference books *Hortus* and *Hortus Second*, among other works. The father-daughter pair traveled around the world together on plant collecting expeditions to places such as Venezuela, Brazil, Panama, China, Japan, the Philippines, Indonesia, and Hawaii. Her exploits were not limited to the botanical: Ethel was the first woman in

Ithaca to receive a driver's license. In 1935 Ethel became the first curator of Cornell's herbarium, the Liberty Hyde Bailey Hortorium, a position she held until her retirement in 1957. She continued to volunteer daily at the herbarium until her death at age ninety-three.

Australian **Ruby Olive Jones Boye** (1891-1990) was the only female coastwatcher in the Solomon Islands during World War II. Born in Sydney, she married Skov Boye in 1919. Skov had previously worked for Lever Brothers on Tulagi and returned to this position in 1928, bringing Ruby and their young son Ken with him. Their second son, Don, was born there, and they relocated to Vanikoro in 1936 when Skov became the island manager for the Vanikoro Kauri Timber Company.

At the outbreak of World War II, a network of coastwatchers was formed to relay radio reports on weather conditions, and later Japanese ship, aircraft, and troop movements, throughout the Solomon Islands. Vanikoro, the southernmost post in the chain of radios, soon found itself in need of a new radio operator when the island's telegraphist departed to join the RAAF. Before leaving, he trained Ruby to operate the radio, and she taught herself Morse code.

The timber company staff left Vanikoro in 1941, but Ruby and Skov stayed behind. Ruby continued to operate the radio as the Japanese began to invade the Solomon Islands, sending reports first to Tulagi until it fell to the Japanese in May 1942 and later to Vila in the New Hebrides (now Vanuatu). Ruby was on call to transmit vital radio messages multiple times a day during the Battles of the Coral Sea, Guadalcanal, and Savo Island.

Meanwhile, Japanese reconnaissance planes patrolled overhead, knowing that she was broadcasting below. She even received personally threatening radio messages from the Japanese: "Mrs. Boye, calling Mrs. Boye on Vanikoro. This is Japanese commander. You get off air pretty damn quick and please to discontinue use of radio. You get right off Vanikoro or we come over and make everything hot for you." Undaunted, Ruby remained at her post despite knowing that she would be executed if captured.

Ruby was officially appointed an honorary third officer in the Women's Royal Australian Naval Service (WRANS) in July 1943, and a uniform was even airdropped to her on Vanikoro. She was honored for her service with a British Empire Medal (BEM) and a personal visit from U.S. Navy Fleet Admiral William F. "Bull" Halsey, Jr. in 1944. After the war ended in 1945, an Associated Press newspaper article even profiled Ruby's brave coastwatcher service, noting that Admiral Halsey had referred to Ruby as "that marvelous woman who runs the radio."

Ruby's husband Skov died in 1947. She returned to Australia and married Frank Jones in 1950, but he died just eleven years later. At ninety years old, Ruby remarked, "Age is a matter of mind, and if you don't mind, it doesn't matter," in an oral history about her remarkable wartime experience as the only female coastwatcher recorded for the Admiral Chester W. Nimitz Museum (now the National Museum of the Pacific War). Ruby lived an active life until she passed away at the age of ninety-nine.

Author and humanitarian **Pearl Sydenstricker**

Buck (1892-1973) earned a Master of Arts degree in English Literature from Cornell University in 1925. While she and her husband were students at Cornell, they resided at the parsonage of the Forest Home Chapel, an adorable bungalow on Forest Home Drive, surrounded by the Cornell botanic gardens. She later received the Pulitzer Prize for her novel *The Good Earth* in 1932 and became the first American woman to be awarded the Nobel Prize for Literature in 1938. In 1933 she purchased Green Hills Farm in Bucks County, Pennsylvania. Now a museum and home to the charity that continues her work, Pearl S. Buck International, I was fortunate to volunteer there as a high school student.

Ornithologist **Frederick Nutter Chasen** (1897-1942) was born in Norfolk, England and served in World War I before coming to the Raffles Museum in Singapore as assistant curator in 1921. He became an authority on the birds and mammals of the region and was appointed director of the museum in 1932. Just days before the fall of Singapore in February 1942, Chasen escaped the doomed city by ship. However, the ship was sunk by the attacking Japanese, and Chasen died at age forty-five.

Aviator **Amelia Earhart** (1897-1937) was born in Kansas and moved around as a child, graduating from high school in Chicago, Illinois in 1916. She then attended the Ogontz School (now Penn State Abington) outside of Philadelphia, but left college in 1917 to become a nurse's aide at a military hospital in Toronto caring for the wounded of World War I. After the war, she entered Columbia University for a year, but left to move to California where she experienced her first airplane flight. She began taking flying lessons early in 1921 and obtained her pilot's license in 1923, becoming just the sixteenth woman in the U.S. to do so. Amelia began setting a variety of aviation records and was one of the founders of the Ninety-Nines, an international organization of women pilots. She became the first woman to fly alone across the Atlantic Ocean in May 1932.

Amelia visited Cornell University on December 6, 1932 as a guest of the Cornell Women's Club of Ithaca. She was given a tour of the campus and city, including the Ithaca Municipal Airport (now the site of the Hangar Theatre), where she met student pilots. In the evening she gave a lecture at Bailey Hall entitled "Flying for Fun" to benefit the Cornell Students' Emergency Relief Fund. She shared anecdotes and film footage of her 1932 solo transatlantic flight and expressed her views on the future of aviation and commercial air travel.

Amelia continued to set aviation records, and in 1935 she became the first aviator – male or female – to fly from Hawaii to California. In 1937 Amelia, along with navigator Fred Noonan, embarked on an around-the-world flight in her specially-modified Lockheed Electra 10E. Departing from Oakland, California, she flew across the U.S. to South America, across the Atlantic to Africa, and on to India, Burma, Thailand, Singapore, Indonesia, and Australia, eventually arriving in Lae, New Guinea. With only 6,500 miles left of the route, she departed Lae on July 2, 1937 for Howland Island; she never arrived. Despite a massive search effort and more than eight decades of speculation, Amelia, Fred Noonan, and her Electra have never been found.

When Amelia spoke of her transatlantic flight at Cornell in 1932, she noted, "I did it for my own personal satisfaction. My flight added little to aviation. . . . However, if the flight interested women in aviation, either as pilots or as passengers, I feel that it was justified." Amelia Earhart's role in inspiring future aviators, aviation enthusiasts, and world travelers cannot be overstated.

Botanist **Alice Eastwood** (1859-1953) was born in Toronto, Canada and moved to Colorado as a teenager. While teaching high school, she taught herself botany and began collecting plant specimens. In 1893 she moved to San Francisco to become a curator of the herbarium at the California Academy of Sciences. During the 1906 earthquake, Alice rescued over a thousand plant collections from the crumbling building. She worked to rebuild the herbarium, collecting new species and publishing hundreds of articles, books, and scientific papers until she retired at the age of ninety.

Nurse **Merle Stephanie Farland** (1906-1988) was born in Christchurch, New Zealand and grew up in Auckland. She became a piano teacher, but felt called to be a medical missionary. In 1938, after training to become a nurse, Merle and a friend, Joy Whitehouse, departed for the New Zealand Methodist Mission run by Reverend A.W.E. "Wattie" Silvester and his wife Moyna at Bilua on Vella Lavella in the Solomon Islands. There, at the Helena Goldie Hospital, the two friends worked alongside Dr. Allen G. Rutter and his wife Elizabeth Rutter, a bacteriologist, to treat the local population for a variety of ailments, including yaws.

As the Japanese began their invasion of the Solomon Islands, Merle refused to be evacuated from Vella Lavella in January 1942 along with the rest of her colleagues. Only Rev. Silvester remained with her at Bilua, and they eventually found themselves behind enemy lines. Rev. Silvester became part of the coastwatcher network and Merle, the only trained medical provider left, soon had ample opportunities to practice medicine. She traveled by canoe throughout occupied territory under the cover of darkness and administered medical care to downed Allied airmen. In December of 1942, after operating behind enemy lines for months, coastwatcher Donald Kennedy asked Merle to relieve him at his post at Segi. After another hair-raising canoe journey through occupied territory, Merle arrived at Segi and began training on the radio. However, one of the first messages she received indicated she was being evacuated. Merle protested, but to no avail. Although she ran the coastwatcher station on her own for three days while Kennedy was rescuing a downed bomber crew, Merle was whisked away on a PBY Catalina flying boat on December 21, 1942.

Merle was taken first to Tulagi and then Guadalcanal, which would not be completely secured until February of 1943. As the only woman among the thousands of American troops on the island, she would have been a curiosity, but when a young man suffering from malaria "recognized" his nurse, she caused quite a stir: a rumor that Amelia Earhart had been found alive spread through the troops! With her tousled brown hair there was some physical resemblance, but the young men who saw her could not have guessed that her courage and adventuresome spirit matched that of the famous aviator, as well.

Merle continued her nursing duties on New Caledonia and Guadalcanal, and later served on the Royal New Zealand Navy hospital ship HS *Maunganui*. Merle was honored for her wartime service with an appointment to the Most Excellent Order of the British Empire (MBE) "for personal courage and devotion to duty while a civilian nurse on Vella Lavella in the Solomon Islands during the Japanese occupation in the rescue of a United States bomber crew."

After World War II, Merle worked for the World Health Organization, specializing in infant and maternal health. Her service took her around the world to places like Ghana, Uganda, Afghanistan, Bangladesh, Taiwan, and numerous islands in the South Pacific. Returning to Vella Lavella for a visit in 1962, she found one of her assistants at the mission hospital had named their daughter Merle in her honor. Merle retired to New Zealand in 1967 and died in 1988.

Writer **Elspeth Grant Huxley** (1907-1997) was born in England and grew up in Kenya on a coffee plantation. She attended Cornell University from 1927 to 1928 as a student in agriculture. During her time in Ithaca she competed on the Cornell women's rifle team, frequently earning top scores in meets with teams from other universities. After marrying Gervas Huxley in 1931, the couple visited Ithaca in 1934 as the guests of Cornell College of Agriculture Professor Bristow Adams. Shortly after, Elspeth published her first book, the start of a long career as an author. She wrote numerous fiction and nonfiction works, including a trio of detective novels set in Africa and memoirs of her African childhood, *The Flame Trees of Thika* and *The Mottled Lizard.* She detailed her year in Ithaca in her 1968 memoir *Love Among the Daughters: Memories of the Twenties in England and America.*

Chief **Ingava** (also spelled Hiqava) of Roviana (18??-1906) was a powerful and influential leader and warrior in the Solomon Islands. Chief Ingava had an adopted daughter named **Pula** who was born around 1880. She was interviewed in 1974 for a doctoral dissertation by K.B. Jackson.

Although Ingava learned to speak some English and was well respected by European traders and colonizers in the Solomons, he was not willing to embrace the missionaries and abandon traditional beliefs and practices. Fearing destruction and desecration by missionaries and souvenir collectors, Ingava relocated an important skull shrine from New Georgia to the tiny island of Kundu Hite in Vonavona Lagoon. His 1906 death and elaborate funeral were reported in *Man: A Monthly Record of Anthropological Science* in 1907. His skull was subsequently added to the shrine of great warriors and chiefs. Perhaps Ingava's skull is still among those remaining on Kundu Hite today.

Writer, filmmaker, and explorer **Osa Leighty Johnson** (1894-1953) grew up in Kansas and married adventurer Martin Johnson in 1910. Together they traveled throughout the Solomon Islands, Vanuatu, Kenya, the Congo, and Borneo filming the people and animals of these countries. They made eight feature films of their travels and wrote several books together. In 1932 Osa and Martin learned to fly and took their two Sikorsky amphibious airplanes on expeditions to Africa and Borneo. George Eastman of Eastman Kodak in Rochester, New York was a patron of their work, and in 1934 they flew to Rochester in their aircraft "Osa's Ark" to present their films. However, the crash of a routine commercial flight from Utah to California claimed the life of Martin in 1937 and severely injured Osa. She recovered to continue their work and published *I Married Adventure* in 1940. Osa visited Cornell University in 1942 to present a lecture at Bailey Hall and screen her film *African Paradise.*

Botanist **Laurence H. MacDaniels** (1888-1986) was born in Ohio and attended Oberlin College. He came to Cornell University in 1912 for graduate studies and earned a doctoral degree in 1917. During the First World War, he worked with the Botanical Raw Products Committee of the National Research Council and the Bureau of Aircraft Production (due to his knowledge of wood). He returned to Cornell in 1919 as a professor of pomology. In 1940 he became the head of the Department of Floriculture and Ornamental Horticulture. MacDaniels conducted fieldwork on bananas in Polynesia and published the plans for a portable plant drier for tropical climates in 1930. During World War II, MacDaniels focused the department's efforts on rubber production, plant materials for camouflage, and food production in Victory Gardens.

Geneticist **Barbara McClintock** (1902-1992) grew up in Connecticut and Brooklyn, New York. She graduated from Cornell University in 1923 with a bachelor's degree in agriculture, concentrating in plant breeding and botany. She then continued on at Cornell to earn a master's degree (1925) and doctoral degree (1927) in botany with a focus on cytology and genetics using maize as a model organism. She remained at Cornell as a researcher and instructor until 1931. During this time, Barbara and graduate student Harriet Creighton were the first to document the correlation between genetic recombination and crossing over of homologous chromosomes. Barbara left Cornell to pursue postdoctoral research at other institutions, including in Germany as a Guggenheim Fellow. She returned to Cornell again, but left in 1936 to become an assistant professor at the University of Missouri. By 1942 Barbara had left this position to become a researcher at the Carnegie Institution's Department of Genetics at Cold Spring Harbor Laboratory on Long Island, New York. She remained there for the rest of her lengthy career. In 1983 she was awarded the Nobel Prize in Physiology or Medicine for her discovery of transposons, mobile genetic elements. As of 2022, she remains the only woman to win an unshared Nobel Prize in this category.

Cultural anthropologist and author **Margaret Mead** (1901-1978) was born in Philadelphia, Pennsylvania and grew up in nearby Doylestown. She graduated from Barnard College in 1923 and continued on to Columbia University where she earned a master's degree (1924) and doctoral degree (1929) in anthropology. Margaret began ethnographic fieldwork in Samoa in 1925 and continued her research at Manus in the Admiralty Islands, the Sepik River region of New Guinea, and Bali in Indonesia. She made multiple expeditions over the decades while serving as a curator of ethnology at the American Museum of Natural History in New York City. Margaret authored numerous books including *Coming of Age in Samoa* (1928) and *Growing Up in New Guinea* (1930). She visited Cornell University to present well-attended lectures in 1941, 1945, and 1952.

Zoologist **Michael W.F. Tweedie** (1907-1993) was born in England and studied natural history at Cambridge. He worked as a paleontologist for Shell Oil in Venezuela before joining the Raffles Museum in 1932 as assistant curator. Tweedie led many collecting expeditions and focused on crustaceans, but was also known for his contributions to ichthyology, herpetology, and malacology. In 1938, Tweedie married Elvira Toby of Hobart, Tasmania, and they had a son and two daughters. During World War II, Tweedie joined the RAF as a camouflage officer. He escaped the fall of Singapore for Java, but was captured there by the Japanese and remained a prisoner for the rest of the war. He returned to Singapore in 1946 to serve as director of the museum until his retirement in 1957, when he returned to England to serve as a natural history journalist and broadcaster for the BBC.

While the other characters Ivy encounters are fictional, some do have elements inspired by real people. Jay's service experience in the Spanish Civil War drew on that of Mexican-born aviator Francisco Tarazona Torán (1915-1989). Helen, Ivy's traveling companion aboard the Pan American Clipper, was based upon Helen Gierding Hagerman, who flew from New Jersey to Manila to be married in 1937 and wrote about her experience in a booklet entitled, "The Bride on the Philippine Clipper." Ito, the Japanese shell trader, was inspired by an actual Japanese shell trader of that name thought by some to be a military spy in the Solomons in the 1920s.

Emerald Asche-Böhrer is, of course, fictional. However, the Nazis did enlist botanists, as well as other scientists and scholars, to further their reprehensible aims through the Ahnenerbe, a collection of research institutes within the SS, founded by Heinrich Himmler in 1935. Emerald's all-too-real namesake, the emerald ash borer, *Agrilus planipennis,* is an invasive beetle that has caused significant damage to ash trees in North America since its accidental introduction in 2002, killing tens of millions of trees and threatening all sixteen species of native ash trees.

The blond-haired people of Melanesia could have been of interest to the Nazis due to their fixation on "Aryan" traits. The recessive mutation responsible for blond hair among the Solomon Islanders was identified in 2012 as a single nucleotide polymorphism (SNP) in the *TYRP1* gene that results in a cysteine-to-arginine change in tyrosinase-related protein 1 needed for melanin biosynthesis, and is distinct from the genetic basis for blond hair in European populations.

Parasitic *Rafflesia* flowers of Southeast Asia, the largest single flowers in the world, could also have been of interest to Nazi botanists due to their use in traditional medicine to treat fevers, help with pregnancy, and as an unlikely aphrodisiac. Today, *Rafflesia* species are facing the dire threats of habitat destruction and poaching for medicinal uses. A new species of *Rafflesia*, *Rafflesia tiomanensis*, unique to Malaysia's Pulau Tioman island, was described in 2021.

Pulau Tioman is also home to other endemic plants found nowhere else in the world. The island's fragile ecosystem is at risk due to overdevelopment and tourism. One popular tourist attraction there is 'Mother Willow,' a strangling fig whose spirit is revered by local people, according to a report by the International Union for Conservation of Nature (IUCN). Work to protect the island's biodiversity is ongoing.

Ivy's original quest, a rare tree found only in New Zealand's Three Kings Islands, is *Pennantia baylisiana,* Three Kings kaikōmako. New Zealand botanist Geoffrey Baylis discovered a single female tree on Great Island in the Three Kings group in 1945. The natural population had dwindled to just one tree due to the introduction of goats to the island. Although the goats have been removed and the tree has been propagated elsewhere by cuttings, only that single tree remains in the wild. The species is critically endangered and at risk of extinction through natural events such as storms and death due to old age.

When asked to explain how they discovered a plant's medicinal properties, Indigenous Peoples from a variety of cultures around the world have often told Western ethnobotanists that the plant spoke to them directly. While the concept of plant-to-plant communication is gaining traction in the scientific community, the idea of plants communicating with people is still regarded as a fringe idea. However, rather than perfunctorily dismissing these claims, perhaps it would be wise to keep an open mind. It was none other than acclaimed scientist Barbara McClintock who said, "Every time I walk on grass I feel sorry because I know the grass is screaming at me." Can you hear the plants?

Kundu Hite, Solomon Islands, 2017

Selected References and Further Reading

Beniston, D. N. (1994). *The Call of the Solomons: The New Zealand Methodist Women's Response.* Wesley Historical Society N.Z.

Djokovic, P. (2017). Calling Mrs. Boye. *Semaphore, 7.*

Edge-Partington, T. W. (1907). 15. Ingava, Chief of Rubiana, Solomon Islands: Died 1906. *Man, 7,* 22.

Jackson, K. B. (1978). *Tie hokara, tie vaka: Black man, white man: a study of the New Georgia Group to 1925* [PhD dissertation]. Australian National University.

Keller, E. F. (2003). *A Feeling for the Organism, 10th Anniversary Edition: The Life and Work of Barbara McClintock.* Macmillan.

Kenny, E. E., *et al.* (2012). Melanesian Blond Hair is Caused by an Amino Acid Change in TYRP1. *Science, 336*(6081), 554.

Lawrence, D. R. (2014). *The Naturalist and his 'Beautiful Islands': Charles Morris Woodford in the Western Pacific.* ANU Press.

Lord, W. (1977). *Lonely Vigil: The Untold Story of the South Pacific Coastwatchers.* Viking Press.

Moore, C. (2019). *Tulagi: Pacific Outpost of British Empire.* ANU Press.

Nay, C. (1939). *Timmy Rides the China Clipper.* Albert Whitman & Company.

Safari Museum in Kansas - Martin and Osa Johnson Safari Museum. https://safarimuseum.com/

Siti Munirah, M. Y., *et al.* (2022). *Rafflesia tiomanensis* (Rafflesiaceae), a new species from Pulau Tioman, Pahang, Malaysia. *Malayan Nature Journal, 73*(1), 19–26.

Acknowledgements

I am deeply grateful to my sister Maria Esposito for her expert proofreading skills, helpful comments, and unwavering support. She always provides just the right words of encouragement when I need them most.

I wish to thank Alex Welsh for her enthusiastic critical reading of the manuscript; Joo Rhee, Kathy Kozak, Patti Duke, and Leina Isno for their kind encouragement during the writing process; and Caroline Bardwell for her support of independent authors.

I am also grateful to my parents, James and Jean Esposito. They were so supportive of my earliest writing projects, and I hope they would enjoy my recent endeavors.

Other people I'd like to thank for making this work possible include:

Anderson "Andy" Giles, Vicky Reynolds-Middagh of Valor Tours, the crew of the MV *Bilikiki*, my fellow travelers, and the people of the Solomon Islands who welcomed us so graciously in 2017. Our "Cruise up The Slot" included stops at Guadalcanal, Tulagi, and Kundu Hite, as well as an impromptu visit to Vella Lavella. This journey, which I'd dreamed of making for more than twenty-five years, led to an unexpected series of adventures far beyond anything I could have imagined.

Diana Hurlbut Murphy and Lori Leonardi, stewards of the New York State Museum's botany and mycology collections, who kindly taught me the art and science of plant and fungal specimen care when I served as a behind-the-scenes volunteer in the museum's herbarium.

Scientists Dr. Robin Wall Kimmerer, Dr. Suzanne Simard, Dr. Monica Gagliano, Dr. Lynn Margulis, and Dr. Barbara McClintock. Their groundbreaking research and writing has been so meaningful and inspiring for me.

The many museums, libraries, and archives that make their collections publicly accessible. I'd especially like to thank the staff and volunteers who digitized the collections of Cornell University, the New York Public Library, the Smithsonian Institution, the National Museum of the Pacific War, the British Museum, the Auckland War Memorial Museum, the Henry Ford Museum, the Martin and Osa Johnson Safari Museum, the Naval Historical Society of Australia, Ngā Taonga Sound & Vision, Australian National University, National Library of Australia, Navy Victoria Network, Singapore National Heritage Board, National University of Singapore, Biodiversity Heritage Library, HathiTrust Digital Library, the Internet Archive, Newspapers.com, and Ancestry.com. It never ceases to delight me that I can easily find what movie was playing in Ithaca on a particular day in 1938 or what someone might have eaten at the Raffles Hotel had they made a journey to Singapore that year. These collections allowed me to travel around the world and back in time without leaving my desk!

Lastly, I want to express my profound gratitude to our plant kin, whose generosity makes life possible for those of us without chloroplasts. I humbly offer this story as a small act of reciprocity for their many gifts.

ABOUT the AUTHOR

Growing up in Pennsylvania's Bucks County, Donna Esposito was inspired by the lives of past residents James A. Michener, Margaret Mead, Pearl S. Buck, and Oscar Hammerstein II. She earned an undergraduate degree in molecular biology with a minor in anthropology from Lehigh University and a doctoral degree in genetics from Cornell University, focusing on chloroplast gene expression. After overseeing a genetic testing laboratory for a dozen years, she made a radical career change to explore her other longtime interests in writing, museums and archives, World War II history, plants and ethnobotany, and the South Pacific.

Donna's first novel, *Flying Time*, was published in 2016, setting off an unlikely series of events that led to her visiting the Solomon Islands, Papua New Guinea, Palau, the Marianas, and Sicily to explore World War II sites. While visiting Guadalcanal, she was involved in the repatriation of an American soldier, missing in action since 1943, and has researched numerous World War II servicemembers to bring closure to their families.

Donna is currently working on other writing projects, including Ivy Linden's next adventure, from her home in upstate New York.

Printed in Great Britain
by Amazon